The Dream in the Heart of the Forest

By David Holly

Herndon, VA

ISBN 13: 978-1-61303-051-6

Published in the United States by STARbooks Press, PO Box 711612, Herndon, VA 20171. Printed in the United States

Many thanks to graphic artist John Nail for the cover design. Mr. Nail may be reached at tojonail@bellsouth.net.

Herndon, VA

Also by David Holly

Delicious Darkness
Kissing Behind the Bathhouse
Stealing the Mayor's Underpants

Dedication

For Kristina, always my first and my final proofreader

A special thanks to Eric Summers and all of the gang at STARbooks Press

Contents

The Dream in the Heart of the Forest

The stranger had been wandering the mountain, lost for three days and nights, uphill and down, his weary feet rustling the fallen leaves, his lightly clad arms raking the brilliant fall foliage. When darkness came, he built a pile of leaves and slept covered with his thin windbreaker. As he pulled his legs toward the core of his body, his blue jeans drew up his crack, displaying the moon curve of his buttocks. Natty Bumppo approached him curiously, sniffed him from head to toe, and then left him alone. On the second morning, ravenous, the stranger found the black walnut tree. Frustrated at breaking his nails on the fibrous husks, he resorted to cutting through them with a sharp stone. He smashed the inner shells between two rocks. Cracking the fifth nut, he hit his finger and swore, but hunger drove him. He persevered, and then he cupped his stained hands to drink water from the steam. If he continued drinking from the streams, he would discover the fevers, accompanied by diarrhea and vomiting.

Standing to urinate against a tree, he revealed a thick penis, hooded and dark. As he refastened his jeans, he had to tighten his belt two notches. That's when he waded into the cold stream and tried to catch a steelhead with his bare hands. Of course, the fish eluded him easily, so he next fastened his gaze upon a rabbit. He threw a rock at the rabbit, and though his aim was good, by the time the missile reached its mark, the bunny had disappeared behind a rock outcropping.

By the third night, the stranger was losing hope. No human voice had disturbed the sounds of the mountain forest; he had neither seen nor heard search planes or helicopters; and he did not believe anyone was looking for him. He passed the evening throwing rocks at the squirrels and songbirds, but the creatures evaded his aim, and besides he had no fire with which to cook them. Once Lenore swooped low over the stranger's head, and he ducked away from her beak. Rising, he picked up a rock and made as if to throw it at Lenore, making my breath catch in my throat, but Lenore soared to the top of a Sitka spruce and watched from on high.

The stranger piled his leaves higher that night, having learned that the ground sucked the heat from his body. In his exhaustion and despair, he fell into a fitful sleep. He slept peacefully until the moon was riding high above the treetops. Then he became restless.

A long moan escaped the stranger's lips. He rolled to his right and thrashed back to his left. With Natty at my heels, I crept toward the stranger as he thrashed upon his leaves, in thrall to some strong dream. I looked closer as he cried out. Up until that moment, I had kept my distance, watching from bluffs and the tops of trees, but when I saw that his cock had hardened so it strained his blue jeans, smeared with earth and tree sap, I was drawn to partake in his sexual dream. My heart pounding in my throat, I squatted and lightly traced his cock with my forefinger. That faint touch was enough to wake him. To my horror, his eyes popped open and he drew his breath with a gasp. Leaping up, I ran toward a tall oak, but he was already on his feet.

"Wait," he called. "I'm lost. I need help."

Stopping and looking in thrall, I realized how pretty he was. His hair was chestnut brown and hung a little below his ears. His face would have been creamy had it not been stained with mud and decaying leaves and the husks of the black walnuts. His jeans were torn out at both knees from a fall, revealing shapely legs. His downy chest was showing through his ripped shirt and his ass appeared round and solid.

I wanted to take him home to my cave; still, I was afraid, and the memory of how it had been when I lived among the people still haunted me. He saw my hesitation. "Come on, man," he pleaded. "I'm starving and I'm freezing." At the word, he hugged himself in the frosty mountain air. "What are you afraid of?"

"You," I said. "You come from the people."

Even in the dim moonlight, I could see his puzzlement. "What people, man? Ah, never mind. I'm not gonna hurt you. Is that what you're worried about? Man, I'm not gonna hurt anybody. Please. I don't wanna die out here."

It was a long two-day's walk to the place where the logging road passed the woods, and another half-day to the stores. In his condition, he would never make that journey. I had to take him to my cave.

"Come," I said, making up my mind. I led the stranger up the trail. He followed, staggering after me. "Don't mind Natty."

"Who's Natty?"

"Natty Bumppo. He's right behind you."

The stranger looked down and saw Natty trotting behind his heels. "Holy shit! Is that a wolf?"

"Natty is my friend. So is Lenore." I put out my arm, and she swooped down, landed, and climbed onto my shoulder.

"That's a fuckin' huge bird, man. Is it a raven?"

As we climbed, the stranger seemed wary of Natty Bumppo and Lenore, but I noticed that once Natty licked his hand, the stranger could not resist touching the wolf's silver head and scratching behind his ears.

# # # # #

"Man, those were good steaks," the stranger said with a half-burp. "The potatoes and roasted corn too." He washed down the last of his meal with two bottles of black cherry ale from the cold stream. "Where did you get this stuff?"

I smiled and shrugged and downed the last of my third bottle. Natty Bumppo had wolfed down his dog food and sat down beside the couch. The stranger glanced at the wolf, though he was less wary by then.

"Not telling, huh?" he said. "Oh, it doesn't matter. Say, what's your name?"

My heart thundered. I had not spoken my own name for ten years. I should have known that if I brought a stranger to my cave, he would want to know my name. "Billy," I finally whispered, hoping that would not be enough to identify me when he went back to the people.

My answer satisfied him. "I'm Russell," he said. "Russell Welk. I was camping with a group of guys this Thanksgiving weekend – that is, until I got separated from them." He thought for a few minutes. "They were assholes. They didn't even look for me, and I'll bet they never told anybody they left me here on the mountain." He set his plate of steak scraps onto the rock floor, and Natty licked it clean.

"Is this Thanksgiving?" I asked. I shivered as I remembered Thanksgiving dinners at my grandparents' house – a day of prayers and spite.

"Yeah, wow, dude, you didn't know that?" Russell said. "I got lost Wednesday evening. This is my third night." He thought for a second. "Thanksgiving was two days ago." He looked around again. "Billy, how long have you been living in this cave?"

I shrugged, and Natty Bumppo turned around three times and went to sleep on the warm fireplace hearth. "Ten years, I guess," I said quietly. "Why did your friends leave you?"

Instead of answering, Russell looked at me in a way that made me feel funny all over. His eyes still locked on mine, his hand slid to his crotch and rubbed his cock through the denim. When I lowered my eyes, he didn't stop. He kept on fondling himself until his cock was hard in his jeans. My own cock was hardening at the same time, but I didn't quite have the nerve to stroke it.

Russell must have seen my cock stiffening, because a half smile formed on his lips. He unfastened his jeans, reached into his briefs, and pulled out his dick. It was thick, as I had noticed when he pissed, with a drooping foreskin, through which the tip poked as he stroked slowly.

"Come here, Billy," he urged. "I'll let you touch it."

Like one lost in a dream in the heart of the forest, I stood up. My cock was jutting out the front of my pants, so I undid them and let them drop to the swept granite floor. It was like a dream. Slowly I pulled off my shirt, and stood naked with my cock protruding.

"You always go commando?" Russell asked, his voice thick with lust. A sudden sensation told me that I had leaked, and I looked down at the long string of pre-cum hanging from my piss-hole. Russell looked at the wet spunk with a lascivious grin.

"That's it," Russell urged. "Show me what you've got."

I had a small carpet in front of the couch, with an oil lamp on the table beside it. The lamplight cast a flickering shadow upon the carpet as I crossed toward Russell. My heart was thundering with fear and desire, but I soon found I had no need to fear. Russell reached for my cock, touching my circumcised dick head with his soft fingers. His fingers lightly explored my cock, feeling it all the way around and down the shaft.

"Don't you want to play with my cock?" Russell asked. I did, and overcoming my shyness, I reached for his hard-on. Russell pushed his jeans and briefs to the floor as I climbed onto the couch beside him, took his cock in my hand, and gasped at the thrilling fullness. Without a word, Russell pulled me onto him so my knees straddled his thighs. He had one hand on my cock, while the other slid around to my ass. I was fondling his cock while his lips moved nearer to mine. Only then did I grasp that he intended to kiss me.

When our lips met, I thought that I would die. Never had I felt such closeness. Only in my dreams had I ever kissed another guy, and I had lacked the imagination to conceive the passion a mere kiss could inspire. I wanted him in every way. I slicked my hand with my saliva and stroked his cock.

Jacking Russell's cock was more exciting than jacking my own. My fist slid up and down his shaft, wringing his foreskin with every stroke until he was moaning around the hard tongue playing within my mouth. His left hand stroked my ass, and the other pounded my dick. Our kiss went on and on; my tongue slipped into his mouth, and he sucked it.

He pulled his mouth away. "Wait. Stop jerking me off. You're making me come too quick." He stopped stroking my cock at the same time. He kissed me again, but he held my hands while our lips met. Then he whispered into my ear, "Have you ever sucked one?"

"Yes," I said. I didn't tell him that it had only happened once, and that it was ten years earlier.

"I like to swallow," he said blithely. "So when you're ready to shoot your load, don't hold back. Pump your cum down my throat."

The utter frankness of his offer made me bold. "Let's suck each other off – at the same time."

"Sure," he said, positioning himself on his side so that his cock was inches from my mouth. "That's what I was hoping for."

He spoke no more, for his mouth grew busy upon my cock. I felt his wet lips on my dick head, which was as hard as oak. He kissed the head of my dick, and licked it with his grainy tongue. His cock touched my lips, so I flicked his foreskin with my tongue. Taking his cock into my mouth was thrilling. I let it slide over my lips until his hooded head was inside my gums. I circled it with my tongue, licking hard on it, and taking it in a little farther bit-by-bit.

5

Once, after I had been humiliated at school and the principal telephoned my family, my grandmother called me a cocksucker. She said cocksucker like it was a bad name. Yet how could something so wonderful be bad? I am a cocksucker, I mused, as I sucked Russell cock, and I never felt so happy.

Russell was moaning as I sucked him, but he never stopped popping his lips over my dickhead. He licked down my shaft, and then lowered his mouth upon it until my dick head entered his throat. I felt him swallow, as though he wanted to take my cock to his stomach. Then he was fucking my cock with his throat, sucking me so deeply that my mind reeled. I tried to do the same with him, but my tongue wanted the taste of his cock. I could not let his leaking cum sneak away from my taste buds.

As I sucked, my senses magnified. I could hear Natty Bumppo snoring; I could hear Lenore's raucous cries from her perch in the Douglas Fir outside my cave door; I could hear Tom and Huck rooting in the vegetable scraps I'd set outside. I could also hear the thunder of my heart and the tiny mews of pleasure that rose in my throat as I felt Russell's cock tighten harder in my mouth. Knowing that he was on the verge of orgasm, I sucked him harder, nibbling at his dick's head and torturing it with my lips.

As I worked on bringing Russell off, I was hardly thinking about how close I was to shooting my own load. I sensed that my dick was growing heavier just as a large squirt of thick jism covered my tongue. Then I was instantly in full-blown orgasm, the storms of pleasure rushing through me with the thunder of orgasm and the lightning crackles of mindless ejaculation. I was coming heavily in Russell's mouth. I wanted to cry out with joy, but I could only suck on the thick cock erupting in my mouth, the great gouts of honeyed jism pulsing down my throat and satisfying me as no other meal ever had.

We finished drinking the last oozing of love's pleasure, pulling apart only enough to lie with our cocks nestled against faces, and we drifted into a deep slumber with Natty Bumppo, Lenore, and Tom and Huck guarding us from harm.

I felt Russell moving, restless where I had him pinned against the back of the couch, my left thigh thrown across his legs. "Are you trying to get up?" I would have happily kept him there forever.

"I gotta use the crapper. Where is it?"

Dawn was throwing pastel streaks against the pale sky as I led him to my outhouse. There was a two-hundred and fifty foot drop just beyond my cave, and I had braced my outhouse so it hung over the edge. My outhouse was spacious for I like lots of legroom while pooping, and it had a door with a star carved in it, the traditional symbol for the men's outhouse. The half moon indicates a women's toilet. The supreme advantage of my outhouse is that it never requires one to dig up the deposits and haul them away. The shit drops two hundred and fifty feet down into the ravine where it is washed away by the frequent flash floods.

"Holy crap," Russell said as I proudly displayed my engineering wonder. "Is it safe?"

"It's anchored to two strong trees and braced against volcanic rock. A two ton bear could go in to take a dump." As if in demonstration of the roof's sturdiness, Tom and Huck peeked over the edge.

"Wow, forget the bear – I nearly pooped my pants," Russell exclaimed. "Those are gigantic raccoons. They must weigh fifty pounds each."

"Tom and Huck are my friends, too." I petted them in demonstration.

When Russell emerged from the outhouse, I led him to the shower, a twelve-foot waterfall that poured into a basin of smooth rock thirty feet in diameter before dropping to a longer fall into the ravine.

Russell quailed when I waded into the basin. "We'll freeze our nuts off."

"It's a thermal stream," I said. "It bubbles out of a hot spring over the rise. Come on in."

Russell and I had fun playing naked under the warm waterfall. As he was washing out his clothes, smelly after three days, I grabbed his cock. It hardened immediately, though we had sucked each other nearly dry just a few hours earlier.

"You like that, don't you, Billy."

"Yeah," I managed, my voice husky with the admission. I was fighting against the old emotional garbage in my head.

"I like yours too," Russell said, showing me what he liked about it until I was also jutting hard under the falling spray. Suddenly, I realized why Russell's friends had abandoned him.

"Did your friends find out you like cock?" I asked.

He hesitated for only a few seconds. "Yeah, some friends those guys were," Russell said, a pained expression crossing his face. "They were goofing around at college, pretending they were gay. I fucked up. I thought they were, and when they invited me camping with them, I thought they wanted me. But they got me up here; then they laughed at me and played tricks at me. One guy even hit me with a rock. Then they left me."

"I guess things haven't changed that much," I said. "My sister used to call me a faggot, and my grandfather called me Nancy. I got ridiculed in high school, beat up too. One day a bunch of guys smeared shit on me in the bathroom. That's when I decided to take off. I was only sixteen, and I didn't want to hustle on the streets. I was done with the people, so I took all the food and blankets I could get and lit out for the forest. One day I found this cave, and I've been here ever since."

"So you're twenty-six now," Russell said. "That's cool. I'm twenty-three. I didn't start college right away, but I've been catching up this year. Until this happened. I'm gonna miss Monday's class for sure."

"I never finished high school."

"How many guys have you been with?" Russell asked.

"Only two."

"Two counting me?"

"Yeah."

"You suck cock real nice for a beginner," Russell said. "You ever take a dick in the other end?"

I liked the direction this conversation was taking. "No, but I'd like to try it. I'd do anything with you."

"Okay, but if I fuck your ass, you gotta fuck me back."

"Sure," I promised. "You've done it before?"

"Oh, yeah, Billy. Lots of times. There's nothing better. Having a man inside of you. Banging your ass. Getting off in you. Oh, man, I love it."

Naked, we sauntered arm in arm back into the cave. As we approached my bed, Russell halted with a stricken expression. "My condoms and lubricants were in my bag," he cried. "I don't have anything."

"I don't have any condoms," I said. "I've never needed them. But I did liberate this bottle of Astroglide the last time I went for groceries." I displayed the half-filled bottle.

"I've always been careful," Russell said. "I don't have any STD's. I've never taken a cock without two layers of condoms."

"I'm healthy," I said, climbing onto the bed. "You don't get sex diseases spanking your monkey in a mountain cave."

"So we're safe to go bareback," Russell said, sighing with relief as he slid his hand over the curve of my ass. "This will be a first for me too." He drew a sharp intake of breath. "Oh, Billy, your ass is hot."

"Hot for you," I purred. "How do you want me?" Russell's cock was rock hard, ready to enter into me. For a moment he could not answer, so I crouched upon the bed, my face nearly in the pillow. "Take me like this," I suggested.

"Okay," he rasped. "Oh, man, this is gonna be good. I like to take it doggy style too."

Then he was upon the bed too, behind me so I could not see what he was doing. I sensed rather than heard him pick up the lubricant. Before I knew it, I felt a slick hand on my ass. "I'm gonna open you up, Billy. I'm gonna open your ass for my dick."

My heart raced. "Yeah. Open me up."

I felt something pressing against my asshole. "Let it in, Billy," Russell said. "It's only my finger. Push with your asshole. Take a deep breath and push hard."

As I pushed, his finger, slick with the lubricant, slid into me. It produced a warm, delicious sensation that flowed through my body. My cock tingled pre-orgasmically, my lips prickled, and my nipples tightened. "Oh, Russell," I moaned. "I want your cock."

"Be patient, Billy," Russell said. "You're going to get it. There's no rush. I'm gonna make it super good for you. You're gonna love it."

"Yeah, make me love it, Russell," I moaned as he twisted his finger. He pulled it out, and I heard him use the lubricant bottle; then he slid it back in slipperier than before. I felt like a hollow tube with a small rod twisting in it.

When Russell pulled his finger out a second time, he reinserted two fingers, which stretched me a little wider. "You're opening up real nice, Billy," Russell complimented me. "This fuck is gonna be wickedly good. Now take a couple of deep breaths and push harder, 'cause I'm gonna give you three fingers."

There was no pain as my asshole opened around his digits. He stretched my hole open to a greater and wider diameter until I was ready to take his cock. Russell knew exactly how far to open me up, but still my heart thundered with excitement when he placed the tip of his cock against my anal sphincter.

He entered me slowly, his cock opening me more pleasantly than his finger had. I was penetrated, opened widely, and probed by that thick cock, and I hummed in my throat with the intense pleasure I felt. My cock was throbbing like a horny ground squirrel and leaking like a half-fucked ferret upon my bedclothes. I sprawled upon knees and elbows, my ass offered and taken.

"Oh, yes, Russell," I moaned. "Oh, yes, slide it into me. Give it to me all the way. My ass is yours, Russell."

He hardly needed any urging, but my eagerness to take his cock excited him further, so that he pushed suddenly, impaling me to the hilt. His pubic hairs were pressed into my spread buttocks. I gasped at the violence of his thrust, though happily delivered and even more happily received.

"Did I hurt you?" Russell asked anxiously.

"No, it felt great," I howled, and Natty on the rocky floor beside the bed echoed my howl. "Fuck me, Russell. Fuck my ass."

Russell pulled back and thrust his cock deep again. I thought that I would come right then. My dick leaked more freely. Russell pulled back and filled me, pulled back and filled me, filled me with his thick cock, opening me wider and deeper with every thrust, though I had taken him all the way from the first.

"Oh, it's good. It's so good," I wailed, trying to meet his thrusts with my ass.

"Yeah, it's good," Russell exclaimed. "You have a hot ass, Billy. I knew you'd like it. I knew you'd love getting fucked."

10

"That's it," I yelped. "Fuck me as if I were a she wolf. Come in my ass."

I was so close to coming that I could not hold out another minute. The fucking was massaging my prostate fiercely, pumping my cum up my shaft. "Oh, Russell, I can't hold out. I'm gonna go."

"Let it happen, Billy," Russell urged. "Oh, man, I'm on the edge. I'm gonna come right along with you."

I gripped his dick with my asshole as the wild tingles throbbed from my anus and into my dick. My orgasm was darker and richer than any I had experienced before. Uncontrollable, breath-stopping waves rushed through me, even as I heard Russell moaning in my ear. My dick bucked, sending a long stream of cum onto my bed.

"This is it, Russell," I shouted. "I'm hard at it now."

"I'm coming too, Billy," Russell moaned, pounding my ass faster as he filled me with his cum. "I'm giving you my spunk right now. It's all yours, Billy."

"Give it to me," I moaned, coming hard. The pleasure was wonderful, yet almost unbearable in its intensity. I thought I would die, and would have died happily to have it go on forever. But pleasure is fleeting, and soon my orgasm quieted to a final spasm of pleasure.

"Oh, fuck, that was intense," Russell said, pulling his cock out of my ass with a popping sound. "Now you have to fuck my ass."

"Oh, give me a minute," I moaned. I slumped forward onto my face. My asshole felt hot and wet and my insides were slippery. I stretched out on my stomach and tried not to leak.

Russell excused himself. When he had cleaned his dick, he came back and sat beside me on the bed. His hand caressed my ass, tracing along my crack. "I want you to fuck me the same way, Billy," Russell urged. "You rest for a few minutes. Then we'll go at it."

And go at it we did. It took twenty minutes for me to recover from that incredible fuck, but when I saw how Russell was offering his ass, the moon curves of his butt spread by his doggie position, my cock hardened. Russell had a hole that needed filling, and my cock was up to the task.

"You don't need to use your fingers on me," Russell said. "Just stick your cock on in. I'm built to take it, and I've been fucked hundreds of times. I open up real easy."

He was right. After I had lubed my dick and pressed the head against Russell's asshole, it seemed as though his hole sucked me in. Before I knew it, my lap was slamming his buns and my dick was encased in a hot, grainy chute that gave better friction than any mouth or hand.

"How about that, Billy," Russell said. "Now you know the secret. Now you know why guys love fucking ass."

I pulled back and rammed him, unable to control my lust. His hot hole burned my dick pleasantly, and the friction tortured my cock head. The idea of being inside of another male and fucking his ass the way he wanted set off explosions of joy in my brain. As I fucked him, I gripped the swells of his ass, and the tactile sense of his curves excited me even more. I found myself humping wildly, so wildly that Natty stood and watched with his wild wolf eyes wondering.

"Oh, man, you're fucking the shit out of me," Russell screamed. "It's great. Oh, yeah, you're a fucking maniac. I love it. Oh, yeah, keep fucking me just like that. Don't stop."

I couldn't have stopped. I was humping him so hard and fast that the momentum itself kept me going. I was a humping cony, my hips thrusting as if all of their own, as ripples of pleasure started once again in my dickhead. If I couldn't slow, I was going to come fast. I tried to retard my speed, but it was as if Russell's ass was controlling my movements. Certainly, I had no control as I bucked furiously against his butt cheeks.

"Ah," Russell wailed. "Oh, Billy, you're gonna make me come. Oh, fuck, man, you're slamming the cum out of my cock. There it goes. Oh, oh yeah, there it goes."

The throes of my own orgasm were claiming me. Had I been able to think, I would have thought my brain exploded. I don't think I was conscious at all at the last, not as the overwhelming orgasm ripped through my body, blasting me like a bomb. Everything was in orgasm, and my whole body was squirting the cum out of my dick and up Russell's ass. I banged him so hard I could hardly hear his howls and wails, even as Natty raised his head and sang the wolfish song he sings to the moon.

After the wild anal sex, Russell and I showered again under the waterfall. I enjoyed washing Russell's butt crack while he washed my cock, after which we switched. I was surprised to see that the sun was hanging low in the western sky. It was late afternoon, when I had thought it still morning. We had butt fucked the day away.

Hungry after our exertions, I led Russell beside the cold stream behind the cave where we selected six bottles of milk stout from my vast pool of chilled beers.

"How come this creek is freezing cold when the waterfall is warm?" Russell asked.

"Different springs. The hot stream passes close to a lava tube. This one comes from deep underground. It's always colder than the devil's icebox."

We cooked hamburgers in my fireplace, along with big potatoes and ears of corn. I melted a pot of butter together with cheese. Natty had his dinner while ours was cooking, though that did not stop him from begging scraps while we ate. When we finished eating, I fixed a pan for Tom and Huck before plopping down beside Russell, who was finishing his second bottle of stout.

For his part, Russell was examining my furnishings as though he was seeing them for the first time. "Billy, if you've been living in this cave since you were sixteen, how'd you get all this stuff?"

"I hike to the stores and take what I need. The people don't even look at me."

"You mean you steal it?"

"I don't call it stealing," I protested. "I take what I need."

"The stores you visit would call it shoplifting," Russell said. "Oh, well, you gotta live. But I can't believe some of this stuff. Like the bed. That highboy dresser. The carpets. The table and chairs. And this couch. How do you shoplift a couch?"

I smiled enigmatically and said nothing. We went outside to watch the sun set behind the snow-capped peaks, and the soft red light made the trees glow like angels. As Russell and I snuggled close, I placed my hand on his crotch. I could feel the bulge of his cock beneath the denim, and even in its drained condition it stiffened noticeably.

"You wanna try it again already?" Russell asked.

"Sure."

"Okay. Let's jack each other off this time."

I ran into the cave for the lubricant. Russell had his jeans off by the time I returned. Like me, he had forsaken the use of underwear as unfitting to life in nature. "I'm going commando, too," Russell had bragged earlier, tossing his briefs into the blazing fireplace, which after several days in the forest was the best place for them.

I screeched to a halt when I saw Russell's naked cock standing tall, thick, and erect in the frosty November night. Without my pants and shirt, I felt cold, but Russell's hot hand soon warmed me. We sat side by side, hardly looking at each other in the darkness, but communing intimately nonetheless. Russell's cock filled my hand delightfully. I stroked up and down his shaft, then toyed with his hooded head, twisting it like a bottle cap, flipping it lightly with my finger, cupping it with my palm. Russell emitted a keening moan as I jerked him and followed my actions on my own cock.

Of course, my cock had no hood, cut away by the malicious religious spite of my grandparents after Mom and Pop drove blind drunk into a tree. Still, the lack of a hood, though a small misfortune, did little to diminish my pleasure at what Russell was doing to me. When he cupped my dickhead with one hand and stroked up with the other, I thought that I would explode. The tingles soon arose in my dickhead, signaling approaching orgasm.

"It's starting," I breathed.

"Mine too. We're going off, Billy. We're jacking off."

I twisted his dickhead, back and forth, while I pounded his shaft. I tried to maintain my control, even while my tingles increased and my dick grew heavier. Russell's cock swelled harder as I cupped his dickhead, and he made mewing sounds that alerted puzzled eyes among the gooseberry bushes. Tom and Huck were watching us masturbate.

I had passed the point of no return; I was committed to come, as was Russell. Nothing could stop us then. We beat the cocks in our hands, giving each other no respite, no moment of pause in the approaching storm. My pelvis contracted as my cum rose in my dick, and the

14

volcano of pleasure erupted. My cum splattered into Russell's hand, decorating his arm clear to his chest. Russell's first salvo took me right on the chin, and some coated my lips. I could taste his cum in my mouth as I continued shooting my load.

When we were finished, we pulled our shirts on against the air and sat on our folded jeans. A layer of ice was forming on Natty Bumppo's water bowl, but still we sat together, naked from the waist down, savoring the night and the scent of our spent semen. Our hands were wet with cum and lubricant but we held hands as we watched the night grow.

As the air grew chillier with snow flurries, the aurora borealis came out, flitting color and light across the sky. I fondled his dick, as Russell fondled mine, and we watched the shifting northern lights until the clouds rolled across the heavens, and the frost crisped the spilled semen upon our bodies. Shivering, we rose and climbed into bed, the cum melting and sticking our bodies together.

In the morning, I awakened to bliss. While I slept, Russell had slowly opened my ass as I slept upon my side and had slipped his cock into me. I woke with a tremendous sensation of fullness, my own cock hard from the banging at my rear, while Russell gleefully bounced his hips against my buttocks.

How he had pushed his cock up my ass without waking me, I could not imagine. Still, it was a wonderful present, and I gripped his gliding cock with my anal sphincter, tightening for him as he pulled back and opening to him as he pushed forward. Considering our position, he was still filling me to the hilt; I felt his soft pubic hairs tickling my buttocks as he drove his cock deep into my rectum.

Then he slid his left arm over my waist and seized my cock, which was already close to squirting. "I'm gonna give you an anal orgasm, Billy. I'm gonna make this one even better than the last one."

Of course, the first one had been good for me, so I expected no less from this fuck. I squirmed my ass back to meet his thrusts, while his left hand pumped my dick. He was gripping my cock so hard, squeezing it so tight, abusing my dickhead so wickedly, that I could not hold out against him.

"I'm gonna go, Russell," I said. "This is it. You're making me come."

"Come, Billy," Russell urged. "I can't hold off either. Oh, man, your ass is so sweet. I'm gonna fill you with cum."

"That's it," I urged. "Shoot it into me. I want it all. Oh, fuck, yeah, here I go."

Russell started hammering my ass faster and faster as his approaching orgasm drove him. Meanwhile, he pounded my dick furiously, creating pleasure in my cock head that sizzled like lightning bolts in my brain. I was aware that he was shooting his spunk into my ass, and my open asshole and my hard cock trembled with a long series of orgasms, while Russell continued massaging my prostate with every stroke, not to mention his unrelenting hand pounding my dick that sent me into a paroxysm of pleasure and the orgasmic explosions overwhelmed me. I shot my cum and received his cum, and for a while that was all I knew.

"How about you come back with me, Billy?" Russell suggested. "You could live with me. Lots of sex every day. We'd have fun."

Natty Bumppo wailed as if he understood. "I can't go back to the people," I said, hugging the wolf reassuringly.

"Not even to be with me?" he pleaded, placing his hand on mine so both our hands were touching Natty's back.

"You could stay here," I suggested. "We wouldn't have to go near the people until the supplies run low. Then we take what we need and come back."

"You want me to be a hermit," Russell said. "I can't do that. Also, shoplifting would be wrong for me. I don't think it's wrong for you to do it, because you'd starve if you didn't. But it would be wrong for me."

"Then you'll go back to the people," I said finally. "Don't tell them about me."

"I won't," Russell said. "I promise." He didn't say anything else for a long time. He just sat looking at me. Finally, he asked, "They must have hurt you pretty bad."

I shrugged again. Suddenly he grabbed me and held me close. My heart was thundering. I didn't want him to go, but I knew that he could not stay. Only I could lead the life I lived. Then he was kissing me hard, almost bruising my lips in his eagerness, and soon we were on my bed again. His cock was up my ass, filling me again with that wonderful sensation. I had never felt so open to anyone.

When he had climaxed, he begged me to fill him again, and so I fucked him on all fours, taking him doggie style the way he liked, and banging him hard. When we finished we washed each other one last time under the waterfall while Lenore watched from a tree and Tom and Huck played on the bank. Then I watched while he dressed, and after a while I dressed. I supposed that I would never see him again, and my heart hurt me, but he said, "Christmas break is coming up fast, Billy. I was supposed to go on a ski trip, but I'd rather come stay with you. If you want me?"

I grabbed him and pulled him close. "Of course I want you," I said and kissed him hard. Then, with Natty for protection and Lenore watching from the sky, we set forth, for Russell had to get back to his college. We hiked through the woods, with me teaching him how to survive along the way.

"You're gonna keep track of the days, Billy?" Russell asked when we stopped for a few hours' sleep and a final overpowering blowjob. "That's exactly twenty days, Billy, and I'll be waiting where the highway intersects the Sandy Trace Trailhead."

Two days after we left the cave, I climbed to the top of a tree and watched Russell thumb for a ride beside a logging road that led to the main highway. Lumber trucks came past frequently, and I waited until a kindly driver picked him up. As Natty and I trudged back up the mountain, I had no doubt that Russell would appear at the trailhead at the appointed time.

("The Dream in the Heart of the Forest" originally appeared in the now out-of-service online periodical *Tommyhawk's Fantasy World*)

Rode Hard and Put Up Wet

Against the northeastern horizon, the Wallowas stood, stark and glaciated, the glistening snows of their peaks reflecting an indigo sky. To the north, the old gods had plunked down the Blue Mountains, piney, steep, and forbidding. As I slowly turned my head, surveying the horizon I spied the shape I had been seeking. A young man stood on the sparse grassland textured with Indian paintbrushes and sagebrush, with his back to me, the fringes on his cowhide chaps whipping in the wind, but his tight cowboy Levi's, which showed off the eloquent curve of his ass so enticingly, were perfectly in place. The rear seam cut a deep groove in his butt crack.

Tipping back my Stetson, I sat upright in the saddle. Ethel, the grey mare the ranch boss had selected, stood motionless as an upholstered chair. "Hey, buckaroo," I hailed.

Slowly the man turned and regarded me, his mouth breaking into an infectious smile as his eyes traveled up from Ethel's hooves to the tip of my Stetson. I felt completely naked, and I was certain that he knew this was the first day I'd set foot on a working ranch, despite the elaborate fabrications I'd penned onto my job application.

"Are you Johnnie Valdez?" I asked, knowing that it had to be him. Who else would be stranded out on the range, so far from civilization?

I urged Ethel forward. Johnnie Valdez stood still, watching our progress with interest. "Yer the new hand the ranch boss was fixin' ter interview?" he asked when we had walked close enough for casual conversation.

"Yep," I replied in what I hoped was an appropriate western inflection. "Just hired on this morning. Boss sent me out to fetch you back to the bunkhouse."

"Spect I'd best mount up then," Johnnie said, his tone leaving me to wonder whether he was mocking my cowboy pretense. I got the distinct impression that he knew I was greener than grass, and my horsy skills had been learned in a Portland riding stable. Still, there I sat aboard an actual horse, in an authentic western landscape, with a brown felt Stetson on my head, tight cowboy Levi's covering my legs, cowboy boots, a checked western shirt, and a carefully knotted yellow neckerchief.

Without asking permission or giving fair warning, Johnnie grabbed hold of the saddle horn that was situated about an inch from my crotch and flung his shanks up behind me. He settled into the saddle, his thighs wrapping around my ass so intimately that I felt my cock stiffening. I didn't let on that I was aroused though, and urged Ethel into a turn.

"Where ya from, tinhorn?" Johnnie asked as we settled into a trot.

"Here and there," I answered vaguely, wondering whether "tinhorn" was a slight. I wished I could see Johnnie's face.

He cleared his throat. "Yer one o' them 'emo' boys?"

How did he guess that? I was into the "emo" scene at one time. Actually a time not that long ago because I still owned a tee shirt that read "I like guys in girls pants," and I still had several pairs of girl's jeans in my closet back in the city. However, I had gone through a series of phases, as my mother called them, but I hadn't discovered my true calling until I saw *Brokeback Mountain*. I bought the DVD and watched the movie about fifty-seven times – okay, exactly fifty-seven times, but who's counting? That's when I started buying authentic western clothes and dressing like a cowboy. That's also when I started riding lessons, and learned a little about the lasso too. I even went to the Pendleton rodeo and watched a round-up.

On the morning Heath Ledger died, I wept for a while. Then I clamped my buttocks tight and began sending out resumes about my vast – though wholly made up – cowboy skills. June arrived before I received a response. Leaving a note for mother, I climbed aboard a bus, rode to eastern Oregon, and passed an interview to become a ranch hand at a real working ranch. I filled out my income tax forms, handed them to the ranch boss, and got put to work on the spot, with the warning that if I didn't work out, I'd be out on my ass faster than a two-peckered bull can piss. I spent the first half hour locating the bunkhouse, the chuck wagon, and the barn; I was wondering how much longer it'd be until lunch when the boss pointed toward Ethel and told me to mount up.

"Go find that goldanged buckaroo Johnnie Valdez and fetch his ass back here," the boss ordered. "I reckon he'll be off a'way yonder."

Of course, I suspected that the assignment was some kind of test, but which of my skills was being examined, I couldn't guess. I rode off in the direction the boss had suggested, still wishing somebody had offered me lunch first. I didn't have to look too hard for Johnnie Valdez. After I'd been riding for an hour, I saw a lone human form silhouetted against the horizon. Why he was out in the middle of nowhere with neither horse nor vehicle, no one had cared to inform me.

"I'm a buckaroo," I answered in response to Johnnie's "emo" question. No sense in these ranch hands getting the wrong idea about me – or even the right idea.

My assertion made Johnnie snort. Without warning, he reached his hand around and touched my cock through the denim. Of course, I was harder than a striking rattler, what with his cock tight against my butt and his chest pressed against my back. Ethel continued to trot, and we were both bouncing up and down in the saddle.

I felt Johnnie's hand fumbling with the fly of my jeans, and without warning, my cock popped out. My mind was in a whirl. What was he doing? Of course, I knew what he was doing, because he had grabbed hold of my cock and was squeezing it hard and fingering the head of it the way I loved so much. But, really, what the hell was he doing?

The enormity of what was happening struck me, and I must have trembled, for Johnnie advised, "When in doubt, let yore hoss do yer thinkin'."

For the life of me, I could not imagine what he meant, but he spit in his hand, slicked up my cock, and jacked it as though he meant it. "That's right, tinhorn," Johnnie said. "I'm all over yore pecker like a chicken on a June bug."

He was sure right about that. He knew how to jack off a cock; he had a tight grip on mine and was pounding the shaft with well-practiced strokes. I thought that I should tell him to stop, worrying that I was revealing myself, but by the time I tried to open my mouth, I was feeling too good to complain.

"Dude, that feels good," I moaned.

His hand stopped. "Dude?" He still gripped my dick shaft, but his hand was no longer moving. "Dude's purt near a fightin' word, greenhorn."

Suddenly I realized how many big city assumptions I had that were bound to trip me up. "Whoops, I meant buckaroo."

"Dude ain't a word we use out here," Johnnie advised, tweaking the head of my cock. "I don't reckon ya know nothing about bein' a real buckaroo. Howsomever, I'm fixing ter learn ya somewhat right here."

"What are you gonna learn me?" I asked, bounding harder in the saddle as his hand commenced to twitching my cockhead again.

"That's the way, greenhorn," Johnnie urged. "Ride it like ya stole it."

Don't spoil his fun – let him play with it, I thought. I'm not saying another word until he's finished. He was jacking me harder, his hand sliding up and down my shaft, and stopping only to thumb the head of my cock. Johnnie knew how to bite deep into my flesh, and he twisted my dickhead as he rubbed his thumb hard over my peehole.

Ethel trotted onward, oblivious to the passion smoldering upon her back. The feeling of fullness inflated my cock. I was getting close to the point when I was going to spurt my load. My cock seemed to lose tension briefly, just before it swelled for the big release. I was skirting the edge of orgasm and ejaculation when Johnnie stopped. He held my cockshaft, which was throbbing for release, held it, and gripped it so tight that the semen could not make its way up my tube.

"Don't stop," I moaned. "Not now, dammit."

"Yer wantin' ter get yore gun off now, pard?"

"Fuck, yeah. You got me right on the verge."

"Yer gonter shoot yore donkey butter all over this pore hoss?"

I moaned in exasperation. "Ethel doesn't give a shit. Finish me off."

Johnnie laughed. Was he only a prick tease? I couldn't believe it. He looked like a real cowboy. Except for giving hand jobs to other guys, which would've been an unusual event on *Gunsmoke*, he acted every inch the cowboy.

"I'll make ya come, but ya gotter make a promise."

"Anything. What?"

"Ya gotter pay me back for this."

"How's that?"

"Ya gotter git my *huevos* off."

22

"I'll be happy to," I said. "After I come, we'll switch places and I'll jack you off."

"Ain't what I meant, pard," he said, giving my cockhead a tweak just to keep me on the edge. Just to make me promise anything. He knew that the head on my shoulders wasn't doing me much good. The head of my cock was doing my thinking, and it had only one idea. It wanted to spit and spit hard.

Johnnie recommenced to jacking my cock, slowly, ever so slowly, too slowly to make me shoot, just slow enough to keep me on the edge. My cock seemed to be growing as it hardened like it had never hardened before. I was afraid I would pass out if he didn't make me blast soon. My balls were in an agony, and my dickhead was a spurt of flame.

"What? What?" I demanded. "I'll do anything."

"Yer gonter gimme yore ass?" Johnnie asked. "I wanter cornhole ya. I wanter stick my buckaroo cock up yore hot A-hole and ride ya, cowboy."

"Yee-haw," I said. "You won't be the first. I'd be proud to have you fuck me."

"Okay, then," Johnnie said. "We'll do it tonight. In the bunkhouse. With every buckaroo on the ranch watchin' how ya take it."

"Holy crap," I gasped. "They'll know that I like it. It'll be the tire iron, for dead sure. Just like Jack Twist. If they don't lynch me."

"Won't be like that," Johnnie promised. "Ya'll see. Ya won't be doing nothin' the rest hain't done. Including yores truly."

"Are you telling me I stumbled into a group of gay cowboys?" I howled. He went to work on my cock again. I was already so close that a few strokes would be sufficient. However, he took it slow, caressing my cockhead, manipulating my sensory organs into pumping every drop of my semen into launch position.

"You can fuck my ass in front of the whole world, if you want," I promised, somewhat rashly, but inspired by my closeness to orgasm. "Johnnie, you can pick me up and frog fuck me on live television," I shouted as the first tingles of orgasm rippled through my cockhead. Ethel broke into a gallop as I whipped up the reins in my sexual frenzy.

The tingles grew in strength. Johnnie kept pumping my shaft and torturing my cockhead. Just as the tightening of my balls drove my semen upward and my muscles poised to pump out my first shot, Johnnie gripped my cockhead in a tight squeeze and placed his thumb over my peehole. The intense sensation was so exotic and so delicious that I nearly toppled off Ethel.

"Oh, fuck," I shouted in the throes of feverish bliss. "You're killing me. Oh, buckaroo, you're killing me. Don't stop killing me."

Johnnie pulled his hand down my shaft again, freeing my cockhead to unload. A thunderous pulsing in my ears accompanied the twisting of my lips as my body contracted and a spurt of wet semen rocketed over Ethel's head. It was a glistening trail that arced through the air and fell into the purplish sagebrush. Other spurts followed, each one rising high and landing among the grasses and Indian paintbrushes.

"Oh, buckaroo," I wailed as Johnnie continued beating my meat until I was utterly drained.

"I've plumb drained ya ter an empty nub," Johnnie bragged into my ear. I couldn't respond. My heart was thundering, and my breath was heaving in and out of my lungs.

"Pull up here, pard," Johnnie suggested. "I gotter wash my hand in the stream yonder."

I looked at his outstretched hand and saw that his palm and fingers were slick with spittle and spent spunk. Glancing down at my own crotch, I saw that I had left not a spot on my Levi's. I halted Ethel and tied her reins to a dead Juniper. Johnnie slipped off with a grace I could hardly hope to match and dipped his hand into the cool creek water. Watching him humming to himself as he washed, I lowered my jeans, readjusted my cock and balls, and made myself presentable. Afterwards, we rode together back to the barn.

Johnnie helped me unsaddle Ethel. She had hardly worked up a sweat, but we rubbed her down, gave her fresh oats and water, and stroked her side before we left her in her stall.

"Let's rustle up some grub in the chuck wagon," Johnnie suggested. "I'm hungrier 'an a wolf in calving season."

The chuck wagon was a long structure with a wide porch with authentic rocking chairs. Most of the rocking chairs were occupied by the ranch's numerous cats, sleeping in the sunlight. A smoking chimney made of red brick signaled the use of the far end of the chuck wagon. The other side was a room decorated with cowhides and horns, a mounted bear that looked real to me, and several long tables.

"Lassoed the son-of-a-bitch myself," Johnnie claimed, cocking a thumb at the bear.

Six hands were sitting at one table, spearing or spooning food from large bowls and piling it onto their plates. Johnnie led me to the group. Everybody was so busy eating that they greeted me with grunts and burps.

"Sit down and chow down, pard," Johnnie urged, taking a place across the table from me. He forked a fried chicken breast off one platter and a couple of pork chops from another. I took the same meats and covered the rest of my plate with an ear of corn, mashed potatoes mixed with mashed carrots, fried onions, creamed cucumbers, and long green beans with nuts and crumbled bacon.

Ole' Dack, the cook, an effeminate man of about forty, who was the oldest fellow I'd seen so far, and would have still looked damned sexy in a thong swimsuit or even the jeans he was wearing, plunked a tall glass of iced tea down in front of me. I sugared it heavily and took a sip. After I'd eaten the biggest lunch of my life, we wandered onto the porch and sprawled back in the rocking chairs. I noticed that none of the men would disturb a sleeping cat, so we were spaced out rather far. Still Johnnie was next to me, and he told me what I could expect in the way of work.

After we had digested our lunch, we spent the remainder of the afternoon roping calves. Johnnie showed me a lot of tricks, and by the time the dinner bell sounded, I was getting good with the lariat.

Dinner was another large meal, though not quite as excessive as lunch. Still we ate steak and big buttered squashes. There was a green salad with tomatoes, and we finished off with huge wedges of huckleberry pie. After we ate, the cowboys hit the rocking chairs again. The cats had gone into the barn for the night, which would protect them from the coyotes and where they could fulfill their natural function of ridding the barn of rodents. As the moon rose and the stars shone with an intensity I'd never seen in the city, the cowboys told stories about the range, strange events, ghostly hauntings, fierce creatures, and lost gold mines.

Apparently, television reception was spotty, and there was no cable out in the wide-open spaces. I had already noted that my cell phone was useless, so I had stowed it away in my personal locker. I didn't tell any stories that night, feeling a bit new and shy. The cowboys cast sidelong glances in my direction, as if they were not too certain of me yet. As the darkness grew close and the coyotes set up a musical cry across the range, the cowboys rose as one and headed for the bunkhouse.

My heart leaped into my throat, for the memory of my promise to Johnnie was borne back to me. Would he really want to butt fuck me in front of the whole bunkhouse crew? The idea seemed too incredible to be credible. Yet, as we passed through the bunkhouse door, Johnnie patted my ass. "This is gonter be purty sweet," he exclaimed.

The cowboys leaned against the wall or slouched on their bunks in pairs as Johnnie pulled me close. The meaning of those sidelong glances and shifting faces was thrust upon me. Every one of the bunkhouse boys had been wondering how I was going to respond. They were waiting to see if I was going to put out or not, whether I was one of them, a lonesome cowboy looking for affection in the only place we could find it. My heart soared with joy, for it was as if I had awakened in paradise.

Johnnie Valdez grabbed my Stetson and tossed it onto a peg. His own sweat-stained hat landed beside mine a mere second before his hand embraced the back of my head as he pulled my lips to his.

"Yee-haw!" the buckaroos cheered as we kissed. My cock stiffened rapidly in my tight Levi's, but it couldn't have been stiffer than Johnnie's. His cock seemed to grow and grow, sliding upward so it formed an extended, chunky bulge beside his rawhide chaps.

Johnnie's hand slid down to my neck and over my shoulders. His tongue was hot and taut in my mouth, playing against my own tongue. I was so hot that I felt as if I would burst into flames. I couldn't see what the other buckaroos were doing – in fact my eyes were closed – but I could hear sighs and whispers, and nothing I heard carried any tone of disgust. These cowboys were appreciating our hot, and wholly homosexual, kiss.

Johnnie's hand slid over my shoulders and down my back. Down he traveled until his hand was squeezing my left buttock, and his fingers were tucking the tight denim into my crack. I pulled my mouth from his and said softly, "Yes, I want it, Johnnie. I want your hard cock up my ass. I want you to fuck me."

A joyous sigh rose to the rafters of the bunkhouse. I was no longer the unknown quantity; I'd just made myself one of the boys. In fact, I was a cowboy who was about to get made.

Johnnie pulled me toward his bed and unfastened my jeans. "Gotter git yore boots off," he said, pushing my ass down.

My cock was pushing out of the fly of my Jockey briefs while Johnnie grabbed one of my cowboy boots and pulled it from my foot. As he stepped forward to grab the other boot, he could not resist giving the head of my cock a quick kiss. Would Bat Masterson have taken a taste of my cock? Or Maverick? Or Paladin? Cock sucking would have added a whole new level to *Have Gun – Will Travel*. Still I could not stop singing to myself as Johnnie slurped at my cockhead before turning his attention to my second boot.

"Git along, little dogie," Johnnie urged when he had me completely naked.

"I gotta undress you," I protested, jumping from the bed and grabbing at his boots. With a laugh at my eagerness, Johnnie dropped onto the bunk and raised his feet. I had him stripped within two minutes. Then I jumped into his bunk again. Johnnie showed me an ultra-sized condom of the extra strength variety and a huge jar of something graphically called Butt Hole Lube.

I grabbed up the jar and discovered that it was water soluble and safe for use with condoms. The back of the jar gave explicit instructions for pleasurable butt fucking. I opened the jar and found it half full, a telltale that it got lots of use.

"It's plenty fer tonight," Johnnie reassured me. "And there's plenty butt grease where that come from."

Johnnie Valdez told me to slip the condom over his cock. I opened the package, lubricated his cock lightly and unrolled the rubber. Johnnie sighed as I wrapped his dick and lubricated the outside with the "butt grease." The excitement of handling his cock was almost too much for me; I just about came right then. And I wasn't the only one excited by Johnnie's hard on. The other cowboys were eyeing it greedily, and some were shooting me envious looks. I winked at one buckaroo's particularly lascivious expression.

"Lay yerself on yore stomach," Johnnie suggested. "Pull up your leg. That'll open up yore butthole right purty."

How could I resist such a sweet-talking butt-fucker? I did as he asked, assuming the time-honored submissive posture of the anally passive homosexual male.

Glad cries rent the night. "Wahoo! He knows how to take it. Wahoo!"

Johnnie stroked my ass gently as he slowly worked his fingers into my crack. Finally, his index finger touched my asshole. He lubed his finger and twisted it gently into me. I sighed with contentment as his finger opened me up. Johnnie worked in more and more of the lube until he had me quite slick. Then he inserted two fingers and twisted them around. My asshole dilated comfortably, and pleasurable sensations rushed up my ass and down my cock. My entire pelvis warmed as my body prepared to receive the delirious bliss of deep anal penetration.

"Pears like yer ready to take my whole pecker," Johnnie observed.

"Oh, yes," I agreed with a happy sigh. "Let's get to it."

I felt the eye of every cowboy in the bunkhouse upon me as Johnnie positioned the head of his cock against my asshole. I felt the pressure of his cockhead against my hole. The heaviness increased as he entered, leisurely and cautiously. His entrance was the gentlest I'd ever experienced, quite unlike my friend Larry back in Portland, who'd fucked my ass all the way through high school, usually by ramming his cock with one mighty plunge.

Johnnie slowly drove his cock into my rectum until his full weight was pressed against my ass. I felt wonderfully full. He was stretching me to my limit, and I loved every inch.

"Oh, you're filling me so good," I moaned. Opening my eyes, I saw one of the watching cowboys take the arm of another and cast a significant glance toward his bunk. Within a minute, they were both naked and lubing up from the jar. Meanwhile, Johnnie had raised his hips so that his cock pulled back to the verge of my asshole.

"Oh," I gasped, and gasped a second time as he lowered his weight so that he fully impaled me again. As he rose and fell upon me, fucking me in that enjoyable, rhythmic, and compelling way, I could see the two cowboys were following our movements. One was atop the other, sliding his cock into the passive buckaroo's submissive ass.

My cock was raging, hard and ready to shoot. Every thrust brought me closer to the edge. "You're gonna make me come again, Johnnie," I promised.

"Yer gonter git yore gun off just 'bout the time I'm a gittin' my gun off, I 'spect," Johnnie confirmed, his voice hoarse with his rising lust. "I ain't gonter hold out much longer."

"Neither am I, Johnnie," I moaned, feeling the deep massage of my prostate through my whole frame. My nipples were crinkling, and my cock grew heavier. Writhing on the blanket, I rubbed my cock against the coarse cloth. Of course, the more I writhed, the closer Johnnie got to shooting his load, and the nearer I came to orgasm. Without warning, I knew that my climax was inevitable. I had been trying to watch the fucking cowboys and listen to the soft sounds of fucking, tugging, licking, and sucking that filled the bunkhouse, but my eyelids were fluttering uncontrollably.

"I'm goin' off like keg o' powder in a lava tube," Johnnie howled.

I wanted to howl along with him, but my lips were drawn back and my tongue was protruding. Every thrust was milking my prostate gland, which in turn milked my cock. My semen had filled my dick and my balls were drawn up tight while my muscles pumped my wet spunk onto the blanket. The coarse blanket was a wonderful irritant on my throbbing cock head, which made my ejaculation even more intense and my orgasm all the deeper.

Slowly, slowly Johnnie raised up and pushed down, squeezing the last thick drops of cum out of his spent cock. I could hardly move, but my cock had spent its all already. I lay in the wet slickness of my own spilled semen while Johnnie collapsed atop me. His cock was still tight and hard in my ass, and his breathing came fast. I could feel the thundering of his heart, along with my own. After a while, he raised himself and removed the condom from his cock. Then he rolled over beside me into my splattered jism. He touched his finger to a wet spot that had adhered to his buttock. He sniffed and gave it a quick taste.

"Ya shore got yer huevos off, pard," he said.

A few of the cowboys stamped their feet and whooped, though many were too close to their own orgasms to applaud mine. Still, Ole'

Dack, the cook, bouncing on a recumbent buckaroo's hard on and beating off onto his lover's chest, called out in encouragement, "Yer all right, pard. A real cowboy knows how to come when he's fucked. Yer one of us now."

And Johnnie added as he settled close to me, "Welcome ter the bunkhouse boys, new buckaroo."

Deep into the restless night, I heard my bunkhouse mates whispering and giggling. Their speech was authentic cowboy speech, but I well knew the actions that accompanied it.

"Remember them two words, Hapgood: saddle sore," one whispered to his bunkmate. "I reckon my thirteen inches is gonter hurt a mite."

Meanwhile another was saying, "Yancy, don't you'll worry none – I've been in tighter spots than yore asshole."

Johnnie snuggled closer to me, and I noticed that his dick was hardening again as he pressed it against my bare ass. Right next to us, one cowboy was sucking another's cock. The one getting sucked advised, "Don't worry 'bout bitin' off more than you can chew, Shane. Yore mouth is bigger'n you think."

I snuggled against Johnnie, his thick cock nestled between my butt cheeks, and listened to the sounds of the night: the howling coyotes, the sighing cowboys, the cries of owls, and the moans of pleasure. Near me buckaroo sucked buckaroo, cowboy fucked cowboy, and ranch hand jacked off ranch boss. I had found my niche at last, and as I drifted into dreamland, I looked forward to many days of roping and countless nights of riding.

("Rode Hard and Put Up Wet" originally appeared in the now out-of-service online periodical *Tommyhawk's Fantasy World*)

Under the Rushes

After talking it over with the people involved, especially Will Branch, I've decided to give a complete account of the events that occurred during April of 2005. I'm only doing this because the news media got it all wrong. The national news turned Will and me into heroes and temporary media sensations, but we didn't deserve much credit. Here's what really happened:

It was the first day of spring break week at Lithia College, so Will Branch and I pedaled our bicycles out to Foggy Fenland, which most people thought was nothing but a marsh, but where we had found a nice spot with a sandy shore where the refulgent sun hit full on. The mire was only four feet deep at its deepest, so it wasn't much good for swimming; however, the spot Will and I had discovered couldn't be beat for sunbathing and other activities that might require a bit of privacy.

Wearing only cutoff jeans with our T-shirts flapping behind us, Will and I bicycled over the elevated gravel road across the sun-drenched bottomland. Our path took us along the edge of the slough where waterfowl of brilliant plumage made their home. Two long-billed curlews were feeding along the rushes, and a great blue heron and several black-necked stilts were wading near the shore. Will and I braked as a family of brown rabbits hopped across our path. One little bunny sat up and regarded our bicycles with amazement.

"Jim Finch, do you smell the wild dill blowing?" Will shouted, breathing deeply. "That scent makes me want to pound your dick until you come like a milkweed."

We dismounted and walked our bikes through the rushes and tall cattail stalks with tops just budding until we reached our spot, a sandy beach basking in the sun and hidden from prying eyes by the tall rushes, scented herbs, and thick ferns.

Will untied the blanket from the rack on his bicycle and spread it on the sand. The picnic basket had ridden behind my seat. I lifted it off and set it on the corner of the blanket. Will was still standing, though he had kicked off his sneakers. He handed me a dare you look, so I unfastened my shorts and hooked my thumbs into the waistband. I slowly wiggled out of my pants until I stood glorious in my hot-pink thong swimsuit. Will's eyes regarded my well-filled pouch with approval.

"Your turn," I said and waited until Will had dropped his shorts, catching them with his toe and draping them over a clump of green reeds. In his golden thong, Will resembled a god of ancient Greek mythology. When I touched his thick cock through the cloth, my swelling dick pulled my thong tighter into the cleft between my perky cheeks. I wiggled my proud ass and felt sexy as hell.

"I can't wait," I urged. "It's been a whole fucking week, Will. Let's do it before we eat."

"Do what, Jim Finch?" Will asked, playing innocent.

I stepped closer until my cock nudged his. "Let's do it now, Will. Right now." I twisted so our cocks rubbed hard. Will moaned, so I stripped his thong down to his knees. His cock bobbed, hardened to its full thickness.

My fingers found the head of his dick, just as they had years earlier in what was the first of a long history of giving each other pleasure. I fingered his dry cockhead with my fingers, stroking the top lightly with my thumb. Then I gripped his shaft with one hand and rubbed my palm over the tip.

"God, Jim, get the lube," Will moaned.

Laughing, I rummaged in our picnic basket. I pulled out sandwiches and bags of chips until I found the bottle that had slipped beneath the black raspberry beer. Will had decided to help me look, and his cock brushed my bare buns. A strange thrill shot through me, as though there was something I wanted – but I didn't know what it was.

We stretched out on our blanket and lubed each other. Will's hand was like an old friend on my cock: he knew how to jerk me off better than I knew myself. It was the same with me – time and experience had taught me the movements that gave him pleasure. When a guy pounds his own cock, he tends to give himself a break. He'll back off sometimes if the pleasure grows too intense. However, when you've got another guy beating your meat, he's not going to give you a break. Even when you beg for mercy, he's going to dig deep into your tingles and make you come harder than you can ever make yourself. At least, that was the way with Will and me.

My lubed-up hand was thumbing Will's dickhead in the way that drove him crazy, while he was stroking hard up my shaft and squeezing the head of my dick. Working at his dick and feeling my own getting ready to erupt into a series of orgasmic thrills, I looked past Will's pleasure-tortured face, his lips drawn back with the delicious agony that was growing within his dickhead, and saw the blue sky framed in the thick green rushes. Little finches, red crossbills, starlings, and a red-winged blackbird were sharing in our sport. The birds delayed their feeding while Will and I tumbled beneath them and prepared to spill our seed.

As the orgasmic ripples grew in my cockhead, a long-tailed weasel ran across our blanket, and the watching birds scolded him for his effrontery. It was if all nature stood in hushed expectation of our orgasmic tempest. We had attuned our bodies to the throbbing excitement of nature, and nature approved.

We moaned, we thrilled, we squirted our hot wet seed, we howled like beasts, wild, free of society's restraint, at one with the rushes, and the soft wind, and the chattering birds, and the waiting weasel. The orgasm was like thunder in my cock from the flashes of lightning in my brain. I knew I was shooting great streamers of semen, and I could feel the hot strands of wet spunk that spurted from Will's cock splattering upon my chest and stomach.

When the climax was past, we lay muttering softly, sounds that made no sense but were abundantly clear, as we rocked our hips lightly and fucked the last drops of semen out of our cocks, into each other's fist.

"Fuck, that was a good one, Jim."

"Yeah," I agreed, unable to come up with anything more intelligent.

"Want to do it again?"

"Of course. But let's eat lunch first."

Will nodded in agreement, for the long bike ride and the intense sex had made him hungry too. When we sat up, the little birds flew away with mistrustful conjecture, and the weasel faded into the rushes. I removed the caps from two black raspberry beers and handed Will his bottle. He looked at my hand, still streaked with his cum, and took the beer from me.

I swigged from my beer before I removed the wrapping from my roast beef sandwich, thick with horseradish and sliced red onion, and took a hearty bite. Then I tore open a bag of cheese puffs and grabbed a handful.

A gaggle of Canadian geese saw me open the bag, even as Will opened the bag of potato chips. The geese were soon surrounding us, behaving for all the world like a group of old friends congregating to share in our riches.

"I doubt this is good for you," I told a goose as he beaked a cheese puff from my fingers.

"Probably worse for us," Will said, fending off two geese with a few chips while he stuffed a handful into his face. "If we keep eating like this, we'll be fatter than the geese."

I grabbed some of his chips. "Nah, we're young. We can eat whatever we want."

We were dressed in our thongs, having put them on before we ate. With the sun already warming our skin, neither Will nor I could forget the day the sun burned our cocks, and we couldn't beat each other off for two weeks. As I was sipping from my black raspberry beer, I noticed that the long-tailed weasel had returned to our blanket and invited one of his relatives along. I flipped them a couple of bread crusts, and within a few minutes, the bold creatures were eating chips from my hand.

"The birds are keeping clear of those guys," Will joked. "I'm surprised the ferocious little carnivores will eat bread and chips. Even the friggin' geese are backing off."

Close up, the weasels were lean and brown with pale yellow bellies. Including their black-tipped tails, they were about twenty inches long. Their eyes were strange, reflecting consciousness that stood between omniscience and nothingness.

Will had a more material impression. "The little buggers look like dicks," he suggested.

Abruptly the two weasels bolted and the birds beat their wings. "What scared them?" I asked, alarmed, but even as I spoke sinister shadows fell across us.

"Will you look at the fairy faggots, Brother Skeet," barked a harsh country voice.

"Looks like our informant was right, boys," came a horribly familiar accent. From occasional samplings of the radio's fulsome drivel, I recognized the tones of Brother Skeet, pastor of the Last Chance Church and founder of "God's Gonna Burn Everybody Who Don't Think Like Us."

I bounded to my feet and saw four pickup trucks parked along the gravel path. Neither Will nor I had heard them arrive, and I wondered how long these depraved, self-selected Christians had been watching us. What I did know was that Jack Skeet and his boys were the most intolerant, homophobic hypocrites walking and that they were extremely dangerous. There were rumors that they had tortured and lynched several men they suspected of homosexuality. It was a documented fact that following each murder Brother Skeet preached a sermon about "them hosexual prevorts what busted Hell wide open."

A redheaded dipshit named Frank Clink, whom I knew from my high school days, pointed at a tall chestnut tree across the path. "That un's got a good limb, Brother Skeet. We can string 'em up right yonder."

Skeet examined the chestnut branch with a critical eye. "It'll do fer a hangin' tree, Brother Clink. But before we send these two faggots to Hell, we're gonna have a little fun with 'em."

"You mean..." Clink spit out a wad of snuff and the other men giggled in anticipation.

"Yeah, just like we did with them other two. We'll fuck 'em before we lynch 'em. Send the fruits to Hell with C-U-M in their asses."

Will had heard enough. Without warning, he kicked Brother Skeet in the nuts, and the preacher toppled with a shriek. Grabbing my hand, Will dragged me into the rushes. "Run, Jim," he urged, though I needed no urging. We ploughed headlong through the reeds, ferns, and cattails, running until our breath gave out, and then we fell to our knees and crawled through the muck. We had abandoned our clothes and our bicycles, so we possessed only the thongs that scarcely covered our dicks and left our asses exposed. Although, I suppose, we were trying to save our asses.

We crawled on our hands and knees for what seemed hours. I might have enjoyed the view of Will Branch in front of me, his bountiful ass cleft by his golden thong, were it not for the hunting cries of our dogged pursuers. Brother Skeet's oaths were the loudest: "Boys, we're gonna get them fuckin' fruits what kneed me in the balls, we're gonna buttfuck 'em 'till they faint, and then we're gonna string 'em up so the whole world can see the wages of sin is death."

"Amen, Brother Skeet," shouted his followers.

"Why do homophobes hate us so much?" Will whispered as we crept desperately through the rushes.

"Because they're queer but can't own up to it – even to themselves," I answered.

"Right on, Jim," Will agreed. "Look how their first thought was to fuck us in the ass. They're the Queens of de Nile."

"Do you ever think what it'd be like to have a dick sliding up your ass?" I whispered, watching his buttocks tighten as he crawled.

"I guess I'd give it a try sometime," Will said. "But not with Brother Skeet's mob."

"I didn't mean we'd put out for those assholes," I said. "I was thinking about butt-banging each other. I'd take your cock anytime you wanted, Will."

For a while, we heard the men's pickup trucks racing down the cinder path and their calls to each other as they beat the reeds. We had been crawling through the mire for nearly two hours when I saw that we were approaching a clearing.

"Hey, Will," I said. "There's a cabin ahead with a big SUV parked outside. Maybe we can call for help."

Taking a quick look for our pursuers, Will and I sneaked to the cabin door. We had never traveled that far down the path, so we had no idea that anybody had built along the shores of Foggy Fenland. The cabin was a single-story dwelling, only about eight hundred square feet in size, though it appeared to be tightly constructed. Its poured concrete base lifted the beams above the marshy ground. The slough found its source in the Foggy Fenland directly behind the cabin.

"They must be duck hunters," I whispered to Will as we stood in considerable trepidation before the door. To knock or not to knock?

Suppose the inhabitants were part of Brother Skeet's bunch? We'd be delivering our quivering asses to our hunters. Standing in only a pink thong as the sun dipped low in the sky above the rushes and a cool breeze rustled the tops of the ferns, I had never felt so chilled, so naked, nor so vulnerable.

Will looked at me, his eyes filled with questions. I drew a deep breath and rapped my knuckles upon the door. Never had a rap sounded so loud, and it was met promptly with a thunderous din as though a thousand dogs were woofing in warning. They sounded like gigantic dogs.

"Oh, crap," Will said as the door slowly swung open. He gripped my hand so hard that my fingers went numb.

"Mustard. Ketchup," came a ringing voice from inside. "Be quiet, boys. Do you want to scare the life out of our callers?"

Suddenly, standing before us was the most beautiful man I had ever seen – even including Will, though I wouldn't tell him so. Our host stood about five-ten, had frosty blond hair cut short, creamy skin, and perky muscles. I could see his muscles clearly because he was wearing only silk boxer shorts. His eyes traveled down our bodies, muddy, mucky, and scratched after our crawl through the bog, lingered over our thong swimsuits, and traveled back to our fearful faces.

"Hurry in, boys," he urged. "We don't want Mustard and Ketchup getting out and rolling in the mud."

Another man stood inside, holding the collars of two magnificent Golden Retrievers. Like his friend, he was good looking, and he was wearing only silk boxers. Once Will and I were inside with the door closed, the man released the two dogs. They promptly sniffed Will and me up and down and indicated that they would enjoy a good wrestle.

"Some men are hunting us," I blurted, stroking the dogs and fending them off at the same time. "They said they're going to rape and lynch us. Can we use your phone?"

"Rape and lynch?" the man who'd opened the door gasped. He glanced at his partner. "Boys, was it Jack Skeet and his bunch?"

"Yeah," Will said. Will and I introduced ourselves. The men told us that they were Hugh and Reggie. Reggie, the beautiful guy who had opened the door, told us to follow him.

"You boys need a shower," he suggested. "After that, we can find a way to get acquainted while we're waiting for Skeet's bunch to show up here."

"You're not gonna give us to them?"

"Hardly," Reggie said. "You boys are gonna have to trust Hugh and me."

Will and I stepped into the shower together, still wearing our thongs. After we'd rinsed off most of the muck, we pulled off our thongs and wrung them out. The warm water was a relief after our ordeal, and we began soaping each other. I was running a soapy washcloth up Will's buttcrack when the shower door slid open and Reggie joined us. My jaw dropped at the sight. Reggie looked even better naked. His dark, untrimmed cock was half-hard already, his gym-sculpted buttocks protruded enticingly, and his purplish nipples were swollen.

"Did Jack Skeet catch you boys jerking each other off?" Reggie asked to break the ice. "Oh, don't play innocent. Hugh and I have seen you in your hidden spot."

"I don't know," I said. "They arrived after we shot our loads, but they might've been spying."

"Yeah, they're sneaks," Reggie nodded. The shower door opened again and Hugh, naked as Reggie, stepped in. Hugh wasn't as strongly built as his partner, but he did have a sweet thick cock. His ass wasn't as muscular, but it was perky and rather girlish.

"Don't you guys do anything but beat each other's meat?" Hugh asked. "Don't you ever suck cock?"

Will turned red and his cock throbbed visibly. I grinned. Will and I had discussed cocksucking, but we had not yet worked up the nerve to try it.

"You haven't lived until you've felt a man's mouth on your dick," Hugh said. Hugh slowly slid to his knees before Will. As the warm shower spray beat upon his back, Hugh touched his tongue to Will's cock. Will moaned as Hugh kissed the tip of his dick.

"Don't you love watching them get hard?" Reggie whispered to me, directing my attention to his own swollen cock. Of course, mine was also soaring. And Hugh's.

Hugh licked down Will's shaft, flicked his tongue around his cock, and up the other side. He gave Will's cock a thorough tongue bath, returning repeatedly to the head where he kissed and licked the rim around the head and the tip. Will's hands involuntarily clasped the back of Hugh's head, pulling the other man's face onto his throbbing erection.

"You ever thought about doing that?" Reggie asked. I thought Reggie planned on sucking my cock, just as his partner was blowing Will.

"All the time," I confessed. With a bolt of excitement, I caught on that he was asking if I wanted to suck his. I was interested, but I hesitated. "I've tried it with a banana."

Reggie placed my soapy hand on his erection. "This is no banana, Jim. Keep gripping my shaft with your fist and go to work on the head with your mouth. You don't have to take it all. Just get a little taste."

Hanging tight to Reggie's cock, I slid to my knees. My hand drifted down his silky back until I was stroking his brawny butt. His cock stood solid before my lips, and I touched my tongue to its tip. The effect was electric – more of a lightning bolt. As my tongue tasted the tip of Reggie's cock, I heard a clap of thunder – the lights flickered.

One taste of his cock was sufficient. I was seduced. I was devoted to sucking it. I kissed the hood, mouthing it with my tongue and my lips. Without warning, without me thinking about it, Reggie's cock was traveling over my lips until I felt the base of his dickhead on the inside of my lips. Reggie hadn't moved, hadn't forced me, hadn't stuck it into my mouth. I had done it myself. I pulled back until it was out of my mouth, and as it brushed the outside of my lips again, I realized how much it belonged in my mouth. I wanted to suck it. I wanted to nurse on it, torment it with my lips, my tongue, my whole mouth, until it erupted and the creamy spunk coated my tongue and slid deliciously down my throat like a rich, sweet cream.

"That's it, Jim," Reggie moaned. "Suck me. Suck me off."

I rolled my eyes upward to see his face, which was unutterable bliss revealed, and over his shoulder I saw Will's face, near ecstasy from the ministrations of Hugh's mouth, yet watching me suck off Reggie with strange delight.

Even as I sucked Reggie, I knew that after this day my relationship with Will would be different. Before, we had made love as boys do, and although we would continue to masturbate each other, we would be open to new pleasures. I foresaw bliss such as I had never known.

However, that speculation only promised future bliss. Reggie's was the present cock in my mouth, and my hopes were wisps of smoke compared to the flesh I was going down on then.

"That's it, Jim," Will encouraged. "Blow him. Suck him off, Jim. Make him come in your mouth."

I sucked more furiously, gripping and stroking Reggie's fine ass with both hands while my mouth formed a hot chute for his dick. "Oh, Jim, you're doing it right," Reggie moaned.

"Ah, Hugh, you're gonna make me come," Will howled. "I'm getting real close."

I felt an electrical tingle and smelled burning sulfur in the shower. A close clap of thunder ripped the sky. Reggie pushed my head off his dick, and Hugh stopped sucking Will.

"Don't stop now," Will yelped.

"It's a thunderstorm," Hugh said. "Didn't you feel that lightning bolt? A direct hit might have killed us. We'll be safer on the bed. Besides it's time to switch."

Mustard and Ketchup were plastered against the bathroom door. When we pushed it open, the dogs leaped fearfully, woofing and yipping. Through the window, we could see wild lightning spears splitting the clouds and striking the ground in long terrible forks. The thunder became a din, and the cloudburst hit the cabin, the rain gushing down the windowpanes so heavily that we could see nothing.

The two dogs dived under the bed while the four of us piled onto it. "I guess that storm will send Brother Skeet and his mob packing," Will proclaimed as he stroked Hugh's cock. Those were Will's last words for a while. He discovered the delicious sensation of a cock in his mouth, and the only sounds coming from him were wet, sucking ones.

Events had pushed Brother Skeet from my mind, and I forgot him again as Reggie began licking my cock. As the storm snarled without, Reggie mouthed my cock and his hands stroked my ass. His fingers explored into my buttcrack while he sucked me, and the sensation of the intimate touch heightened my pleasure.

"Oh, Reggie, that's fucking terrific," I groaned. "Oh, yeah, you're sucking me so good."

Meanwhile, Hugh was encouraging Will, who was sucking as if he'd been born to the task. "That's the way, Will. Oh, fuck. Like that. Work the rim with your lips and tongue. Ah. That's the way. You're a natural cocksucker."

Inspired by the praise, Will rose to further heights, driving Hugh nearly mad with pleasure. I couldn't believe that Will and I had been such dunces. Yes, years of beating each other off had been great, but we could have been mixing masturbation up with some serious mouth action. "Just wait until next time, Will," I declared, my voice nearly a shriek as Reggie tongued my cock toward the edge. "We're gonna use more than our hands. Even what we talked about earlier."

The picture of Will and me sucking each other's cocks and of fucking each other in the ass was too much. I howled, "Oh, I'm getting close, Reggie. I'm gonna get my rocks off in your mouth."

Reggie stopped sucking immediately, and Hugh pulled his cock out of Will's mouth.

"Why'd you stop?" I yelped. I was in pain. I had been close to the jumping-off place, the moment when I was going to orgasm no matter what, and Reggie had stopped with my dick teetering on the periphery.

"Nobody gets to come yet," Reggie proclaimed. "We're all gonna go off at once."

Hugh beamed. "We'll link up a four-way."

The rain was still coming down hard, though the thunder and lightning had ceased. The dogs remained under the bed as the four of us shaped a square. In the new arrangement, Hugh sucked my dick, I sucked Will's, and so on. That cock I had jacked to orgasm so many times was projecting toward my mouth. My eyes crossed in trying to look at it. I felt Hugh taking my cock into his hot mouth. Slowly I closed my lips around Will's dick and touched my tongue to the tip. He tasted of salt and musk.

Will made a low sound of pleasure in his throat. We were all so close to shooting our loads that I knew we would come right away. We'd gone to the edge of orgasm and stopped, and as we linked, we were a potential vortex of hard throbbing cocks, sucking mouths, contracting muscles, and rising semen. Will was leaking his seed onto my lips even as I took him into my mouth.

Hugh's mouth was a hot, wet, sucking chute. He sucked me hard and fast, until I found my own head matching his rhythm on Will's cock. Will was thrashing as he sucked off Reggie. Opening my eyes, I saw Reggie rocking in utter abandon, and I knew that he was coming in Will's mouth. Will had to be swallowing the ejaculated spurts; where else could they be going but down his throat and into his stomach?

That vision was with me as my cock tingled heavily. The tingles in my cockhead grew into an intensity that stopped barely short of pain. The pleasure was rhythmic and enormous. Then my muscles contracted, shooting my spunk into Hugh's mouth. I tasted something sweet and salty, wet and slick, and I knew that Will was pumping his cum onto my tongue. However, my own orgasm and ejaculations were so intense that I was hardly aware that I was swallowing Will's dick cream. I could only rock and thrust, nodding my head vigorously on Will's cock, abusing the head of his cock with my lips and tongue as I shot salvo after salvo of wet spunk down Hugh's throat.

The rain had stopped by the time we staggered into the kitchen. Will and I had dressed in our thongs again, while the other guys had slipped into their boxers. Reggie prepared gargantuan mugs of hot cocoa to which he added generous dollops of Bols crème de cacao and crème de menthe, and he set out a platter of colossal oatmeal cookies swollen with hazelnuts, black walnuts, and pecans, and dried apples, cherries, dates, raisins, and pineapple. "Hugh and I baked these earlier," he said. "Before we knew that anybody was coming."

We laughed at the pun, which seemed clever while we were all delirious from the incredible sex. We ate cookies and listened to the eaves dripping. Lured by the odors and our voices, Mustard and Ketchup ventured from under the bed. I slipped them a few bites though Reggie warned us not to gratify the beggars. I noticed that he broke his own rule.

While we were sipping from our mugs, Mustard and Ketchup bellowed a warning and rushed to the door. My heart leaped into my throat, and Will turned pale. Parting the curtains, I saw four pickup trucks stopping in front of the cabin. "Is there a back door?" I gasped. I had been having so much fun that I had completely forgotten about the indefatigable Brother Skeet and his flock.

"I've been expecting those boys," Reggie said.

"Persistent bastards," Hugh mused. "Probably hid out in their vehicles during the rain and then charged up this way. We'd better get changed."

"What?" I gasped.

Reggie regarded Will and me with a steely gaze. "Remember when I asked you to trust us?"

"Yeah," I gulped, hardly able to believe that Reggie and Hugh would hand us over to Brother Skeet.

"This is it," Reggie said. "I need you boys to go out there and stall Skeet and his crew while Hugh and I get dressed."

Will and I exchanged a mind-melding glance. After we had sucked cock together, we had to trust Hugh and Reggie with our lives. Squaring my shoulders and tightening my buttocks, I pulled the door open, and Will and I stepped forth into the glare of the searchlights on the pickup trucks. Horns blew with malevolent glee as the preacher and his men fixed their lights upon our nearly naked bodies, our dignity preserved only by our minuscule swimwear.

"Who-ee, we got the tootin' fruits now, Brother Skeet," Frank Clink shouted, and his brethren echoed his malice. "Amen. Glory Hallelujah. Amen."

"It's 'bout time. Get them thongs off 'em and bend 'em over the back of the truck," Brother Skeet shouted. "And see if there's more fairy boys inside that cabin. Boys, it's a good night for a bonfire."

"We're gonna burn 'em at the stake?"

"Damn straight. Give 'em a taste of Hell 'fore they get there. Help ol' Satan recognize his own."

We had to stall them for a few more seconds. I couldn't think of anything, but Will raised his arm with an accusatory gesture, pointed at Brother Skeet, and intoned, "I have said to corruption, Thou art my father: to the worm, Thou art my mother and my sister." I could never have come up with a cooler quotation.

Brother Skeet's flock stopped, gape mouthed, uncertain, looking to their leader for guidance. Jack Skeet looked as though he were about to shit out the entire New Testament Apocrypha. Even I had never realized that Will could command such a dramatic presence, much less quote verbatim from the Book of Job. After a befuddled silence, Brother Skeet shook himself and screeched, "Lay hold of them faggots and search the cabin."

Rough hands seized Will and me, while two of the crew charged the cabin door. They had reckoned without the dogs, however. Mustard and Ketchup jumped against the luckless simpletons and knocked them backward down the porch steps. Behind the dogs came two men wearing state police uniforms. Reggie was holding his service pistol in one hand and a collection of handcuffs in the other. Hugh was brandishing a shotgun.

In less than a minute, Brother Skeet and his bunch were the ones bent over their pickup trucks while the two officers frisked and cuffed them. Will and I smiled beatifically as Reggie read the vigilantes their rights and placed them under arrest for attempted murder, attempted rape, attempted sodomy, possession of illegal weapons, possession of illegal substances, attempted kidnapping, assault, and assorted hate crimes. We laughed out loud when Reggie assured Brother Skeet that he would be spending the night in a secluded cell with the meanest, toughest butt fucker in the county jail.

A van from the jail arrived immediately, for it turned out that Hugh had alerted the sheriff before he ever climbed into the shower with us. Deputies had been watching the road, and when Brother Skeet and company moved in on the cabin, the law swooped down upon them.

After we watched the van carry Brother Skeet and his men off to jail, Hugh and Reggie drove Will and me back to our spot. Our bicycles were wet but undamaged, but our shorts, T-shirts, blanket, and picnic basket were soaked. Two reddish-brown muskrats were raiding the bags of soggy chips and the remains of our sandwiches. Still, the air had a clean smell. Wild geraniums had opened with rose and purple blossoms, and the rain had sprouted new growth on the quail plants, the winecup clarkia, and the naked bloomrape. Above our heads, a hunting owl hooted.

Will and I wrung out our cutoffs as best we could and slipped them over our thongs. Reggie patted my ass as it disappeared into the wet denim. "Guess you don't want to sneak into your dorm in a pink thong."

We loaded our bicycles and other stuff into our new chums' SUV. As we drove up the path, we saw a mule deer with grayish fur and new antlers watching us from the willows. Farther on, a bobcat, identifiable by his short tail, darted across our path.

"Glad we didn't disturb him while we were crawling through the rushes," Will quipped.

"Better a bobcat than Jack Skeet," Hugh commented.

Hugh and Reggie were reluctant to take credit for the arrest, and I wondered whether it was safe to be "out" if you were a part of the state police. The next morning, the media credited Will and me with capturing the gang. The *Lithia Ledger* headlined COLLEGE STUDENTS CAPTURE VIGILANTE KILLERS. Suddenly, we were heroes. That afternoon we received a call inviting us to a special celebration at the White House where the president would honor our bravery in a Rose Garden ceremony. We were scheduled for pick up by Air Force One for a ride to Washington with President Bush.

The next day, however, Will answered the phone, listened with an increasingly bothered expression, and announced, "It's all off. The White House. The Rose Garden. Air Force One. They refused to give a reason."

Grinning, I pointed to the campus newspaper's headline, printed just an hour earlier. The bold type read GAY STUDENTS TRAP CHRISTIAN HOMOPHOBE RAPE SQUAD. It was a truth the Bush White House couldn't swallow.

The case didn't come to trial until August, after Brother Skeet's church had gone bankrupt paying for his defense. Will and I testified, as did Reggie and Hugh. Brother Skeet's lawyer cross-examined us vigorously to no effect. In the end, the jury found the whole bunch guilty, and Judge Cross sentenced each one to twenty-five-to-life. Judge Cross even assured Brother Skeet that he would gladly sentence him to lethal injection if evidence surfaced of his other rapes and murders.

Will and I became the two most famous students at Lithia College, but our new fame didn't make us forget our friends. Every weekend we bicycled along the slough to the Foggy Fenland. Sometimes we met Reggie and Hugh at our favorite spot, and other times we went directly to the cabin where Mustard, Ketchup, and their owners greeted us with joy.

("Under the Rushes" originally appeared in *Best Gay Erotica 2010* from Cleis Press)

Sam's Turn

In April 1977, I was living in the old frat house on Biscayne Bay next to Krome University. My fraternity brothers were downstairs watching a late afternoon rerun of *The Carol Burnett Show*. The day was tropical as only a spring day in South Florida could be, meaning that my third floor room was about ninety-five degrees. However, the Atlantic breeze cooled the sweat on my face as I hunched over my unmade bed with Red's cock stretching my asshole.

"Yeah. Fuck me," I whispered so the guys down below wouldn't hear. "Red, you're sticking it to me real good. Fill me up, ass fucker. Oh, yeah." My knuckles were white from clutching the unmade bedclothes.

Hard and fast, Red slapped his hips against my butt cheeks. His hands gripped my hair, pulling my head back as he tugged. "Fred, you've got the tightest hole I've ever fucked."

Red's compliments provoked me to greater heights of ecstasy, but they also filled me with fear. What if the guys should hear us? I could imagine no greater catastrophe than having them learn that I was gay, and not only gay, but actually getting my ass reamed in the frat house.

"I'm taking it, queer boy," I sighed, gripping his slippery cock with my anal sphincter. "You're a horny homosexual stud, Red." (Red and I thought it liberating to use explicit expressions like *fill me up, ass fucker* and words like *queer, fag,* and *homosexual* during sex).

Red started humping even faster. The fucking felt so good that I bit my pillow to keep from screeching with joy. My asshole gripped his stout cock. His cock's head pressed my joy buzzer with each stroke, sending ripples of pleasure over my body. (Looking back, I'm almost embarrassed to admit that we referred to our prostates as joy buzzers).

"Oh," I grunted. I gripped the bedclothes, clawing the bedspread and biting my pillow.

With a piercing wail, Red shot his wet load into my ass; then he collapsed with his boner still buried in my rectum.

"Hell, Fred, you're a sweet butt fuck," Red gasped, shrill in his enthusiasm.

"Shhh," I cautioned, my heart beating fast. My fraternity brothers frequently joked about homosexuality, but I had no idea how they might react. Most of the guys sounded open to the idea of a blow job, but they also used words like *faggot*, *sissy*, and worse. I had even sat with them while the television news reported on the new gay rights movement in Miami. Beyond a few rude jokes, none of the guys commented on the reports. As a result, the thought getting caught terrified me, even though the risk was stimulating. Somehow, fucking in the frat house made it all the more exciting, even better than calling each other *gay* or *homosexual*.

Miami had become the scene of contention about homosexuality. There had long been an unorganized gay population, but they had never faced down oppression or prejudice. A former Miami mayor once closed all the gay bars, deeming them a menace to children. When I was in elementary school, a police officer came to our assembly and warned us about the homosexual menace. Since I had become that menace, I felt like a stranger in a strange house. Then I had taken Red in my bedroom.

I first met Red at the gym. My gym clothes consisted of white cotton: a white tee shirt, jockey briefs, and gym shorts from my high school days. A few months of doing squats had rounded my ass so the rear of my white shorts poked out like an invitation.

As was my routine, I was pushing my butt back as far as it would go, the out-the-window thrust, while I finished three sets of squats. In my mind's eye, I fantasized that the other guys were drooling over my ass. Then my dreams came true; Red approached me from behind.

"Nice buns, guy," a strange voice whispered, and a strange hand gave my ass a surreptitious pat. I just about shot a load into my briefs as I whirled to see who was molesting me. I saw and stood utterly numbed with shock. He was beautiful, with long red-golden hair and dreamy features. His skin was creamy and his sculpted body was shapely without looking brutal.

Red's cock had swelled in his abbreviated gym shorts. He didn't have a full boner, but his dick was signaling his interest. An hour later at the home of his aunt and uncle, he tongued my asshole until I was squirming. Then he fucked my ass, reaching around to jerk me off while he pumped. I drove back to the frat house with a silly smirk plastered upon my face and a wet, gooey present up my ass.

We fucked in his room almost every day. Then one day I invited Red to visit me at the frat house – cautioning him not to reveal our secret. Overcome with passion, we ended up fucking furtively over the guys' heads.

Red had also been thinking about the day we met. "I'm glad I picked you up at the gym and turned you out." Red was no more a felon than I, but he liked using prison slang. He made gay sex sound dangerous and masculine.

When I laughed, Red started stroking my dick again. "Now, let's think about turning out your fraternity brothers."

"Holy shit!" His suggestion nearly made me poop.

"Yeah, how about the guy in the next room? The one with the brown hair who comes traipsing down the hall in his bikini."

"Who? Sam?" I said, raising my ass so he could get a tighter grip.

"You only got one other guy on this floor, don't you? And he's got an ass as cute as yours? And he's old enough to be legal?"

"Yeah. But Sam?"

"Yeah, Sam. Let's fuck him, Fred. Let's turn him out until he's a horny fuckin' faggot just like you."

"And you, queer butt."

"And me," Red agreed with a happy grin.

I shook my head. "I don't know about Sam."

"He's gay, whether he knows it yet or not. Look at that bikini he wears."

"Are you kidding? Most guys wear Speedo swimsuits today. After Mark Spitz won the Olympics you know. I wear one too – as do you. I saw it in your drawer. Look at the pants you wore over here. Seamless Cheeks. Just like most guys wear. Sam's fashion statement doesn't mean he'd gonna wanna put out."

"I know about guys, Fred. I spotted you clear across the gym."

"Takes one to know one, Red."

"Fuckin' A, Fred. So let's do Sam."

"What if we approached him and he blabbed like a little bitch?"

"Maybe he'd be doing you a favor, Fred. You've got to come out of the closet some day."

A cold fear swept over me at the words. Coming out of the closet was the most difficult thing I could imagine. Meanwhile, Red kept rubbing my cock, his thumb tickling the rounded head, even as he continued his argument.

"Fred, these are the seventies. It's a new world. There's a gay rights movement now. There's even a Transsexual Action Organization, and GAA staged events during the Republican and Democratic conventions. We're getting power. A few months ago the Dade County Commission passed an ordinance outlawing discrimination against us."

I trembled again. I knew that Red was right, but I also knew that the political state was not as rosy as he claimed. As soon as the Dade County ordinance passed, the orange juice goose Anita Bryant and her gaggle of evangelical loons commenced honking for repeal.

Red released my cock. He went into my bathroom, washed off his cock in my sink, and brought back a soapy washrag. Red cleaned the oily lubricant out of my crack and washed my asshole with the soapy rag. I loved being Red's favorite fuck, and I didn't want to share his thick cock with Sam.

"Where is Sam?"

"He went to the beach. With his girl friend. He's into all that cunt-fucking shit. I can't believe that he's gay."

"Fred, you're gonna have to lay it out to Sam and your other fraternity brothers. They can't be so closed-minded. These are the seventies, dammit."

A cold sweat broke out on my forehead. "Red, I want to be a lawyer. Homosexuals aren't allowed to become lawyers – not in Florida. My fraternity brothers must never know. Never."

Sam had started playing with my cock again as we cuddled naked on my bed. "Fred, don't you realize that my aunt and uncle know what's going on when we shut ourselves up in my room? I have no secrets from them, and you shouldn't hide the truth from anybody either." He paused for intentional dramatic effect. "You ought to call your parents and tell them too."

Red's urging me to divulge my darkest secret made me horribly uncomfortable. "Red," I said. "My parents are kinda lame. Do you know what my mother would say if I asked if you could spend the night?"

"What?"

Acting in my own voice, I said, "Hey, Mom, do you mind if Red stays over?"

Switching to a falsetto, I answered, "Of course not, Freddy; I don't mind your little friend sleeping over."

Little friend tipped Red into gales of uproarious laughter. "Oh, not so little, Freddy," he boasted, stroking his cock. Red just didn't get that my parents still thought me a kid. I was almost twenty-two. Red was twenty. And Sam was nineteen.

Outside, a car kicked up gravel. Red jumped to the window. "Sam's back." Red's cock was still half-hard. I couldn't tear my eyes from his protruding tube, still hot from fucking my butt hole. Red also had a yummy ass. His creamy, albeit tanned, butt was rounded; it stuck out in a jaunting manner that made me want to kiss it. In fact, I had kissed it.

I climbed out of bed and slid my hand over Red's butt cheeks. Red shivered with pleasure as I moved my hand. Falling to my knees, I spread his cheeks and touched my tongue to his hole. I licked around the rim before I slid my tongue into his sweet hole.

"Oh, yeah, lick my ass, Fred." Red paused to wiggle his ass; although, he kept staring out the window. "Sam's cute. I wanna fuck him." He paused thoughtfully. "Have you ever thought about fucking him, Fred?"

The question jolted me, because I had thought about it. I pulled my tongue out of Red's ass, and he turned to meet my eyes. "How many times have you flogged your dolphin and shot your cum in that direction?" Red pointed to the wall that separated Sam's room from mine.

"A hell of a lot," I confessed. "Of course, I've thought about fucking Sam's sweet ass. Or sucking his cock. Or the reverse." Oh yeah, I sure had thought about it. However, I had never suggested any such thing to Sam. And I'd never heard Sam say anything that would indicate in the remotest way that he would be interested in gay sex. Plus, we'd both made lots of statements that put down faggots.

Red turned back to the window. "Sam's wearing his bikini. A purple sunset pattern. I love how the Lycra clings to his cock and ass."

The way Sam slammed his car door proved that he was pissed off about something. I looked over Red's shoulder, pressing my hard cock against his buttocks. Sam had already disappeared through the front door. Soon we heard him stomping up the stairs.

"He's pissed."

"Yeah, females will do that to you," Red agreed.

I stuck my head out my door and called to Sam. He had become even more of a hunk lately. Most college students pack on fifteen pounds of fat during their freshman year, but Sam had grown more muscular and – dare I say it – more curvaceous. His solid ass packed his Speedo, which rode up his butt crack. The sight of his tempting anal cleft stiffened my cock. Hung like a racehorse, Sam packed the front of his bikini too. His thick cock and big balls made a bulge in the thin Lycra.

"What are you so pissed off about, Sam?"

"That bitch. She got me all hot, and then she wouldn't put out. Girls must lie awake nights thinking up ways to torture guys."

I didn't make any conscious decision. In spite of my fear, I heard my mouth saying, "Sam, come to my room for a second. There's someone I want you to meet."

Sam looked down at his skimpy swimsuit. "Maybe I better change."

"Shit. If it's good enough for the beach, it's good enough for us. Come on."

Sam innocently strolled through my doorway and froze with his mouth agape. He looked at me standing naked, my cock still half-hard. Red lay on my bed, his solid erection pointing toward the ceiling. Two naked guys in a bedroom reeking with spilled cum.

"Sam, this is Red. I met him at the gym. Red likes guys."

Sam's mouth dropped wider. An army could have fucked his mouth-hole. My heart stopped beating – Sam might shout an accusation and my fraternity brothers would come running. Then I looked down. The front of Sam's bikini was stretching. The outline of his trimmed cock head through the thin material made me drool.

Sam finally shut his mouth. Then he opened it again, "So, have you guys been jerking off, or what?"

Red grinned at Sam's growing hard on. "No, Sam, we weren't jerking off," Red gloated. "I fucked Fred." He paused to watch the effect. "I stuck my cock up Fred's horny ass, humped his hole, and shot him full of cum."

Staggered, Sam looked to me for confirmation or denial. My face was burning, but lying would have been fruitless. "It's true, Sam. I take it up the ass."

Sam's swimsuit tore with a ripping sound. I gawked at Sam's naked cockhead emerging from the rent fabric. A more resilient soul, Red reached for Sam's cock and ran his finger over the smooth dick head. "Wanna join us, Sam? Your girlfriend left you with blue balls. We'll give you some relief."

"I...ah," Sam grunted weakly.

Red turned Sam and kissed the back of his neck. Sam sighed with infinite longing when Red's hands roamed over his bulging ass cheeks. After seeing Sam's reaction I jacked my dick toward Sam's face.

"You know you want it, Sam," Red coaxed.

"Look, Sam. I'm jerking off. You don't wanna waste my hot cum, do you?" Still jerking with my right hand, I spit in my left and rubbed Sam's cock.

Red kissed down Sam's spine while Sam stood speechless but lusting for gay sex. Sam's cock was firm and throbbing in my hand. I slid to my knees and licked his dickhead, rubbing my tongue firmly over the rim where his foreskin had been cut away. I opened my mouth for the head of his cock. It was nice, like a big lollypop, and Sam moaned with rapture as I tongued his tortured dick.

All this while, Sam's cock had still been sticking through his torn Speedo. Ripping the bikini down the back and casting it aside, Red drove his face into Sam's ass crack. Sam started like a spooked rabbit and drove his cock deep into my mouth, but as Red kept licking, Sam began to rock his hips forward and backward. It was obvious that the sensation was driving Sam nuts.

Sam started fucking my mouth like a wild man. He humped his hips, riding Red's tongue and my lips. Relishing Sam's sexual aggression, I mouthed his cock for full value. He was leaking a thin pre-cum, a taste that lingered on my tongue while I went all the way down his cock until its big head was thrusting into my throat. I discovered I had a natural ability to fuck Sam's cock with my throat.

"Oh, suck me off, Fred," Sam burst out. "Suck me until I shoot. I wanna get my ass fucked. I didn't know it before, but I know now."

He was loud. I wanted to shush him, but Sam clenched his hands behind my head so I couldn't stop sucking him off. "Yeah, lick up my ass crack, Red," Sam yelled at the top of his lungs. "Stick your tongue up my ass. That feels so fucking good. I like it. I wanna get my ass fucked."

My lips were pressed into Sam's crispy hairs. His dick got firmer as I sucked it, tensed, ready to unload. I pulled back to tongue bathe his cock head.

"Oh. I'm gonna squirt," Sam hollered. "I'm gonna shoot my cum into your mouth, Fred. Keep licking my ass, Red. Lick my hole while I shoot off in Fred's throat. Here it comes."

Sam's cock bucked, and a wet gob covered my tongue. I swallowed the fresh jism as the next spurt splattered into my mouth.

"Fred. I'm shooting off in your pussy mouth. Oh, fuck, yeah. Swallow my spunk, Fred. Eat my cum." Shot after shot of Sam's fragrant cum squirted, and I swallowed every drop.

When Sam's heavy ejaculation ceased, I held his cock in my mouth until he had oozed his last drops. I licked his cock until it started going soft. But it only went a little bit soft, just enough so it could recharge. Sam was as horny as a three-balled tomcat, and although he'd gotten off a load that eased the worst pain, plenty more cum was boiling in his balls.

Standing dizzily, I gripped the old dresser. The woodwork spun, and I laughed. "Fred's cum drunk," Red affirmed. "Sam, do you remember offering us your ass?"

"Uh, yeah, I guess I must have said that."

Red started walking Sam toward my bed. I guessed that was my cue to butt out. I assumed that Red wanted to get his cock into Sam's asshole, but I was wrong. Red surprised me. "Fred hasn't got his rocks off today, Sam. How about letting him fuck you up the ass?"

Sam looked at me. "I'm scared, Fred. I want it. I want your big cock up my ass. But I'm scared."

Staggering to the bed, I grabbed Sam's sexy ass. My dick was throbbing to release its load. I whispered, "Sam, I want to push my wet cock up your tight hole and fuck you full of my cum."

"I'm scared, Fred."

"There's nothing to be scared of, Sam. I love getting fucked, and you will too."

"I'm scared that I'll turn into a homosexual."

Red laughed so loud that I thought the whole house would come running. "Sam, you're already queer. You are a homosexual. You're always going to be a homosexual. Now it's time to start acting like one."

Sam made a mewing sound in his throat. He wanted it. He needed it. I slid my fingers into his crack and fingered his asshole. "Just imagine my cock going up your ass, Sam. It's gonna feel so good. So warm and so wet. It's gonna fill you. You'll love it. You won't be a slave to your bitchy girl friend anymore."

Sam's ass was suddenly burning my fingers. His whole body flushed as he broke down and cried out, "Oh, yeah, fuck me, Fred. Fuck my horny ass."

"I'll fuck you, Sam. But I want you to do something while I fuck you."

I had lubed my index finger with the jar Red had brought, and I pushed it all the way up Sam's ass. While he was still attempting to form a reply, I gave him a prostate massage.

"Oh, Fred. What are you doing? I never felt anything like that."

"You've got a joy buzzer up your ass, Sam. I've got one too, and so has Red. That's why men like to get fucked. It feels so fucking good when a thick dick hits your buzzer."

"I'll do anything. Anything. What do you want me to do?"

"I want you to suck Red's cock while I'm fucking you." Red's huge pecker would keep Sam from shouting out.

"You wanna make me a cocksucker, Fred?"

"Yeah, Sam. You'll suck cocks real good. Giving blow jobs is fun."

"Okay, Fred, I'll suck Red's cock." Sam bestowed Red with a trusting smile, and Red smirked knowingly.

55

Bending Sam over the bed, I lubed my cock. Then I shot more lubricant into Sam's asshole and worked in three fingers at once. I stretched his asshole until I had four fingers holding him open. I slicked his rectum until a hotshot pilot could have flown a Boeing 727 up his ass.

Sam couldn't hold his tongue while I finger-fucked his virgin hole. "Oh, Fred," he shouted. "Open me up, Fred. Fuck me until I come."

My dick was so rigid that I feared it would split. I couldn't wait any longer, so I pulled my fingers out of Sam's ass and slid my cock down his crack until I pushed against his brown hole. Sam wailed with joy as he felt my cock. "Stick it in, Fred," he screamed. "Stick your butt fucking cock up my horny ass." He didn't resist for a second. As I pushed against his ass, he pushed his asshole open. Oh, how Sam submitted to sodomy – he wanted to get fucked.

"You're taking it, Sam," Red assured him.

Sam moaned loud enough to be heard in Fort Lauderdale.

"Does it hurt?" I asked.

"It's nice. Push it in. Fuck me hard." Red started laughing then, and I could hardly resist cracking up myself. Even so, I was too interested in penetration to succumb to humor. I kept sliding my cock into Sam's ass. He got my thick nine, because I didn't stop until there wasn't any more to push in. Sam was sweating, but whether from pain, or fear, or joy, I couldn't tell until he began shouting again. "Oh, Fred, I'm so full. I'm full of cock," Sam shrieked. "Oh, you big ass fucker, you've got your whole cock up my ass. Oh, yes. Yes. Fuck me. Fuck my queer ass."

I tried to stop his mouth as I pulled my cock back and slid it in again, humping his tight hole. His ass fit close around my cock, and I was surprised at how grainy it was. It rubbed my dick with coarse friction. I had never felt anything like Sam's ass. Beating off was never as good.

"Oh, Fred. Oh, fuck, Fred," Sam groaned. "That's so fuckin' good. Yeah. Fuck me hard, Fred. I'm your dog, Fred. Ream me out."

"His dog?" Red howled.

My heart thundering, I slammed my dick home, harder and harder, as Sam begged for more. Red watched with an eager grin as he waited for Sam to suck him off. "Shut him up, Red," I urged.

Red fed his dick head into Sam's mouth. "Suck on this, Sam," Red ordered. "Suck me off, cocksucker."

Sam's head started bobbing up and down on Red's cock while I humped him hard and fast. Meanwhile, Sam squeezed my cock with his asshole. I couldn't believe that he could pinch down so hard. He was bringing me off fast, and I couldn't stop it. Not that I wanted to stop my wild orgasm. I wanted to make it last, but I had to blast my cum.

"Ah, Sam. I'm gonna do it in your ass," I whispered hoarsely. "Oh, Sam, I'm gonna shoot you full of spunk. This is it, Sam."

Waves of pleasure vibrated up my dick. The overwhelming thrills filled my whole midsection as the powerful orgasm carried me on its swells. I felt the first muscular contraction as I blasted a big wet spurt into Sam's rectum. Waves of pleasure beat against me as I shot burst after burst of hot cum into his bowels.

Sam never stopped milking me off while I came. He pinched with his asshole until I thought that he'd wring off my cock, but I let him milk me dry. When I pulled my dick out of his ass, Sam gave Red exclusive consideration. A look of incredulity settled on Red's face as if he couldn't believe what Sam was doing to him.

"Oh, Sam," Red howled. "Oh, you wonderful cocksucker, I'm gonna die. You fuckin' magnificent cocksucker." He never heard me trying desperately to shush him. I hoped that the television was covering the noise.

Red's eyes squinted and blinked uncontrollably as the mighty orgasm ripped through his cock. His mouth drew up like that of a man who had been gut shot. "You cocksucker. You're killing me. Fuck. Don't stop."

"What are you doing to him, Sam?" I whispered as Red began to resemble a victim of zombification.

Sam continued to bob his head furiously as Red moaned, gasped, and grunted. He wasn't capable of any human noise, so powerful was the orgasm that Sam gave him. I could see Sam's throat working as he swallowed Red's cum.

Finally, Red collapsed backward on the bed with a mighty, "Ah." Sam took his mouth off Red's dick and looked at him. Then he looked at me. "How was it?" Sam asked.

"You're a natural born gay boy. Just like me."

Red recovered his breath. He sprawled on the bed staring at Sam with wild eyes. "He's more than that," Red said. "He's fuckin' insatiable. I never had a blow job like that in my life."

"He milked my cock off with his ass so I thought that he was gonna kill me," I chipped in.

"I have felt the truth," Sam announced.

"Huh."

"Goodbye, girlfriend. Hello, Gay Liberation."

"Have you lost your marbles?"

"It's sex euphoria," Red pronounced. "Sometimes it happens to guys like us. I've seen it before. You've been going along trying to fit in, trying to be straight, trying to conform, but all the time you knew something wasn't right. It wasn't working for you. Then, Blam! You get a taste of the good sex – I mean gay sex – hot guy-to-guy fucking and sucking. Next thing you're announcing your sexuality to the world. I did the same thing."

"I didn't," I said.

Sam pulled up his bikini, which did little to conceal his nakedness considering the cock-sized hole in the front and the significant rip in the rear. "I'll be back in a second."

"Where are you going?"

"I thought I'd just nip downstairs and spring the news on the guys. They won't have to take my girlfriend's calls anymore."

"No," I gasped. "I haven't come out yet. They don't know about me."

Before I could stop Sam, he was out the door. I could hear his voice from below. "Hey, guys, anybody want a great blowjob? I'll suck your cock. I'm gay, and so is Fred."

Stricken, I looked to Red for answers. "What are we going to do now?"

Stifling a leer, Red pretended to give the question serious consideration. Finally, he asked, "What's the difference between a straight guy and a gay guy?"

"Huh? What?"

"About six beers. I guess you'd better send out for a few cases."

With an anguished moan, I buried my face in my pillow. Red patted my ass and laughed. My heart thudded as I waited to hear what would happen next. Strangely, the only sound issuing from below was a loud nonstop slurping.

(A version of "Sam's Turn" originally appeared as "Sam Feels the Truth" in the now out-of-service online periodical *Tommyhawk's Fantasy World*)

Love Has No Ears

Later, I could never pinpoint the instant that I fell in love with Archie Davis. Archie and I were students at Coral Shores High School on Plantation Key, which was small enough that everybody knew everybody, but we were never friends until senior sailing class.

In those days in the Florida Keys, students wore cut-off jeans and tee shirts to class, so we didn't change for sailing. Every morning around 9:00, our class of senior boys and girls trooped across the ball field and down the slope to the shore. The reef, a quarter mile out, made our patch of ocean smooth as bathwater. The warm waters of the Atlantic swished gently against the dock where we launched the sailing dinghies the school provided.

Coach Stout evaluated our abilities during the first day of class and partnered the strong with the weak. I was afraid she would stick me with Jill Mendoza, who was nice enough, but her big ass threatened to swamp the boat, and she sweat profusely.

My heart leaped into my throat when Coach Stout looked at me, glanced at Jill, and then said, "Dave, I'm going to pair you with Archie."

Archie sweat too, and he had a nice curvy rump, but his ass wouldn't sink the dinghy. Getting paired with him was the dream of a lifetime. I had been admiring Archie from afar, not only because he was a skilled sailor, whereas, I was fair at best. I vaguely realized that he embodied the undefined image I'd been jerking off to for years. He was not tall, particularly, but he was nicely shaped. He had the reddest hair I have ever seen on any human being. Combined with his green eyes, his coloring and mannerisms made him almost cat-like. He moved with a fluid grace.

The first day that he and I cast off our dinghy, I was holding a bag of grass that I'd bought from Elaine Albury, whose family had the best pot patch in the Keys – the stuff they grew was damned near lethal in its psychedelic properties. A bunch of seaweed had attached itself to the rudder and Archie was trying to clear it. He was bent over the back of our dinghy, and the sight of the seam of his cut-offs pulling up his crack emboldened me. I cranked up a joint that would put a Havana cigar to shame, fired that sucker up, and took a mighty toke.

"Do I smell...," Archie said, his voice trailing off as he turned and saw the magnificent doobie.

Archie took a toke that would have harelipped half of Southeast Asia, and our dinghy sailed wildly toward Tavernier Key. "We're not supposed to land," I advised, hoping in my drug-induced state that he would want to land and explore.

"Fuck it," Archie said, stoned after one hit off the potent shit I'd laid upon him. He took another toke, guaranteed to knock his socks off – had we been wearing socks. "Man, I'm fucked up," Archie confessed as our dinghy shot toward the mangrove shrouded island, off limits to students from our high school.

"We're about to hit the reef," I shouted, releasing the pin in the daggerboard and pulling it up.

"This is good shit," Archie said, even as some instinct caused him to lower the sail. We slid over the sandy reef and hit the inlet gently, and I tied us off to the mangrove roots.

Archie looked around wildly as he realized we'd stopped. Still he took another hit off the joint. "Let's explore," he suggested.

"Explore, yeah," I managed, being more stoned than he. Exploration was my design, though perhaps in a sense he had not yet considered.

As we climbed onto the path through the mangroves, I copped a feel of his generous rump. "Wow, man," he aspirated in his wrecked state. "That's my fuckin' ass."

"Yeah," I agreed. "It's nice."

Someone had blazed a trail by placing planks over the mangrove roots. We walked the planks until we emerged from the mangrove swamp to the sun-drenched dune at the center of the island. The center was a long, narrow oval of sea oats growing out of the coral sand. Key lime bushes, hibiscus, coconut palms, banana stalks, and two flowering flamboyant trees softened the isolation of the clearing.

The joint had burned out, but we were so wrecked already that we did not relight it. Of course, we were ravenous. Archie investigated the banana stalks and returned with a bunch of finger-sized bananas, creamy and succulent. We sat down side by side amid the flowers and the exotic grasses while we ate. From the mangroves, a bird rattled a tropical sound, while at the far end of the key, a woodpecker went merrily to work.

The pot had destroyed our inhibitions. I pulled off my tee shirt and shorts. My cock was hard and eager for release. Archie looked at my erection with wonder, as if mine were the first he had ever seen. Slowly, hesitantly, he touched the circumcised head with the tip of his forefinger. As he made contact, he shuddered and his stoned eyes gleamed. I knew, instantly, instinctively, that he wanted my dick.

"Let's jerk off," Archie suggested, pulling off his clothes. He was wearing white jockey briefs under his cut offs, and his cock was so hard that he had trouble getting the waistband over it. I was amazed at its thickness, rising so magnificently from the blazing red hair of his crotch. I tweaked the head between my thumb and forefinger.

"Let's jerk each other off," I corrected. "I'll beat your meat while you beat mine. See who can make the other guy come first."

Archie's breath came rasping with his lust. "Okay," he said, spitting into his hand and seizing my dick with a will.

There is no other sensation on earth like having another guy jack you off while you're stoned out of your gourd from a monster reefer. Archie's fist squeezed my dick. He drove his hand down into my pubic hair before sliding up and over the head of my cock. For a second I was so enthralled that I could not grasp his dick or even form any coherent thought. Then the sight of his thick cock standing so eagerly awakened me to my duty. I spit into my own hand and grasped hold.

"Oh, Dave," he moaned, as I teased his dickhead and squeezed his beautiful balls. His balls were tight and smooth, indicating how full of spunk he was. I was careful not to squeeze enough to hurt, but enough to milk.

We were both so stoned and so horny that ejaculation came quickly. Deep throbbing tingles rushed though the head of my cock. "This is it, Archie," I yelped. "I'm gonna squirt."

"Me, too," Archie gasped. "Let fly, man."

His cock stiffened even harder in my hand, and I distinctly felt the throbbing buck as a great squirt of hot jism shot from his cock and arced through the air. My own orgasm was claiming my whole body. My lips curled back and my nostrils flared, as the deep pleasure that was almost painful in its intensity claimed me. Still my hand squeezed Archie's cock and my fingers twisted his cock's head.

"Oh, wow, I've never had it this good," Archie blurted as blasts issued from his cock. Meanwhile my spunk was leaping from my cock and splattering Archie's chest.

We collapsed side by side as our orgasms stilled. When we had caught our breaths, we looked at each other and laughed. "My cum is running down your arm," Archie giggled. "You got some on your shoulder too."

"That's okay," I said. "You ought to see how I decorated you. It's all over your chest and stomach."

"We better get cleaned up," Archie said – way too late.

"Boys," a voice called through the mangroves. "Dave. Archie. Are you boys on the key?"

"Shit, Coach Stout spotted our boat," I swore. "We're screwed."

There was no other way but to pull our clothes over our semen streaked bodies. I wiped my arm with the inside of my shirt, which made us snicker in spite of our apprehension. We checked each other's exposed skin for telltale signs before we made our way back along the path through the mangroves. Coach Stout was waiting beside our dinghy, since she was too afraid of snakes to attempt the passage through the mangrove roots.

"What have you boys been doing? Don't you know that Tavernier Key is off limits? You weren't supposed to go ashore."

"We were blown ashore," I said, which was an obvious fabrication.

Coach Stout sniffed the air. "Have you boys been doing drugs?"

"Drugs? Us? Never!" I protested, shocked to my core. I hoped that the coach would not notice the bulge the bag of pot made in my shorts. For his part, Archie was still too wrecked to respond.

The coach escorted our boat back to the school's dock. Soon we rejoined our classmates who were tripping lightly up the path to the school. Jill caught me and whispered, "What happened?"

"Nothing."

"Don't bullshit me, Dave," she chided. "You and Archie are stoned, and you both reek of C-U-M."

64

"You're hallucinating," I scoffed, buying her silence with a joint. "Besides, how do you even know what cum smells like?"

"I got three brothers," she explained, as if that explained anything.

From that day on, the coach kept her eye on Archie and me. We didn't get another chance to land our sailboat on an uninhabited island. Still, we became the best of friends. Two nights after our adventure, I slept over at Archie's house. His parents didn't suspect a thing as Archie and I spent half the night pounding each other's cock.

But if his parents didn't suspect, and my parents didn't either when he slept over with me on another night, the rest of Coral Shores High was buzzing. Everybody knew for a fact that Archie and I were a couple of "fags." Jill swore that she hadn't mentioned the smell to anyone, which convinced me that she had blabbed.

"You've heard what people have been saying about us?" Archie asked.

"Yeah," I admitted. "I've heard. Who gives a shit? They've got a proverb in Haiti: 'A hard cock has no ears.' My dick doesn't care what people say. And neither does yours."

I was afraid that Coach Stout might reassign Archie and me once the rumors reached her ears, but she was either open-minded or stubborn – I could never figure which one. Nevertheless, she kept a close watch during class time.

Graduation was still some months off when Archie's birthday rolled around. "Guess what I'm getting?"

"A boat?" It wasn't a difficult guess. Archie's father owned a boat dealership, though he mainly sold powerboats.

"A sail boat. A twenty-five foot sloop – with a cabin, Dave." His eyes were blazing with excitement.

We tested out the cabin on her maiden voyage. On Friday afternoon, we sailed through the channel into the Bay of Florida and anchored beside a deserted key. We smoked one of my giant doobies, downed half a bottle of Ripple Pagan Pink wine, and considered ourselves sophisticates. Stoned and slightly buzzed from the wine, we built a campfire on the beach and roasted a big T-bone, four ears of corn, and a couple of potatoes. We ate on the beach, lingering until the sand flies drove us into the water.

"Shit, my fuckin' wallet is soaked," Archie complained, stripping off his cut-offs and tee shirt. His briefs were transparent in the water, so he stripped them off. Not to be outdone, I threw my clothes into the boat. My cock was hard before I touched Archie.

We were standing in blood-warm water up to our stomachs. The rising moon left a path of luminescence upon the surface, and beneath we could see our protruding cocks. Suddenly Archie pulled me to him and pressed his lips to mine. I opened my mouth to receive his tongue, and he promptly slipped it in. I had never felt anything so exciting. For weeks and weeks we had been jerking each other's cock, but that was our first kiss.

We ended up back in the cabin of his boat, got more stoned, and tried sucking cock a little, before we ended up jerking each other to orgasm. Then Archie did something wild. He tasted the cum I'd ejaculated onto his hand. As he grinned lewdly with his tongue protruding between his teeth, I chanced a taste of his spunk. Cum wasn't anything like I had feared, but I took only the one taste – then.

We made out for a while after we ejaculated, which made me feel good in ways I could not express. The notion that our relationship wasn't only about the sex was important to me, and I thought that it was important to Archie too. At least, he acted that way, and at school neither of us tried to hide the truth. Of course, we were getting teased and harassed a bit, but we were in the Florida Keys, not on the mainland, and a sense of "everybody goes to Hell in the tropics" prevailed. In a way, we were accepted.

A month before graduation, we sailed toward Key West. We stopped at an unnamed key somewhere off Big Pine. Three key deer stood along the shore, looking as if they had never seen a human. Colorful flamingoes were standing knee deep in the water, and allspice bushes were putting out a fragrance. Archie and I cooked meat, onions, carrots, potatoes, and parsnips on long wooden skewers. I'd scored more grass from the Albury family, even though they'd raised their price to an outrageous twenty dollars an ounce. After getting high, we sipped Boone's Farm Apple Wine and ate directly off the skewers.

The trade winds were keeping away the mosquitoes and sand flies, so the beach was nearly paradisiacal. We ate until we were stuffed; then we smoked another joint that knocked us halfway to Krypton. Archie had loaded some of his comic book collection, so we read the second *Giant Superman Annual* and the first *Giant Batman Annual*.

In my stoned condition, I could not understand the simple plot of the comic book, but I identified with the caped crusader. Mostly, I liked Robin, whose green briefs looked incredibly sexy. Archie and I were naked, as usual, and sporting boners inspired by the grass and the comic book characters. Suddenly, Archie gripped my arm. "I want us to do the big one, Dave," he murmured.

"The big one?" I was still lost in the comic book world.

"I want you to fuck me, Dave," Archie breathed. "Fuck my ass."

The thought of sliding my cock into Archie's ass was almost too much for me. Of course, that's what I had wanted all along. Every time I saw him bend or squat in those cookie-cutter cut-offs my dick had thumped with desire. But there was something else I wanted, something deeper, darker even, something unspoken. "Okay, Archie." I hesitated for a full minute. Then I said, "But after I fuck your ass, I want you to fuck mine."

Suddenly Archie's hot hands were cupping my butt cheeks. "Yes, Dave," he moaned. "I want to. Yes, I do. I want to fuck you. I want to come in your ass. Just like I want your cum in mine."

Archie's erection was poking my lower abdomen as he stroked my ass. I placed my hands on his rounded buttocks, squeezing them like delicious melons. "Let's do it now," Archie said, his lips moving close to mine. We kissed hard, sucking tongue, until our need grew so great that Archie flung himself down on our blanket. Beside his towel, he had hidden a tube of lubricant, which he handed to me.

I slicked my dick, resisting the urge to grip it too much and ruin the moment. Then I squeezed a glob onto my forefinger and touched it to Archie's asshole. "Yeah, Dave, slide it in," he urged. "I want it."

With a growing sense of wonder, I slid my finger into his grainy hole. He was tight but I soon had him lubed and loosened. "I think you're ready to take my dick, Archie."

"Yeah. Let's find out what it's all about, Dave."

I slipped the head of my dick into him. "Oh, god, it hurts," he shrieked.

"Do you want me to pull it out?"

"No!" he shouted. "Okay, yeah, just for a second. I'm gonna change position."

When I pulled my cock out of his ass and raised my weight off of him, he pulled his right leg up nearly to his chest. "That should open me up," he offered. "Try it again."

I slipped my cock into him rather cautiously, remembering that I was going to be next, but that time he did not cry out. "That's better, Dave. I feel full, but it doesn't hurt. Is it in all the way?"

"No."

"How about you go deeper?"

I had been having trouble not pushing in deeper because his hole was tight, hot, and potent with friction. Just pushing in nearly made me shoot my load. I let gravity pull me downward and I drove my hips forward until I was smashing his round buttocks.

"I'm in all the way, Archie," I advised. "I'm gonna pull back a bit and hump you."

"Yes," he urged. "Oh, man, I think I'm gonna come."

I raised my hips and pushed down again slowly. Archie moaned as I lifted a second time. "Are you all right."

"Don't stop," he urged. "It's really good, Dave."

I humped him a little faster, pulling my dick up farther and riding home. Archie was gasping and moaning all the while, and I thought sure I'd killed him when he gave a sharp gasp, followed by a low keening sound. His asshole throbbed and contracted as though he were milking my cock. The familiar tingles started in my cock head, and my whole cock grew heavier. I was on the verge of orgasm.

"I'm gonna come in you," I said.

"Do it, man," Archie said. "I just got off."

Only then did I realize that I had butt fucked my friend to orgasm. The thought was so exciting that I crashed through the barriers of release in a second. Pleasure better than any hand job could deliver rushed through my groin. My muscles contracted and sent my first spurt into Archie's ass. Delirious waves of orgasmic trills rushed through me. I could feel my own asshole dilating as I unloaded, and still I bounced upon Archie's hot round ass until I had milked my cock of every drop.

My heart was pounding and my breath was coming in gasps when I finally rolled off him. Archie straightened his leg and lolled upon his stomach, holding my cum in his ass. Yet as he turned and looked at me, I saw in his emerald eyes a flash of triumph and a gleam of joy. He had taken my cock, just as he had taken my cum, and he was pleased with himself.

I stepped into the surf with a bar of soap and washed my cock. Then I returned to our beach.

"Are you ready?" Archie asked.

"Yeah," I gulped. "I thought you'd want to rest a minute."

"I can come twice," Archie bragged. "As you well know."

"How do you want me?"

"Same way I took it," Archie said. "I read that it's the best way for the first time."

"Ah-ha! You planned this."

"Yeah," Archie said with a smirk, as I prostrated myself and angled my right leg in the position that had worked for him. I couldn't see Archie, but I supposed that he was lubing his cock. Then I felt his hands on my ass, and I felt his finger pressing against my asshole. "Take a deep breath, Dave," Archie suggested. "That's what the book recommended."

"Archie, I've got to read that book." I drew a deep breath, and Archie slipped his finger into me. It felt great. He fingered my ass, working his finger this way and that, stretching me open, withdrawing to squeeze in more lubricant, and then pushing into me again. After a couple of insertions, his finger seemed to get bigger.

"I've got two fingers in you, Dave. You're ready to take my cock."

So he slipped it into me, and I discovered that it really is better to receive a cock. After my outstanding orgasm and ejaculation, I did not orgasm then – not that night – but later I would experience the same pleasure I had given Archie. In fact, the next afternoon I was bending over the rail of the sloop while Archie was banging me hard, when I suddenly knew that I was going to come. The orgasm did not begin in the head of my cock, but in my rectum, and it traveled up my cock, and when I ejaculated, the contractions were deep and dusky and carried the pleasure of the forbidden.

Every weekend for the remainder of the school year, Archie and I camped out on his boat (as his mother described it), and we took each other to heights of sexual bliss. But beyond the sex, there was our companionship. We cuddled and told each other everything, until I knew Archie far better than I knew my parents – if I knew them at all – and he knew everything I had ever done and pretty much everything I had ever thought. Before long we were finishing each other's sentences, so intimate were we. We even answered for each other in class, which became a school joke, but the humor was generally good-natured.

One guy alone tried to bully us, but we ganged up on him, and he found that his own friends were not as supportive as he had hoped. The confrontation ended without a punch being thrown. Five years later, that bully came out of the closet and became a major force in the Act Up group.

After graduation, Archie and I spent an idyllic summer. Then I went on to college, the same my father had attended, and where he had graduated from law school. Archie went to junior college, and we only saw each other during my breaks. "Let's never part for long," I urged during spring break after passionate love play on his sloop.

Perhaps love has no ears, just as the Haitians say about a hard penis, so Archie did not hear me, nor did I hear him. Our parting came shortly thereafter, in the turbulence of the times: the Vietnam draft, drugs, Nixon, Watergate, the years of Reagan, and the advent of AIDS. The hideous descent into folly and deeper disappointment. My first love, my first of many lost loves, if ever you read these words, know that I hear your voice yet speaking to my heart – but a hard cock has no ears.

("Love Has No Ears" originally appeared in *Best Gay Love Stories 2009* from Alyson Books)

Archie's Tongue

Through our senior year, Archie Davis and I were inseparable to the point that everyone scented the flowering of our relationship. However, this was the Florida Keys where a gay fling was considered a minor peccadillo (though worthy of rich gossip), even among high school students. Farther north where the Bible Belt buckled, we would have been shunned, battered, investigated, and jailed.

In our high school's sailing class, the coach teamed Archie and me up, and on our first voyage together, we beached on uninhabited Tavernier Key, smoked a joint, and ended up jerking each other off. Over the next few months, we discovered the pleasures of anal sex, fucking each other with the innocent freedom of the 1960's. We even sucked each other a bit, but nothing we did prepared me for what happened on the night of the Fourth of July.

Archie's father, who owned a boat dealership, had presented Archie with a twenty-five foot sailing sloop for his birthday. That vessel saw a lot of action during our voyages around the Bay of Florida. We explored little islands, camped out, befriended key deer, and developed our sexual intimacy. Then, on Independence Day, while fireworks were blossoming off Tavernier Point, Islamorada Yacht Harbor, and the Tea Table Bridge below Lower Matecumbe, Archie Davis placed his lips on my asshole.

We had anchored off an unnamed key, cooked a supper of burgers and baked sweet potatoes over an open fire, and ate naked on the warm coral sand beneath swaying palm fronds. As the sun sank into the Gulf of Mexico and night blooming jasmine scented the air, we discovered that our cocks had erected themselves. Setting aside his can of Bush beer, Archie fingered the swollen head of my dick. "No need to ask what you're thinking, Dave," he said.

No need, indeed. His cock was as hard as mine. I gripped his thick shaft and began diddling his dickhead.

"Hold off, Dave," Archie said. "I want to try something we haven't tried before."

I could not imagine what that might be.

"Roll over," Archie suggested.

I rolled onto my stomach and pulled up my right leg. However, this was nothing we hadn't tried. Archie had fucked my ass about twenty times by then, and I had fucked his tight butt an equal number. We had been topping each other for months. However, it wasn't his dick that I felt against my asshole; it was his mouth. Archie pushed his face between my buttocks. His long red hair brushed my butt cheeks as he drove his nose and mouth into my crack. His tongue darted out and touched my anal sphincter.

An explosion of joy filled me. Only kings, potentates, emperors, commanders, caliphs, rajas, pharaohs, czars, mikados, sultans, negasus, sherifs, and werowances could feel what I felt then. As Archie licked around my asshole, my cock nearly exploded. I was in raptures. I had a sense of power, deep erotic power, and the power mingled with a sense of adulation. Archie idolized me. He adored me. He worshipped my ass.

I sighed with euphoric contentment as Archie rimmed around my hole. He licked up my crack until his tongue bathed the small of my back. Then he licked downward until he reached my ball sack. As he bathed my butt crack, he became more urgent. His lust to drive his tongue into my secret place grew upon him. I felt his exalted need, and for a moment, I thought that our consciousnesses had merged. I was Dave, jubilating from Archie's oral ministrations, but I also felt what Archie felt. Somehow, I tasted the enchantment of kissing another boy's asshole, though I had not done it myself.

Archie continued ravishing my anal cleft while his enchantment grew. He rimmed around my hole for a long time while my body tilted on the verge of rhapsody.

"Oh, yes, Archie," I gasped, and he sensed my hedonistic soul's desire. With aching transport, he opened my anal sphincter with his tongue and pushed inside. Nothing I had ever experienced, including the joy of having his cock and his expended semen inside of me, prepared me for the gay beatification. I was Dave the Blessed, bewitched, enraptured, and paradised. Titillating, thrilling, intoxicating tickles transported me.

"Archie!" I yowled, sounding more like a wild thing in heat than a human being. Words fail me; overused metaphors such as "banquet of the soul" or "cockles of my heart" could not describe the ecstasy that was so much more than the purely physical. Archie's mouth was on my asshole – His tongue was up my ass – Such profane terms to describe a sacred action.

The contractions and dilations of my asshole as I passed through shuddering orgasm, a sexual punch that grew from the delectable scent of violets into the prankish joy of throwing a rock through a windowpane, met Archie's firm tongue like a game of Truth or Dare. Archie drove his tongue deeper and held it in place while my orgasm grew and heavy spasms shook my groin. My cock flung my semen upon the warm sand. As my orgasm stilled, a cloud sailed across the face of the moon and a tropical bird warbled from the mangroves.

Afterward, Archie slipped his cock into my ass. He humped me, and I met his motions gleefully. But even as I received his wild dick ride, I knew I could never give back the gift he had given to me.

Since then, hundreds of men have touched their mouths to my asshole before they drove in their cocks. Most of the time, I feel a shadowy echo of the ancient thrill, but only an echo. When Archie licked me, he was doing it because he genuinely loved my asshole and made love to it with his tongue. Thus, when men kiss my ass before fucking me, my mind harkens back to that strange Fourth of July, that final night of innocence, when Archie Davis placed his mouth in my anal cleft and I discovered that I was born to command that men worship my asshole before I granted them the pleasure of filling my booty.

("Archie's Tongue" originally appeared in *Brief Encounters* from Cleis Press)

Kenny's Key

When the offshore breeze captured my sail, I felt a heady release that was almost orgasmic. The Sunfish responded merrily to the gentle wind, speeding me across the lightly rippled surface of the blood-warm bay. I slid over sandy bottoms bright with parrotfish, spotted rays, and queen angels. The exhilaration of the hot tropical sunlight, the clear green water, the westerly gusts, and the exotic sea creatures turned my thoughts from Brady's pitiless voice mail message.

Almost turned my thoughts – yet I could not help remembering the last time Brady and I had made love. He nailed me face down in the submissive position, as usual, while he hammered his cock into my ass. I felt the tremendous sensation of fullness while he gleefully bounced his hips against my buttocks. My own cock was hard from the banging at my rear entrance, but I wasn't close to coming. Brady thrust hard and fast, his tempo increasing as he came close to orgasm.

"Oh, yeah, I'm gonna shoot it to you now. I'm gonna fill your ass with spunk."

"Wait," I breathed, "let me get there too," but he started pounding my ass faster and faster as his approaching orgasm drove him. He was shooting his spunk into my ass before I had a chance to participate in his ecstasy.

"I'm going, Dan," Brady crowed. "Oh, man, I'm filling you with cum."

We were doing it bareback, as always, because we had sworn to be true to each other always, so there could be no risk. When Brady finished, he pulled his cock out and ran to the bathroom to wash. I rolled onto my side, willing my enjoyably tortured and dilated asshole to tighten, and feeling the wetness of the lubricant and Brady's hot cum inside of me.

My cock was still hard, so I began to jerk off alone and rather sadly. Brady returned from the bathroom, and before I could come, he broke the terrible news.

"That was the last one, Dan."

"Huh?"

"Your last butt fuck from me. I've met someone else."

"What?"

'You gonna have to move out, Dan. Tomorrow."

"What the fuck? I live here."

"Not anymore. You gotta be out by noon."

"Where am I supposed to go? Goddamn it, Brady, I've been helping you make your house payments."

"Yeah, but my name is on the deed. And you're gone, Bucko."

Had he considered that final fuck to be a comfort fuck? A mercy fuck? Or was I merely the fucking asshole of the moment? Who the fuck knew?

The moment spoiled, I gritted my teeth as I tried to banish Brady's image from my thoughts. To forget his ready smile. His self-deprecating humor. His desire to please me in the kitchen, if not in bed. Literally tossing caution to the winds, I let the breeze carry me where it would, even as the yellow Florida sun caressed my nearly naked skin. Not until I attempted to return to shore did I realize that I had gone too far.

Desperately, I tried to tack as the hotel employee had shown me, but the vagrant wisps of wind only carried me farther from the placid beach where I had launched. I was no sailor, the Sunfish was not equipped with a radio, and I had not brought my phone. I did not even have a shirt to wave. I could have stripped and waved my Speedo – it was fire engine red. However, no matter how much notice my red swim briefs attracted close up, they were far too miniscule to catch anyone's eye from that ever-increasing distance.

"It's the easiest boat to sail," the hotel's beach boy had assured me, eyeing my package. He continued giving me instructions before committing me to the gentle waters of the bay, but my attention was only half on what he was telling me. I did not listen, so eager was I to get away from everybody for a while, and as a result, my survival depended on a thirteen-foot boat with a single sail, a rudder, and a daggerboard.

Still, the bay's surface was hardly rippled, the cockpit was self-bailing, the Sunfish was impossible to swamp, and the horizon was dotted with small islands. Despite my incompetence, I wasn't afraid that I would sail out of the Bay of Florida into the Gulf of Mexico. Nagging doubts that Mexico might be my destination made me try again to turn the boat and tack back to Islamorada, but the breeze spun me toward a long key with a sandy beach sleepy under coconut palms. When I hit the sandbar, I lowered the sail, raised the daggerboard, and kicked up the rudder. The Sunfish grounded easily, and I heaved an immense sigh of relief.

As I wobbled out of the sailboat and pulled it farther up the beach, I sensed someone spying on me. I felt terribly naked and vulnerable to human predators. I whirled in time to see a bronze shape pull behind a red-blossomed hibiscus.

"Hello," I called tremulously. "Sorry to intrude. I guess I'm shipwrecked."

I heard a faint rustle of the tropical foliage, and a flutter of the wind through the coconut fronds. As I directed my suspicions toward the red flowered hibiscus, a reddish-brown shape emerged from behind a nearby bush with brilliant yellow double blossoms. I had never seen a key deer before, but I knew it from pictures. He was a tiny buck, less than thirty inches tall. He tripped shyly forth on his delicate legs.

"Hello, little fellow," I called to the deer, certain that he was not the form I'd glimpsed. Human eyes were watching me. Steeling my sinews, I stared into the red-flowered hibiscus as though I could penetrate the foliage with my gaze. "You don't fool me. Show yourself."

The hibiscus rustled and the mangrove-climbing bougainvillea shook as the single human watcher made up his mind. After a cautious pause, a vision of gorgeousness hove into view. The islander was about my age, a guy who had been living half wild, but to my eyes he was like a god or the genie of the island. His windswept hair was deep brown, though sun lightened in streaks that no stylist could duplicate. His skin was almost golden, and his eyes were dark pools of unspoken desires.

He was wearing cut off jeans, the front full with his cock and balls. His ass protruded, so the seam of his cut-offs shaped the perfect valentine. His bare chest protruded just enough to attract, pleasingly muscled and bronzed. He must have inherited his ass from Narcissus and his cock from Zeus. To my eyes, he was beautiful, special, vulnerable, kingly, subversive, defenseless, dangerous, and sublime.

"Fuck me," I gasped.

"Hold still," he warned. "Don't move while my protectors examine you. If you haven't come to hurt me, then you don't need to be afraid."

Two narrow fellows were slithering across the coral sand. The snakes were five feet long, thick of body, and decorated down their backs with large sinister diamonds with brownish centers and cream-colored borders. Their tails ended with obvious rattles. The god of the island's warning was unnecessary; I could not move to save my life. I stood frozen in terror as the two rattlesnakes circled me, one passing between my feet and rubbing my bare ankle with his keeled scales. I was too scared to piss when one climbed my leg and poked his deadly head into my crotch.

For the space of a minute, the diamondback rattler and I were staring eyeball to eyeball. From that close encounter of the serpentine kind, I can state that he had vertical catlike pupils. He also had dark stripes running down from his eyes, lighter stripes on his snout, and deep facial pits. As I tried not to fidget, I grew more fascinated than terrified. His physical beauty, for all its mortal threat, drew me toward him. In a wild moment, I considered touching his head.

Smiling as though the snakes were a couple of friendly kittens, the god approached. "Now we'll show the boys that you're my friend," he said, bringing his mouth to mine and kissing my lips hard. His tongue was like a dagger of fire that entered my mouth.

I forgot that two rattlesnakes waited in striking distance and a little key deer watched with bashful eyes. I pressed closer to the beautiful shape, rubbing my swelling cock against his as my tongue slipped into his mouth. That kiss was no short peck. We must have maintained the kiss for three minutes, if it wasn't infinity. I discovered that my arms had slipped around him, almost of their own volition, and I was caressing the exquisite mounds of his ass through the tight worn denim. My cock was so hard that I was close to spontaneous ejaculation.

Slowly, reluctantly, he pulled his mouth from mine. "I'm Kenny," he said, as though he needed to introduce himself after that soul-shattering kiss. "This is my island. I call it Kenny's Key."

"I'm Dan," I muttered, stepping back to take a closer look at Kenny. During the kiss, I had forgotten about the rattlesnakes, and I nearly stepped on one's rattles. The reptile gave his tail a nervous shake, and my heart leaped into my throat.

"Careful, Dan, you almost stepped on Moe."

"Huh."

"That's Moe," Kenny said, pointing toward the diamondback with the rattling tail. "And Curly," he added pointing toward the other rattlesnake. "They're my friends; they protect me." He knelt and stroked the key deer. "This is Larry. He's my friend too."

I let the tame deer sniff my hand before I petted his side. "He sure is friendly."

"Only with me," Kenny said, "or with my friends." He took my hand and drew me along a trail that led away from the beach. Larry followed, as did Curly and Moe.

"Do the snakes ever bite anybody?" I asked. I was still a bit apprehensive about the rattlers.

"Some mean boys used to drive their motorboats out to torment me," Kenny said. "They threw rocks at me. Moe bit one of them, so they don't come anymore."

"Why'd they do that?"

"I tried to kiss one of them. I didn't know that he wouldn't like it. Nobody comes to the center of my key unless I've kissed him."

"You can kiss me whenever you want," I offered. As an afterthought I asked, "Did the boy die?"

"Nah. He bled, swelled up a little, and went home crying for his mommy."

"But he didn't die?"

"At the hospital the docs cut his leg off." Kenny shrugged. "No big deal."

Kenny lived in a house he had constructed of wood, with a roof of palm fronds. The house sat on a grayish coral outcropping, lost anchor lines anchoring the walls into the rock. The house, taking up six hundred square feet, was larger than those jungle huts Hollywood had fashioned in the American psyche. To the side lay Kenny's well-ordered garden, which included a row of pineapples growing on stems. Past the outdoor fireplace and table, he cultivated rows of key lime, lemon, and papaya bushes. Two massive mango trees sheltered the house, and a grove of banana stalks offered a windbreak.

Kenny released my hand and cupped my left buttock. "Nice," he said. "You have nice buns."

"So do you," I said, checking him out again. Up close, he did not appear so godlike, and my imagination may have enhanced his attributes. Still, he was beautiful, desirable, and obviously available.

"Come into my house," he invited. Stooping slightly, I poked my head through the door that he was holding open. The interior was not what I had expected. A silk Chinese carpet covered the floor, and sitting on the carpet was an expensive couch. Heart wrenchingly beautiful watercolors of local settings hung in frames on the plastered and papered walls. A four-poster double bed with a nightstand stood behind a wide beaded curtain. There was no electricity, of course, nor any sign of a bathroom or a kitchen. I would learn shortly that those were both outside.

"Holy shit," I exclaimed. "How long have you lived here? Where'd you get this stuff? How'd you get it out here?"

As the questions sailed off my tongue like a runaway boat, Kenny laughed. "I've lived here for seven years, Dan. Since I was eighteen. As for the furniture, my boyfriends brought it. The watercolors I painted myself. I have friends who sell them."

Larry, the deer, remained outdoors, and, to my relief, so did Moe and Curly. The rattlesnakes took positions on both sides of the door, coiled, and watched for intruders. I looked out at them, so terrible, yet so beautiful, so lethal with potential, and for a second I lost all control. My cock was hardening in my Speedo. I knew, but I did not know how I had pulled Kenny close to me, or how my fingers had unfastened his shorts and pushed them down. As I had already guessed, he wasn't wearing underwear. Still, then I simply knew that his cock in my hand was growing thicker, like a snake itself, unhooded, uncoiling, and ready to strike.

Kenny brought his mouth to mine again, his tongue warring against mine. His cock was leaking a thin stream of watery musk. My right hand was stroking his cock while my left explored his ass. I had not exaggerated the protrusion of his rump, and stroking those enticing mounds was nearly enough to make me ejaculate prematurely.

Kenny's naked cock was soaring, bulky, and erect in the light made green by the leaf of mango, while his sun blessed hand explored the swelling in my swim briefs. His cock filled my hand agreeably. I stroked up and down his shaft, and toyed with his hooded head, twisting it like a bottle cap, flipping it lightly with my finger, and cupping it with my palm. Kenny emitted a low moan as I jerked him and followed my actions on my own cock.

I found myself slipping to my knees and touching my tongue to the tip of his cock. My lips slid over Kenny's cockhead. The tip rode along the surface of my tongue, his leakage tasting sweet and salty at once. I pulled my mouth back until his cockhead was barely brushing my lips. Then I proceeded to fuck him hard and fast with my mouth.

"Oh, yes, Dan," Kenny moaned. Then, "No, wait." I stopped in mid mouth stroke, fearing what he might say. However, I heard, "I want to do you at the same time. I want to suck your dick too."

Kenny pulled his cock from my mouth and pushed me toward the couch. My ass hit the cushions. Kenny pulled on my legs, so that my rear lifted, and stripped off my Speedo. My cock, free of the confines of my swimsuit, rode free, hard, and ready. Kenny pushed me onto my side and joined me on the couch, his mouth close to my soaring cock, and his own dick touching my lips.

Then Kenny was kissing the head of my cock while sliding his hand across the curve of my rump. Again, I touched my tongue to the tip of Kenny's cock, and a thrill shot through me. My lust sharpened as my lips closed around the smooth skin of his swollen dick head. Slowly I moved my wet lips over it. My cock was inside Kenny's mouth and I heard the low, keening sound issuing from his throat, almost a purr of pleasure. Outside, Moe and Curly wiggled their rattles as their reptilian intuition sensed our libido.

It was the most exciting dual blowjob ever. Perhaps it was the phallic appearance of the snakes guarding the door as we sucked, but I had never been so thoroughly inflamed. My cock was near orgasm within a minute, but before I could ask that Kenny hold off, I felt his cock stiffen harder in my mouth.

My cock seemed to grow heavier, while Kenny's swelled tighter. It made a burning shaft riding along my tongue, and I tasted his semen. Deep ripples of pleasure grew in my cock's head, and I committed to ejaculation. I was going to shoot my spunk down Kenny's throat at the

81

same time he was blasting his load into mine. The power of the cocksucker was upon me as I rocked my head upon Kenny's cock and rocked my hips against his lips. His tongue and lips tortured my cockhead as my orgasm increased.

We passed through the mind-blasting stages of orgasm and ejaculation. I was writhing and slithering as if I were one of the snakes. I was swallowing the thick cum that Kenny spurted and spurting my own onto his tongue. I pulled my lips back as his ejaculation slowed so the final ooze could paint my lips. Then, satiated, we sniffed the rich scents of each other's crotch, as we lay sweating and drawing deep breaths.

Finally, we sat up, side by side, our hips touching. I fingered Kenny's cock, still wet with my saliva. Even as it rested, recovering for another explosion of semen, I could feel its potential. Kenny's cock reminded me of the thick rattlesnakes.

"Why don't they bite us?" I asked.

Kenny looked surprised. "I told you. Moe and Curly are my friends. They would never hurt me. And after what we just shared, they will protect you too. You swallowed my cum; that means I'm a part of you now, just as you're a part of me."

As we sat fondling each other's cock and talking about the spectacular blowjob we'd shared, Kenny abruptly turned his head and listened. "I heard a motor," he said. "We'd better check."

He grabbed his cut-offs and pulled them on. "I wear these only around the shore," he whispered. "Otherwise, I don't wear anything."

I had already guessed that from his tan. I stepped into my Speedo and followed Kenny across the yard. Moe and Curly slithered along beside us.

The boat turned out to be a passing cruiser that showed no interest in Kenny's Key. It passed through the channel and out into the bay. Satisfied, Kenny led me to the beach where the Sunfish waited upon the sand.

"Why did you come here?" Kenny asked, sitting down on the side of the hull.

"To your island?" I asked, dropping my ass down beside his. "The wind blew me. I'm not a good sailor."

Tired of patrolling and not wishing to be excluded from the conversation, the rattlesnakes joined us. The late afternoon sun was beating down, which made the snakes sleepy.

"Why did you come to the Keys?" Kenny corrected, his fingers tickling my cock through the thin fabric. "Do you have a boyfriend waiting for you?"

Curly shifted in his sleep and rattled his tail. Then he changed his position so his snaky head was resting on my bare thigh. Would anyone ever believe that my leg could make a pillow for a diamondback?

"I had a boyfriend, Kenny," I confessed. "We broke up. Four days ago. I was living with him, had been living with him for three years, and, without warning, he told me that he'd met another guy. He told me I'd have to move out the next day."

"The bastard," Kenny exclaimed.

"Yeah," I agreed. "A few hours ago, it would have hurt to talk about it. After what we just did, Brady's betrayal is no longer bothering me. Anyway, I moved my stuff out that night, slept at a hotel, and caught a plane to Miami. I rode the bus down to Key West for a night, and then I rode back up to Islamorada."

"So you haven't heard from him?"

"I called him this morning," I admitted. "I got his voice mail. He had already changed the message. A few days ago, his voice greeted callers with 'You have reached the residence of Brady and Dan.' Today I heard 'Brady and Charles.' The way he so casually changed that message tore my heart out, so I decided to try the Sunfish – without knowing how to sail it."

Shifting Curly, Kenny placed his hand on my bare thigh. A shy smile played upon his cock-empurpled lips. "Would you like to stay here?"

"Oh," I said, thinking about my dead end job at the college bookstore. My few possessions were in storage. In effect, back home I was homeless. Kenny offered a choice between paradise and perdition. Still, I wasn't certain that Kenny was offering true love – or loyalty – or sexual exclusivity. He had mentioned boyfriends – perhaps numerous boyfriends who visited the island for fun and games.

"What about your other boyfriends?" I asked.

"I'll share them with you," he offered hedonistically. "The more guys fucking and sucking, the better. I love gay sex orgies." His voice grew even more suggestive as he asked, "Have you ever played choo-choo?" By way of demonstration, he wiggled his prominent rump. "Every guy plugged into the guy in front of him. Get enough guys for a full circle and everybody's plugged."

Heathen sex games! Cocksucking contests! Wanton promiscuity! Circle jerks! Pagan gayboy orgies! Lord of the Flies fuck-fests on a tropical island! Why didn't such thoughts dismay me? Never would I have considered group sex with Brady. Maybe that had been the problem.

"I'll stay," I said suddenly. "But how about this boat? Shouldn't we notify my hotel? If I don't get back soon, they'll alert the coast guard – if they haven't already."

The deer Larry scratched his behind on a palm tree and watched me quizzically. Absently, I laid my hand on Curly's head and stroked his scaly skin, still hot in the setting sun.

"Is there anything at your hotel you must retrieve?" Kenny asked.

I waved a hand toward my brief swimsuit. "Uh, my clothes. A toothbrush. My razor."

"I have a razor and a toothbrush. We can share them," Kenny offered. "As for clothes, I like what you're wearing. Here on Kenny's Key you won't need anything else."

"What about the sailboat?"

"We'll set it adrift. The offshore breeze will carry it northwest."

"Everybody will think I'm drowned."

"Yeah," Kenny affirmed, fondling my rump, "but you won't be drowned. You'll be safe with me."

We waited until the deep red had diminished into purple before we set the Sunfish adrift. The picture of Brady receiving a call about my demise did not displease me. I was feeling like Tom Sawyer on Jackson's Island as Kenny led the way back to our house.

Supper consisted of red snapper baked over an open fire, brown rice with cheese, several vegetables, and salad. We drank a rose wine, which suffered nothing for not being chilled. We ate at the outside table lighted with citronella torches to ward off mosquitoes. After dessert, a delicious fruit tart, Kenny suggested a stroll on the beach.

I picked up my swimsuit, but Kenny raised his hand to the rising moon. "You won't need your sexy swim briefs in the dark."

Soon we were strolling, naked, hand in hand under the coconut palms over sand still warm from the day's sunshine. We stopped and kissed long in the moonlight, and Kenny stroked my bare ass with his loving hand.

"You have a wonderful rump."

"Yes," I said. "Ready to receive your cock."

"You'd like my dick inside of you?"

"Oh, yes."

"Will you return the favor? Can you give as good as you take?"

"With you I can."

"The let's do it."

"We need condoms," I said, thinking of Kenny's boyfriends.

Kenny had an impish smile as he showed me what he held in his free hand: two condoms and a bottle of lubricant.

Kenny laid me on my back with my legs drawn up so we were face to face, and he placed his cock head against my asshole. I opened readily for him, and as he pushed inside I felt the familiar pressure, but joyous then, as he drove deeper into me, and the light of our physical connection sparked in his eyes. He was still filling me to the hilt; I felt his soft pubic hairs tickling my buttocks as he drove his cock deep into my rectum.

Every plunge of his cock was a thrust of pleasure, and even though I was gripping the branches of a spicebush, my cock felt as if a thousand hands were jerking it and a thousand mouths were sucking it.

Riding through raptures, my face to the yellow moon and the whirling stars, I decorated my stomach and Kenny's with my semen, even as he humped my hot ass with his erupting dick. And all the while, Larry watched from the bushes with his soft slow eyes, and Curly and Moe guarded us from any who would do us harm.

("Kenny's Key" originally appeared in the now out-of-service online periodical *Tommyhawk's Fantasy World*)

Out-Island Cruising

The white beach went on forever, and sand scalloped down to the green shallows kissed by the Atlantic waves. Shells dotted the beach. Washed up horseshoe crabs and starfish expired beside plumes of wild sea oats. The sky was a mold of gelatinous blue punctuated with white puffs.

Yet, I was bummed; I was eighteen years old, and my future looked grim. The hawkish establishment was pointing its talons at me. The ambitions of powerful men threatened my survival. Non-conformists faced destruction, disgrace, prison, death, or worse.

Such were the dismal prospects clouding my thoughts when I spied the boy leaning against the coconut palm. The curving palm trunk shadow obscured his face, but he looked to be my age. He was decked out the same swimsuit I was wearing, a Lycra Speedo bikini in a purple and green tropical print. He had been watching the fishing craft manned by the native Bahamians, but he turned in time to catch me staring at his crotch.

A designing grin twitched upon his wide mouth, "What's your bag, man?" he asked casually.

Balling his ass was my bag – or vice-versa. However, the year was 1967, I'd graduated high school just a month earlier, and I'd only experienced sex with one other boy – my best friend, Rick. Rick and I had spent our senior year engaging in a little kissing and jerking each other off. We didn't go any further down that road unless you count the night Rick and I scored some mind-altering pot and ended up giving each other the 69 side-by-side.

Rick had greater inhibitions about being gay, but he was also more wrecked. He forcibly undressed me and pushed me down on my bed. His lips touched the tip of my cock, and his tongue slipped around the hood. His warm mouth closed around my dick, and I felt him going down my shaft. As he took me deeper, his thick boner jutted toward my eyes.

Before I could think, I kissed the helmet of his dick. Rick was sucking harder and varying his pace. I squeezed his helmet with my lips as thrills rushed through my dick head. I sucked his helmet and let my lips slide down his shaft. His cock was only halfway along my tongue when I tasted thick syrup. Rick moaned around my dick as he came in my mouth. My ripples throbbed down my cock, and the spasm shook me. I was coming in Rick's mouth and swallowing his spunk. Sadly, we only scored that pot the one time.

By the time I boarded an airliner bound for Nassau, Rick was in basic training. He came from an Air Force family, and his old man had seen to it that Rick shipped off only days after we graduated from South Dade High School in Homestead, Florida. Whether Rick's old man suspected that his son was fruity, I never knew. Rick's old lady suspected, because she once remarked that she favored rearing a soldier to spawning a faggot. They wasted no time getting their son away from me. For Rick there was never a question of "coming out." Not in a 1960's agricultural town dominated by Homestead Air Force Base. Not in a nation rioting about race, battling for gender equality, rending itself over military conscription, and gambling its soul in Asia.

Although, my sense of loss and betrayal waxed heavily in my thoughts as I stood on that Nassau beach, the stranger lounging against the palm tree was stacked, and his hair was dark black, almost bluish black, and his face was downright pretty. His Speedo left nothing to the imagination; he had sprung a boner.

"Your dick is up," I remarked.

He glanced down, surprised at my forthright statement. My own cock was swelling. I surveyed the beach, but no one was near enough to see our erections.

"So is yours, man."

He was so close I could have touched his cock. "I'm Tom. I'm from Florida."

"I'm Dove," he said, placing his hand on my arm. "From Ohio."

"Dove? Is that your real name?"

"We don't use our given names."

A light dawned. "You're a resister?"

"I graduated high school before I had to register. Before the draft board caught up with me, I hitched a boat ride, made some connections, and changed my name. Are you registered, Tom?"

"They got me in high school," I admitted. "On the morning of my eighteenth birthday, the principal called me to his office. Some birthday present – a gung-ho school counselor was ready with the Selective Service Registration Form. But I have a plan." I drew a deep breath. "If they call me in for a physical, I'm going to claim I'm a fairy. They don't want homos in their army."

Dove surveyed me from toe to top. "Don't kid yourself, Tom," Dove said. "Last year a boy from my high school went to his draft physical wearing his sister's panties and cheerleader outfit."

"What happened?"

"They drafted him and hazed the shit out of him in boot camp. He was killed his first week in Vietnam."

"What a bummer," I said, beset with helpless outrage. "It was a set-up."

Dove nodded. "I'm glad you're a fairy, Tom. I'm one, too. My old lady told me it's because a cow kicked me in the head."

"Is that what causes it?" I asked, going along. "There's a lotta cattle in Homestead."

"Then we both got kicked," Dove said joyously. "Oh, Tom, we're gonna have such good times." He grabbed my shoulders and kissed my lips lightly. The kiss shot through me like a thunderbolt. My right hand slipped behind his head. His raven hair was thick and slightly coarse with a touch of sea salt. I met his lips hard.

We kissed until we spied approaching tourists. Our warring tongues had left our cocks throbbing. "This friggin' island is too crowded with establishment thinkers," Dove said, flicking my erection. "You gotta come to Funky Town where you'll be safe."

"You're not hiding out in Nassau?" I asked stupidly.

"Not a chance. New Providence is filthy with rich gamblers and tourists, the bastards profiting from the war."

"So what are you doing here now?" I asked.

"I came to score some supplies," Dove said, picking up a faded tee shirt and ragged cut off jeans. "I have a little boat."

My heart broke to see Dove's bulging swimsuit disappear into the denim. However, his cutoffs were tight and showed his moon-shaped ass to its best advantage. After he dressed, I found the sea grape bush where I'd doffed my cutoffs and sandals.

Posh tourist hotels hugged the beach and beyond them lurked the casinos. The part of town where I'd been staying was quite different. Dove and I passed aged wooden houses brightly painted in primary colors, then faded into pastel tints. Many were hard to see behind the overgrown foliage blowing in blossom or bract: Royal Poinciana, jacaranda, trumpet vines, poinsettia, frangipani, hibiscus, bougainvillea, and croton. Some houses bore gris-gris charms. On one porch, three solemn children wore their clothes inside out. Their mother had recently died, so relatives dressed them to fool the mother's ghost when she returned to claim her children.

The scent of night blooming jasmine still hanging heavy in the morning air, we walked to the guest house where I had spent the night. I had blown Florida with only the threads on my back and a duffel bag containing a few toiletries and my swimsuit. I grabbed my bag.

Dove was waiting around the corner. "Is it cool?" He had warned me that my landlady was a known police informer.

"She's satisfied. She screwed me out of five bucks."

Dove motioned me to follow. He had an enticing ass that I would have followed anywhere. We hurried down a shady street, lined on both sides with Royal Poinciana, which the natives called flamboyant trees.

"Don't freak out over anything you hear," Dove suggested. "We're going to church."

"Hanging with JC and the boys wasn't what I had in mind."

"That's where we score food we can't grow, toilet paper, medical supplies, and shit."

"Do they know we're draft dodgers?" I asked.

"Man, don't say draft dodger," he whispered, glancing around. "They know."

We turned down a street dotted with neat vegetable gardens and flower beds surrounding blue timber-frame houses with pastel pink, yellow, or green shutters and window frames. The yards were fenced with white pickets and trellises covered by bougainvillea with red, orange, purple, or yellow papery bracts.

The Island Gospel Church sat far from the Paradise Island casinos, tourist hotels, and golf courses. This rustic fabrication opened to the outside air on the leeward side, and bougainvillea with green and white variegated foliage and soft pink bracts climbed its whitewashed wooden slats. A woman dressed in a bright print island dress and sporting the incongruous coif of a nun's habit rounded the corner.

"Hi, Sister Inez," Dove said.

"We were starting to worry," she said, her voice wary. She shot me a dubious look. I made to introduce myself, but Dove interrupted.

"This is Elf," he said, whipping a nickname out of his ass.

"Did anybody send you, Elf?" Sister Inez asked. Until that moment, I had not fully comprehended that I had lucked into the underground railroad for draft resisters.

"No," I said. "I just graduated high school. I don't want the government to send me off to kill men, women, children, and their household pets."

My answer satisfied Sister Inez. "I'm glad you're here, Elf. You can help with the supplies." She turned to lead us into the pastor's office.

"She's a real Catholic nun?" I whispered. "This doesn't look like a Catholic Church."

"It's an Assembly of God," Sister Inez answered. She had fantastic ears. "Christians work together in the field – those with social conscience."

A tall, sandy-headed man of forty blew in. He looked us over before shaking hands with Dove and me. I had the distinct sense that he read us right down to our concealed swimsuits.

Sister Inez introduced me.

"Elf, I'm Jim Hunt. Call me Brother Jim." A chameleon ran up the leg of Brother Jim's khaki pants. He carefully cupped his hands, caught the reptile, and gently placed it on the branch of a red-blossomed hibiscus bush that was pushing its tendrils through the open window.

"Brother Jim, these boys shouldn't stay long," Sister Inez urged.

"You're right," he said, slapping his forehead. "Ike and Julius have loaded the Skuzz Bucket, but Sister Grace wants the boys to sample her key lime pie before they leave."

Sister Grace turned out to be Brother Jim's wife. While Dove and I were forking down two huge slices of her pie and washing the pie down with cold milk, she told us she was a Quaker. I wondered if she had influenced her husband, who was ordained by one of the more conservative Pentecostal churches, toward the peace movement. Whatever the case, these people changed my opinion of Christians. I'd been brought up in the Florida bible belt, and had always considered Christians to be intolerant, racist, and downright mean. Brother Jim, Sister Inez, and Sister Grace were entirely different.

The Skuzz Bucket turned out to be a rusty Datsun truck. Dove and I climbed into the back for the short ride to the shore. We had to squeeze between a bunch of boxes filled with canned food, sacks of rice and noodles, toilet paper, and items of personal hygiene.

"Why was Sister Inez wiggin' out when she saw me?" I whispered.

"If the Bahamian fuzz caught the Christians aiding us, Sister Inez, Brother Jim, and Sister Grace would get kicked out of the Bahamas and sent to the mainland U.S. where they'd be arrested, tried, convicted, and sentenced to ten years in a federal penitentiary. I don't know what the Bahamian government would do to the two black cats Ike and Julius, but their fate would not be pretty."

"Do you think Brother Jim knows about us?" I asked.

"He knows we're evading the draft."

"I don't mean that."

"You're asking whether he knows you want my cock?"

"Yeah, among other things." I copped a feel of his butt. Dove stuck his ass out and gave it a wiggle.

"Brother Jim knows everything," Dove said. "Not that he approves. Jim Hunt is a true believer in the Protestant Bible, but that means that he thinks that sin is sin. To a real Christian, our sucking cock or fucking butt is no worse than siphoning gas out of somebody's car or stealing a fortune from an old couple's retirement plan or foreclosing on some poor slob's house. He cares about the harm people do. He doesn't think that people should kill – not for country, anything."

"Are we going to do that?" I asked.

"Siphon gas?"

"Suck cock? Fuck ass?"

His lascivious grin was brighter than the weird hot light of the Bahamian sun. "Have you ever sucked one?" he asked back.

I told him about my experiences with Rick, including the time we went down on each other. "Have you sucked cock, Dove?"

"I've done it all, Elf. I got laid at thirteen," Dove confessed. "My Uncle Ralph, who was twenty, put the move on me. I was ready – I'd been teasing the horny bastard for months."

The Skuzz Bucket slowed with a high-pitched squeal as the worn-out brakes engaged. The two black cats, Ike and Julius, jumped out, and Dove led us to a twenty-two foot sharpie anchored just off shore. Far Out was crudely painted on the stern. Far Out had a cabin that slept two, a tiller rather than a wheel, and three dull-red sails. Once we finished stowing the cartons from the Skuzz Bucket, I shook hands with Brother Jim, Ike, and Julius, and climbed into the cockpit.

Watching Dove's cutoffs lift his butt while he raised the sails was a treat. I managed to steer our craft away from shore, but my eyes remained fixed on Dove's buns straining the denim as he bent. The prospect of sex with him filled my thoughts as the sharpie lifted, and we hauled ass over the surface. That I was committing the federal offense of draft dodging barely troubled my mind. Once we were underway, Dove pulled off his cutoffs and worked in his Speedo.

"Outasight!" I commented. Keeping one hand on the tiller, I skimmed off my shorts and tee shirt. When he had the sails catching the wind, Dove patted the inside of my thigh, checked the compass, made a course correction, and sat down beside me. I touched his cock and pressed my lips to his. He kissed me lightly but lifted my hand from his cock.

"I hate to bring you down, Elf, but I gotta steer," he cautioned, putting the seal on my new name. "You can navigate. When we reach Funky Town, you can ball my brains out."

"Let's grab a quickie now."

"You see how calm the water is?" he asked, pointing toward the sandy bottom twenty feet below. "That can change." The bottom dropped out as we slid over a blue hole. It was vivid reminder that if we crossed the outer banks where the extensive shelf upon which the Bahama chain ends so abruptly, we'd pass over a canyon wall plunging one mile into the deep. There giant mantas, sharks, swordfish, and sailfish did their fishy thing, and no shallow bottom calmed the white foaming waves of the dark Atlantic. High ocean waves filled with sea monsters were nothing I wanted to brave in a twenty-two-foot sharpie.

Dove tacked near to the wind. He handed me the nautical chart and showed me how to read the compass. New Providence was already out of sight. The lonely expanse of greenish water filled the curving horizon. I was shocked when Dove mentioned that our trip would take seven hours.

"We're not going into the Gulf Stream?" I asked nervously.

"The Stream is off that way," Dove said with a gesture. "We'll be staying within the waters protected by Eleuthera and Cat Island. Our biggest danger is a summer squall. They spring up in the afternoon, and one would be a real bummer."

I shivered in spite of the hot sun piercing the water. However, the bottom was only thirty feet deep below, and the water was a shade of blue/green found only in dreams.

"Are there many cats on Cat Island?" I wondered.

Dove laughed. "Captain Catt was a pirate who hid out on the island when he wasn't running down merchant ships, slaughtering their crews, and kidnapping their cabin boys."

"What did he do to the cabin boys?"

"The pirates of the Caribbean were a homosexual brotherhood," Dove said. "They swore vows of sodomy. Butt-fucking made them loyal to each other."

"So the cabin boys got prodded."

"Having a tight virgin asshole was a lifesaver."

"Should we get boarded by pirates," I suggested, "I'm not your crew."

"You're a cabin boy," Dove finished.

As I daydreamed about pirates and cabin boys, we passed a small island, hardly more than a sandbar. Beneath us, swam colorful parrotfish that ate the coral, butterflyfish, angelfish, a scrawled cowfish, and one magnificent queen triggerfish – a psychedelic denizen of the salt water. It was glistening gold with blue stripes, and beautiful filaments trailed from its fins. We passed so close above a spotted ray that I stroked its back, and the creature shivered with pleasure.

No humans inhabited the tiny sand-covered bars of coral limestone, some lush with coconut palms and mangroves. Off the leeward edge of one island, pink with nesting flocks of flamingoes, Dove asked me to take the tiller.

"You want me to steer?"

"I gotta take a whizz." He pulled down his Speedo and pissed over the side. Treated to my first view of his thick cock and his naked half-moons, I turned the tiller too far and sent us flying toward the island. Two sand sharks separated as we passed over them.

"Elf, man," Dove admonished grabbing for a handhold. "You gotta steer straight." In my excitement, I'd nearly dumped him overboard. The remainder of our voyage consisted of one long sailing lesson.

Late in the day, an island unnamed on our nautical chart appeared. It was composed of a creamy sand beach surrounding twin hills that rose over a hundred feet. On the windward side, the beach ended in a long row of Casuarina pines, which made a ghostly sound as the wind whispered through their feathery needles. Small doves pecked at something in the sand, their little heads bobbing like toys. Behind the pines lay a dense jungle, and again a shiver rippled up my sunburned back.

As we rounded the island, the glow of the late sun illuminated a half-moon beach, awake with rustling coconut palm fronds. Bluffs stood behind the beach, dotted with coral grottos and caves. Frangipani scented the air. Dove leaped from the boat. As I handed him the anchor, I saw seven weird aquatic creatures bearing down on him. I shrieked a warning, but Dove greeted the monsters with delight.

"Elf, meet the ladies," he urged. The ladies were wild pigs that had swum out to meet us. Dove patted each bristled back and promised goodies once we had hauled the supplies ashore. When I dropped into the water, the pigs surrounded me, friendly as dogs.

By the time Dove and I had brought the first cartons to the beach, Funky Town's Flower Children were there to help. Most of these dope-smoking hippies were American boys avoiding military service. A few were as gay as Dove and I, some liked both sexes, and the remainder grooved on chicks. Nevertheless, even though most of the chicks had come with their boyfriends, nobody in Funky Town was straight. The

Flower Children were peaceful people who dug each other's thing. As one head said, "Sex is a gas, man. Mouth, tail, or twat, it's copasetic."

A bare-breasted chick in a bikini bottom laid on Dove and me a hand-carved bowl of fried breaded conch topped with squeezed lime and sided with two joints. We lit up, and nibbled the appetizers while the Flower Children carried the cartons up the hill to the village they called "Funky Town." The wild pigs crowded around as we smoked. We shared our conch fritters with the ladies and with a friendly iguana that sat on my bare foot.

We smoked the joints and tossed the roaches as if Mary Jane grew all around us. It turned out that it did grow all around us. As we trudged up the hill, I saw tall marijuana plants blowing in the trade winds. The inhabitants cultivated vegetables and herbs too, but the marijuana gardens enthralled me.

On the encircling bluff stood Funky Town, a ramshackle jumble of dwellings constructed of driftwood and palm fronds. Funky Town presented a haphazard appearance, though some of the huts boasted decks and towers. Poultry wandered freely among the dwellings. One freeloading rooster begged scraps throughout the meal.

Rough picnic tables formed a rude communal dining area. No walls surrounded the tables but a high roof of bamboo and palm fronds protected the diners from the frequent tropical rains. Nearly fifty flower children crowded their asses together at the tables. Kerosene lamps provided light. Those who had the weekly kitchen rotation served celery stalks, green onions, red peppers, lobster salad, mutton snapper, yellowtail, rice, pigeon peas spiced with thyme, and coconut bread.

As the stars filled the sky, we cranked up cigar-sized joints while "Some Velvet Morning" rasped from a battery-operated radio, followed by "Itchycoo Park." I was sitting beside Dove, smoking, and listening to music. Around me rose the mewing cries of Funky Towners gripped in sexual extremity. I turned toward Dove. Our lips met. My cock swelled, and when I placed my hand on Dove's crotch, I found him ready.

"What's your bag, man?" Dove whispered lovingly, his hand rubbing my cock.

"Fuck my horny ass, Dove," I said, and licked his ear. "Give me my first butt fuck." Willing to oblige, Dove displayed a lubricant concocted from coconut oil.

"I'll do you the way my Uncle Ralph fucked me the first time. Stand up, hold onto that coconut palm, and stick out your ass."

My heart was beating fast as I followed his instructions. "Keep your legs close and stick out your ass," Dove commanded. We were already naked, so Dove had only to slick my asshole with his finger. The coconut oil was slippery on my asshole. I pushed to let him in.

"You must want it, Elf," Dove whispered. "You're opening your ass."

"Yeah."

"Stick out your ass as far as you can. I'm gonna push in my cock."

"Do it, man."

I felt a tremendous pressure in my ass, so I pushed hard against it. I felt the fullness of his cock and griped the palm tree for balance. Dove pushed all the way into me, delightfully, painlessly, and exuberantly.

"Fuck me," I said.

Dove drew back and pushed. He banged me slowly, he banged me swiftly, he kept the pace. I could only push back my ass to meet him, but each thrust was wonderful. I felt a deep sensation, not just the delicious feelings produced in my dilated asshole, but something so deep that I could not describe it.

"What a show," shrieked one delighted flower child. "Look at the boys fuck."

Dove reached around and grabbed my cock with his lubricated hand. He started jerking me off, giving me a first-rate hand job. Rick had jerked me that way, and Dove knew every trick. All too quickly, I was committed to orgasm.

"I'm gonna come in your ass, Elf."

"I'm coming too, Dove."

Deep spasms shook me as Dove's tight fist flogged my dick. My muscles contracted, tightening my asshole as the pleasure milked jets of cum out of my cock. I saw my spunk arc and splatter against the tree. It continued until I stood shaking with Dove's hands still holding my dick and ass.

"I love you, Elf," Dove murmured in my ear.

"What a fuckin' show," the chick shouted again. "Gay boys jack off and have anal orgasms. Outasight!"

The hens provided eggs for breakfast, and we had wonderful pancakes. Most of what we ate we grew on the island or caught in the sea. We never speared the ladies, for they were family, but once we had to trap a feral boar that had gone ape shit crazy. It was a bum trip, but after we killed him, we smoked him for four days and he provided a lot of tasty pork. Lunch often consisted of macaroni-and-cheese and shellfish. Rock lobsters were plentiful, along with grouper, red snapper, and yellowtail, not to mention the random green turtle. Conch was a daily staple.

Dove was the official master of the ship, so I became his mate. Once a month Dove and I made the long sail up to Nassau to pick up supplies. We would spend one day sailing to New Providence Island, sleep in the boat's cabin at anchor, and the next morning we would walk to the Island Gospel Church, and make the return trip. Additionally, we made frequent voyages to other islands to obtain driftwood or to explore.

One night after we had secured fresh batteries for the radio, we dropped tabs of Yellow Sunshine. Donovan was singing "Hurdy Gurdy Man." A squall had passed earlier, leaving the sky starless black. One of the chicks was into boys doing other boys, so she talked me into balling her while Dove impaled me. Even tripping, I was more into Dove's dick filling my ass than I was into the girl.

"I'm shooting off into your ass, Elf," Dove moaned, humping my butt hard, which got me off.

"You're making me come too," I breathed.

"What a gas," the chick howled into the dreaming darkness. That experience was the closest I ever came to heterosexuality, but it wasn't that close.

We celebrated every holiday, and though the Christians helped support us, we thought of ourselves as pagan. We held colorful and raucous parades on New Year's, Groundhog Day, May Day, All Hallows Eve, Yule, and a host of other holidays including the solstices and equinoxes. The community turned out, dressing in costumes designed from donated clothing, shells, coconuts, and lost feathers. We played homemade bells, drums, and tambourines, everybody smoked a ton of pot, and each festival concluded with a cluster fuck in the surf. We declared Valentine's Day Free Love Day, and each flower child shared pleasure, but Dove and I were only into each other.

Funky Town lasted for two years after I arrived, supported by our efforts and those of the far off Christians. The work was always light, the food was always tasty, and the sex was always spectacular. The community's orgiastic revels by moonlight or under the sun never grew old.

We heard rumors of U. S. Federal Marshals sending undercover spies to root out draft dodgers, and of U. S. Coast Guard cutters circling remote islands. Without warning one afternoon, a single-engine airplane flew low over our island. Cream's "Tales of Brave Ulysses" was playing on our radio while Dove and I were balling in a hammock stretched between two coconut palms. I had already shot my semen into Dove's ass. We had changed positions, and I had pulled my legs up so he could fill me face to face when we heard the approaching engine.

"Don't stop, Dove," I demanded, and he drove into me. I clearly saw the low-flying pilot's stunned expression when he witnessed Dove's tanned ass slamming up and down and realized that he was seeing two boys fucking. Squeezing Dove's cock with my asshole, I flipped the pilot the bird.

"What's he doing?" Dove demanded. His cock was massaging my prostate just right on every stroke. I tightened my legs around his ass pulling him deeper into me.

"Keep humping, lover," I urged.

Between the pilot's first and second pass, the residents of Funky Town bolted into the jungle or concealed themselves in the coral grotto. Nevertheless, our palm-thatched shacks were clearly visible. From such a low altitude, the pilot could have counted the chickens that scratched around town. Terrified by the noise, the ladies tore into the marijuana patch and destroyed the crop. That plane signaled our last day in paradise.

Brother Jim provided us with forged Canadian passports and arranged passage on a trawler that dropped us off on a bleak shoreline below Halifax. We traveled across Canada, assuming various identities until we pretended Canadian citizenship. My given name disappeared, and I became a new man.

I did not return to the United States when President Carter pardoned the draft refuges, nor did I ever write to my family. My passport proved that I was a native Canadian citizen, and I saw no reason why anyone would ever question my origins. I attended college, secured a doctorate in history, and ended up teaching at a college in British Columbia.

I made one journey to Washington, D.C. There I scanned the Vietnam War Memorial for Rick's name, hoping against hope that it wouldn't be there. When I did find it, my vision fogged with the tears filling my eyes. Rick had been killed in action in early September while Dove and I were butt fucking among scampering lizards on the out-island beach.

As for Dove, we drifted apart during our sojourn in Canada. We tried, but we had forged our love under the hot Bahamian sun and our passion could not hold in the colder climes. I still have my old Speedo, but its pattern has faded away and the cloth tears to the touch. Sometimes I lift it from the tissue paper and stare at it in wonder. Beneath it, I find my Florida driver's license and draft card. Then I think of Dove and remember our great days in Funky Town.

("Out-Island Cruising" originally appeared in *Best Gay Love Stories 2010* from Alyson Books)

Paradise, Chérie

Haïti

The passengers' spirits were sagging as the Aeropelican plane struggled into the sky above Miami International Airport. Minutes earlier, the flight crew had requested those in first class to stand in the rear so the antique airliner's nose would lift. Confident that he would not die before his vacation, Ray Martin sat in his second-class seat watching the fear-strained faces of the young men bunched precariously in the aisle. Gazing out the airside window before boarding, Ray had noticed that much of the pilot's window was covered with silver tape. He had boarded anyway, trusting that the winged scrap heap would hold up for a two hour flight.

A college kid, not quite twenty, rubbed his ass, taut in beige chino jeans, against Ray's armrest. Ray could feel the heat of the kid's moons, so he copped a surreptitious feel. The kid never noticed, caught as he was in the contagious dread that had gripped the sweating passengers. Never before had they been asked to stand during take-off. The stewardesses tracing the sign of the cross on their chests and the stewards kissing their boyfriends goodbye did nothing to relieve the tension.

However, not all passengers were affected by the general malaise. "As soon as we get down there, we're gonna suck some big black cock," announced a blond man to his bearded traveling companion.

Ray turned his head in disgust, repulsed not by the suggestion of sucking cock, which he considered a kind act, but by the preference for color. To Ray, cock was cock, and a partiality for hue smacked of racism. Indeed, Ray's own appreciation of cock rose above all considerations; he loved cocks long or short, thick or thin, dark or pale, hooded or trimmed.

Still, Ray had his own prejudices; he was choosy about the shape of the male *derrière*. In contrast to his love for all cocks, he liked only men with perky asses, men with round butts, men with bulky butts, men with bubble butts, men with muscular butts, and even men with fat

101

butts. He wanted men whose asses stuck out; hence, his interest in the youth hunched against his airline seat.

Once the plane had climbed to altitude, the first class passengers returned to their seats. Other than the odd takeoff, the flight was uneventful. Stewards and stewardesses served bags of chips and funny little sandwiches and tropical drinks containing a hint of rum. The plane passed through a dense cloud cover as it crossed the southernmost Bahamas, but the skies were clear as it approached the Land of High Mountains.

Ray's welcome involved a horn-blaring, balls-out taxi ride to the faded gingerbread grandeur of the Hotel Oloffson, which Graham Greene described as "fragile and period and pretty and absurd, an illustration from a book of fairy tales." Greene also wrote that with the hotel's "towers and balconies and wooden fretwork decorations it had the air at night of a Charles Addams house."

Shaken by the taxi ride, Ray downed a *Majik Rhum Barbancourt* on the verandah. The bellman found him, received his dollar tip with a soft *mèsye*, and handed Ray the key. A few minutes later Ray surveyed his room and found his walls decorated with two paintings and an exquisite woodcarving. In the paintings, Ray recognized the styles of Castera Bazile and Télémaque Obin. Through the window other enticing shapes caught his eye, so he tossed his clothes on the bed, pulled up his tropical print swim briefs purchased in Miami, and headed for the swimming pool.

Simbi

Ray halted, awestruck from his eyeballs to his sandals, when he saw me reclining upon my *chaise longue*. I had my head turned to one side, so I caught his reaction as his eyes traveled from my raven hair, down my creamy tan back, and lingered over my prominent rump, which my crimson thong split so delightfully. His eyes did not travel farther than my rear; else he would have seen shapely thighs and calves, a golden ankle bracelet, and well-formed feet.

My skin and shape are a product of my genes; my grandparents were the most gorgeous people of their day. My mother's father was a full-blooded Cherokee, and he married my grandmother, a native of the Ivory Coast and fiercely black. My father's mother was a Korean–Irish mix and her husband a high-yellow quadroon from New Orleans. Their characteristics were blended and enhanced in my parents, who passed to me an ethereal physical beauty, a gift, and yet often a bother.

Torn between pouncing and fleeing, Ray was sidling crabwise toward the sparkling blue water. He couldn't help behaving like a pair of ragged claws, and I was used to extraordinary reactions. Beauty such as mine is often a curse, for men fear that I am unobtainable and their hopes and insecurities war within them. Frequently, I must take the initiative, which I did by pulling him toward me with a smile.

"Hey," Ray announced unimaginatively. I could feel his eyes burning the curves of my rump. "I'm Ray," he said, as his rapt stare warmed my ass.

"Welcome to paradise, *chérie*," I said, rolling onto my side. "I am Simbi." I waved to a passing waiter and ordered two *Ayiti Planteurs*. Then I swung my feet to the cement and patted the seat beside me.

"Do you live in Haïti?" Ray asked, sitting. I slid closer until our hips touched.

"I live here," I said enigmatically. "Did you have a pleasant trip?"

Ray told me about his harrowing flight and his wild taxi ride. I clunked my tongue in commiseration until our drinks arrived.

"This is good," Ray said, his hand briefly touching my thigh.

I caught his flighty hand and brought it back to my thigh again. "Be careful," I warned. "It will sneak up on you?"

"Do you mean the rum?" Ray asked. "Or something else?"

"Ah, *chérie*, when is *rhum* simply a drink?"

Vaudou

Ray's mind was in a whirl. After their second rum punch, Simbi had taken him by the hand and led him to his suite, luxurious far beyond Ray's room, pulled off his thong, and stretched face down on a tropical print comforter on a brass bed. Almost mindlessly, Ray had lubricated his cock from the tube beside the bed and slipped it between the golden mounds. Simbi sighed with contentment as Ray entered and proceeded to hump his ass enthusiastically.

Their first fuck accomplished, they stood in Simbi's shower, kissing and groping, washing each other, and playing beneath the spray. "I'm glad you came," Ray said. "I love making a man come."

"It was a magnificent fuck, Ray," Simbi said. "You filled me with much satisfaction."

Simbi reached for a gigantic towel, dazzling with tropical birds, and began drying Ray. He concentrated on the American tourist's cock and slid the towel between the cheeks of his ass. He dried the tousled hair and styled it with his own comb. Then he applied a scent that he had purchased from an *oungan*. The *vaudou* priest had promised Simbi that the scent would bind a man in lust until Simbi released him.

After helping Ray dress, Simbi dressed himself. He knew that Ray was spinning from the rum and the sex, and most essentially, from the hex. Styling his own hair, Simbi blew a kiss to himself in the bathroom mirror. Once out of the bathroom, he found Ray dozing in the rattan chair. Simbi smiled, climbed into the chair with his new lover, and cuddled up with him.

As Ray's head cleared, he surveyed Simbi's art collection. He saw an 1954 Wilson Bigaud, a Rigaud Benoit, two Philome Obins, a Jasmin Joseph, two Hector Hyppolites, and a lone Murat Brierre sculpture in metal from an opened oil drum. The cornucopia of expensive art made Ray wonder about Simbi; he realized that he knew nothing about his new lover. Was Simbi only a happy, passing fling experienced on an Haïtian vacation, or was he more than that, Ray wondered. As in all matters of love and lust, the answer eluded him.

Simbi

Our golden sun dipped behind the high mountain peaks, painting the sky with a deepening red. As the bright hibiscus and pastel bougainvillea faded with the light, the reverberation of a blown conch shell echoed across the Haïtian hills. At the call of the conch the voices of a thousand dogs gave a musical cue to the deepening night, and the sound of the drums began. The drum is the soul of Haïti, evoking the glories of our past.

People proud in deprivation and poverty drank thick rum from iron kettles still in use from French colonial days. The scent of burning cane fields wafted through the night and into the open windows of my car. My driver Antoine asked if we had a destination in mind.

"*Oui*," I told him. "Take us along the *rivaj*."

As Antoine drove, Ray and I cuddled in the back seat. The trade winds brought a hint of spice and the rustle of palm fronds. The moon was casting a long streak of silver upon the rum-dark Caribbean. After a time, we pulled into the courtyard of an open air bistro, which despite its lack of pretension, served food that reflected my taste for luxury. Next door came flashes of the swirling white robes of *mambo* priestesses dancing for the *lwa*.

Seated at the long trencher table, I ordered two Prestige beers. The waiter knew my generosity, and he hastened, pouring the chilled beer into our glasses.

"This beer is sweet," Ray complained, making a face.

I laughed. "Perhaps the sweet taste of the *Ayitian* beer will grow on you, *chérie*." Turning to the waiter, I ordered *gombos en salade, filets de poisson à la sauce de coriandre, croquettes de fruit à pain*, and *délice tropical en coconut*.

As we dined, a meringue band serenaded us, their sounds mingling with the *vaudou* drums, the cries of the dancers, the wash of the waves, and other sounds of the Haïtian night.

"This is so romantic," Ray breathed, staring into my eyes. "I wish this night could last forever."

"The shortness of the night makes the night sweet," I replied. "Yet for a little while, the sweetness is ours to share."

Ray

A million roosters were crowing in the dawn by the time Simbi and I arrived back at the Hotel Oloffson. Simbi said something in *Kreyòl* to his driver Antoine, who answered in the same soft, melodic pitch, French and oh-so African in tone. Once again, I wondered who was this strange man who had captured my heart – not to mention, my cock.

"Perhaps I should go to my room," I suggested, hoping that he would insist otherwise.

"Come share my bed, Ray," he invited.

Five minutes later we were naked, and I was sucking his creamy cock. Simbi propped his shoulders upon two pillows so he could watch me suck him. I smiled with my eyes as my tongue traveled down his shaft and his thick cock head reached the back of my tongue. Behind Simbi's head hung Wilson Bigaud's painting of bountiful Eden. As I sucked Simbi, I felt as though I were taking all of Haïti into my mouth, Simbi's cock stiffening into a flash of art, color, and music.

As Simbi moaned and twisted with rapture, his warm semen filled my mouth. His sweet cream was fit to top the dessert that had concluded our dinner, and I drank it down. As his ecstasy stilled, the long night took its toll upon him, and he fell into a deep and happy sleep. Licking love's last, I slid in beside him and was asleep within seconds.

The hot Haïtian sun was blinding me, streaming through the open window. I heard Simbi in the bathroom. A second later he emerged wearing his thong, and he tossed me my swim briefs that I'd worn barely an hour. "Jump into your bikini," Simbi suggested. "We'll breakfast by the pool."

Sipping the Haïtian coffee plucked wild from mountainsides, I studied the plate of highly peppered eggs and the impossibly thick slices of deep-fried French toast. I had never tasted food so good, and throwing caution to the trade winds, I dug in. The waiter placed a folded newspaper in front of Simbi. I looked at the foreign headline and asked, "What's it say?"

Simbi pointed at the words. "The headline reads: "President Ford Saved from Assassination."

"That happened a few weeks ago," I said. "One of Charles Manson's women."

"*Non, chérie*, this is a new attempt," Simbi replied. "Also by a female. *Koute.* 'September 22, 1975: Sarah Jane Moore fired a shot at President Gerald Ford as he departed the Saint Francis Hotel in San Francisco. Oliver Sipple, an onlooker, grabbed Moore's arm and prevented the bullet from hitting the president. Secret Service agents pressed the president into an automobile and swept him away to safety.'"

"A man from San Francisco saved Ford?" I asked incredulously. "A gay man?"

"The newspaper does not say."

"It wouldn't," I said bitterly. "I'll bet that Oliver Sipple is a homosexual. I wonder whether the president will even send him a 'Thank You' card."

Rhum

After their breakfast, Simbi led Ray on a tour through the colorful streets of Port-au-Prince. Fending off beggars and prospective guides with a single word *ale*, the couple passed shops painted in primary hues, stopped to gawk at dainty gingerbread houses, stepped over the numerous and treacherous open sewers, bypassed entire families bathing and washing their clothes in any source of running water, thwarted vendors of miraculous supply, and patronized the art galleries. Once Simbi learned that Haïtian art fascinated Ray, they toured the museum and the major galleries. Le Centre d'Art was open at number 17, Rue de la Revolution, and there for thirty dollars American, Ray purchased a small Franklin Joseph Jean oil painting on masonite.

From Le Centre d'Art they boarded a brightly painted tap-tap named *La Puissance Divine*, paid their gourde notes bearing the likeness of Papa Doc Duvalier (about 20¢ American), and ended up sitting on both sides of a rapier-thin *madanm* holding a white goat.

The tap-taps of Haïti are rolling works of art, privately owned small pick-up trucks, vans, and mini-busses, brightly painted with flowers, religious symbols or stories, and scenes from Haïtian folklore. A tap-tap's name reflects its owner's creed, driving skill, thoughts, or sweetheart. Tap-taps take their name from the method passengers use to communicate with the driver; when a passenger wishes to disembark he or she taps on the side of the vehicle. Haïtians require less personal space than people from more developed nations, so sitting on the lap of a stranger is not uncommon.

La Puissance Divine carried Ray and Simbi up the mountain road to Pétionville, where the pair disembarked and walked through the market. The tap-taps to Kenscoff were lined up along the street, and Simbi indicated that they should board *Ti Chérie*, a truck with wooden benches in the bed. *Ti Chérie* was already packed with fifteen souls, so it would depart soonest. Several passengers made way for Ray, and he scrunched his *derrière* onto the bench. Simbi planted his ass on Ray's lap. *Ti Chérie* carried no goats, which was a relief to Ray since the previous goat had chewed the corner of the paper package containing his painting. However, the chickens were a nuisance.

"We get off just past the Baptist Mission," Simbi said, bouncing on Ray's lap as *Ti Chérie* bounded over the gigantic potholes and fallen boulders. "It's a dirt road. Not as good as this one."

"Where are we going?" Ray asked, pulling his painting away from a pecking beak. The chicken regarded Ray with disdain.

"A *rhum* factory," Simbi said.

Shortly, they were walking down a road of white sand under the hot Haïtian sun, past beggars and peddlers, and down cement steps into the dim light. When the two men's eyes had adjusted, and they had found a shaded nook on the balcony, and they had seated themselves on stools made from rum barrels, an ancient retainer hurried to serve them. Without asking, he brought two glasses of fruit-flavored rum. "I am Felix," he said with a flourish. "I bring banana."

"Do you want to sample all of the flavors?" Simbi asked.

"How many are there?" Ray gulped.

"Too many to count," Simbi assured him. He glanced at the shot of rum. "*Pitit*, Felix," he told the waiter.

Ray sampled the banana-flavored rum and set his glass on the edge of the balcony. He could see the old equipment used for distillation, while Simbi told him that the parts had been hand carried up the mountain many years earlier and assembled on location.

"Lemon," Felix said, handing them glasses with half the amount. As anise, apricot, cocoa, coconut, coffee, hibiscus, mango, mint, orange, papaya, and spice followed, along with unflavored rums, and special rums including a potent white, Ray began to feel as though he were swimming over the panorama of cloud shrouded mountains spread out before him.

"It's beautiful," he breathed, shifting as the alcohol seemed to have settled in his buttocks and his feet. He heard the children crying for pennies as a tap-tap passed on the road below. "And heartbreaking."

"*De 'ye' morn gin morn.*"

"Yes," Ray agreed. "Everybody knows that proverb. What can you do?"

"I can fuck your gay ass, *chérie*, until you come like a monkey."

Ray had, of course, meant the question rhetorically, and while Simbi's response seemed a non-sequitur, still Ray was encouraged to give it a try. The eyebrows of Felix, who had arrived with nougat-flavored rum, rose as the orbs beneath widened – whether in shock or interest, none could guess. However, as Felix pocketed the generous tip Ray slipped him, he tipped Ray a suggestive wink and wiggled his hips.

Simbi

I mounted Ray, taking him anally, on the floor of my suite. He had dropped to his hands and elbows like a good Haïtian man, and I drove my thick cock into his hole. When he cried out, I thought that I had hurt him.

"*Mwen regret sa, chérie*," I said.

"Don't be sorry. It's good," Ray moaned. "I almost shot my load." As I pulled back and pushed my cock deeper into him, he yelped, "Oh, yeah, fuck me like that."

I reached for his cock and stroked him with each thrust. "Oh, Simbi," he moaned. "Give it to me, Simbi."

Even the rum we had consumed could not dim our desire. When Ray came, he wailed loud enough to set a hotel maid hammering at my door. Ignoring the din, I humped him harder until the waves of orgasm rushed over me. I pounded him until I was spent, never stopping even when I heard the door pop open and then shut even quicker.

After the event, we napped together, cuddled like spoons with my cock nestled placidly between Ray's mounds. We did not arise until midnight. We dressed, took a light supper in the moonlight, and then went to a popular club where we danced until the roosters were crowing.

Ray's week in Haïti passed far too quickly. On our last night together, I treated him to a restaurant in Pétionville. Eschewing the tap-taps, I again had my chauffeur drive us up the hill. Lighting the hillsides were the fires of many ceremonies, commemorating the living gods of Haïti, and the pulse of the drums sent a throbbing excitement through our veins.

The restaurant was patronized by the upper crust of Pétionville society. I had made a reservation, and our table was waiting us. Our entrée was *salade de pamplemousse*, followed by *poulet à l'ananas et au coco with frites de manioc*. *Le dessert* consisted of *tourment d'amour with liqueur au café*. After the meal, we drove higher to the ridge of Kenscoff. There we stopped. Bathed in the music of the drums, we looked out over the lighted city of Port-au-Prince, its poverty and squalor hidden so that only its beauty remained.

There in the moonlight we made love for the last time. Naked I bent with my hands on my knees while Ray took me from behind, his breath hot in my ear as he filled me rhythmically. Too weakened to stand, I sank to my hands and knees, and we came in the traditional Haïtian manner.

Ray

Simbi wanted to have Antoine drive me to the airport, but I preferred to take the tap-tap. It seemed simpler. I felt a pang of guilt after our week of lovemaking, for I knew that I might never return to Haïti, and I doubted that I'd ever see Simbi again.

I climbed aboard a tap-tap named *San Limit* just outside the Hotel Oloffson, its driver assuring me that we would reach the airport in time. We had a long wait while he made certain to collect as many paying passengers as possible, and I arrived at the airport in time to learn that my flight was overbooked and I wouldn't have a seat. When the plane took off, the counter closed, leaving the stranded passengers to fend for themselves. No more planes were due out from Port-au-Prince that day, so I waited again for a tap-tap.

I reached the hotel in the early evening. Carrying my bag in one hand and the painting I had purchased under my arm, I sauntered around toward the pool. The pool lights had just come on, and colored flood lights illuminated the palms, hibiscus, bougainvillea, and crotons. In the fairy light, I saw Simbi sitting at a table. He was wearing his crimson thong, but he had already picked up another tourist. The young man's hand was resting on Simbi's thigh, and I could tell that they were deep in conversation. As I watched, they arose and walked arm and arm toward Simbi's suite.

A pang shot through me. Turning away from the hotel, I found a taxi and demanded that the driver take me to the airport.

"*Aeropò*? There no *avyon* now, *moun*," he said.

"It doesn't matter," I said.

I wasn't the only passenger waiting for the morning flight. Most benches were already occupied, but I found a free one and staked a claim to it. A guard was walking around with a rifle, which he would frequently aim at the runway to pick off imaginary invaders. I smiled at him as I slipped him five dollars. He patted his rifle, a gesture that I hoped promised an offer of protection.

In the morning, I caught an Air France flight to Miami. As my plane lifted above the mountain ranges, I thought of Simbi and smiled. The sharp pang I had felt had been merely the pinch of a passing imp. I was leaving him, so hoping he would pine for me was the height of egocentricity. As my plane soared above the clouds, I was carrying a happy memory that I would cherish ever.

("Paradise, Chérie" originally appeared in *Tales of Travelrotica for Gay Men*, Volume 2, from Alyson Books)

The Second Impulse

The hot water and fumes were making me light-headed. Sulfurous bubbles were bursting the pond's surface like farts from the underworld. Shifting away from a bubble, my hand touched Jeff's bare ass. A thrill shot through my dick head, which I masked by saying, "I'll bet this pool is radioactive."

"No," Larry said. "Well, slightly. Not enough to hurt us."

My face must have given me away. Chip's hand brushed the head of my cock. "Ben's got a hard-on," he sang out.

I felt my face flushing. My first impulse was to blame my condition on the hot water. I scarcely knew these guys, and I didn't know what they'd think about my dick getting hard while we four crouched buck-naked in the small geothermally heated mineral-water pond.

Larry and Jeff snickered at my discomfiture, and laughed harder when Chip added, "You think he's got a hard on for our asses or our cocks, guys?"

My embarrassment was acute, but Jeff took mercy on me. "You're not alone, Ben," he said, rising abruptly from the milky mud suspended in the greenish water. I found his swollen cock head protruding within an inch of my lips.

My first impulse was to pull away, and not because there was anything wrong with Jeff's dick. It had a thick, juicy look, though the heat of the water had made it look a bit boiled and shiny. Jeff's circumcised head flared away from the shaft, and it seemed to be puffed up as if it wanted to spit at me. His pee hole had a wide slit, hooded with a tiny flap. The thought of the rich cum that would spurt from that hole emboldened me to an act I would never have dared had I not been half-dazed by the fumes.

My first impulse was to pull away, but it was my second impulse that I followed. I touched the head of Jeff's cock with my lips. As I kissed his cock head, I closed my eyes so that I could not see the guys' reaction. However, I could not close my ears so I expected to hear them say something. Their only response was utter silence. Amazed silence? Stunned silence? I could hear the bubbles of gas breaking the surface, and the wind blowing down the blighted slopes. I could hear the hissing of the steam plume that vented not too far from our pond, a grim reminder of the volatile nature of the land we were occupying.

Better judgment told me that I should not suck Jeff's cock, especially with Chip and Larry watching, but my judgment was faulty due to the poisonous air, and naked impulse made me touch my tongue to that delicious cock. My lips formed a circle, a tight opening, through which the head of Jeff's cock passed. The weight of his cock head inside my mouth almost made me come. I felt a throb through my entire pelvis. My asshole contracted and dilated in the hot water as my hands arose from the pool, almost as if they had a will of their own, and slid sensuously up Jeff's thighs. His hamstrings were tight from hours in the gym, and his buttocks were nicely rounded.

Gripping his ass with both hands, I took Jeff's cock deeper into my mouth. His buttocks were so firm that I could massage them as if they were melons while I licked the underside of his dick head and down his cock shaft. I fucked his dick with my tongue, controlling position with my head and by pulling his butt toward my mouth. As I traveled his cock, I found that I was taking him deeper, deeper and closer to my throat than I had ever taken any other man.

Not that I had vast experience. Jeff's was only the third cock I had sucked up until that time. When I was younger, I sucked Brother Slim's dick a couple of times, which is when I found out how much I love men's jism. Brother Slim was the youth pastor at my parents' church, and when I started rebelling, my oblivious parents encouraged me to go on Christian outings with Brother Slim. The "outings" consisted of visits to Brother Slim's sleazy little apartment in downtown Sioux City where he showed me a lot of magazine pictures of men sucking cock or taking a big one up the ass. Then he taught me how to suck his dick, though Brother Slim never returned the compliment. (Brother Slim wasn't all that slim, either, being somewhat "corn-fed," as we used to say back in Iowa). However, his cock was thick and his semen tasted better than custard.

I pulled back on Jeff's cock and popped my lips over his dick head, worrying the circumcised rim especially, while flicking his pee hole with the tip of my tongue. Jeff gasped when I did that. I nibbled just a little, too, but not too much. I used my teeth just enough to excite him, to stimulate him to pump every drop of his semen into my mouth when he finally did come. I was careful not to bite or frighten him. I bit Captain Allen once, and he didn't care for it at all.

Allen Waverly was the guy my parents hired to paint our house one summer. My pop was a big-time Republican, and "Captain Allen" was our precinct captain in addition to being a professional house painter. Captain Allen usually worked with a helper, a high school boy named Springer. I always wondered about their relationship, because the first time I saw Captain Allen on his ladder my gaydar pinged as though it was scanning incoming nuclear missiles.

Springer was the most gorgeous African American male I have ever seen, captain of our high school swim team – I attended every practice just to watch Springer swish toward the pool in his brilliant green Speedo. Captain Allen was about ten years older, but no less gorgeous. Still, he was about a hundred times more masculine than Springer, who had an ass like a girl's and a mouth like black cherries. Captain Allen favored faded cut-off jeans and white tee shirts. His tight shorts and shirts showed off his powerfully developed figure, not to mention his most remarkable asset, the big cock that formed an impressive bulge in the front of his shorts.

I hadn't sucked a cock for a couple of years at that time, not since Brother Slim had gotten into the teensiest bit of trouble when he propositioned an undercover vice cop and ended up moving to another town (and probably another church where he could find more young males and introduce them to the joys of fellatio).

The day my parents left town for a three-day state Republican convention turned out to be the same day that Springer couldn't make it to work due to a sick grandmother. I hurried down to the yard to greet Captain Allen, and he was overly friendly as usual. However, he disappointed me when he climbed up his ladder and went to work painting our house (a lackluster white, of course, to match our picket fence).

I went up to my room. My window was open to let in the breeze, for the day was hot. I stretched out on my bed and thought about Springer for a while. Then I thought about Captain Allen. My cotton shorts were bulging by that time, so I slipped my hand into my waistband and started playing with my dick. I fiddled with it dry for a few minutes before I knew that I was going to have to jerk off. I pulled off my shorts and my tee shirt too, because I like to masturbate completely naked, spit into my hand, and started my long-practiced stroking.

I was picturing Captain Allen, and though I must have heard the ladder moving against the side of the house, I paid no attention to the sound or to the sudden appearance of a set of rungs directly in front of my window. I kept jacking my cock, faster and harder, and I was getting close to the point of no return when I saw Captain Allen's head appear at my window. The next instant his eyes met mine, he saw what I was doing, he paused briefly, and then he climbed up another two rungs so that his crotch was centered upon my window.

Then Captain Allen did something amazing. His hand lowered into my range of vision, pulled down his zipper, and let his cock bob free. He was hard as a rock. I had stopped beating my meat when Captain Allen hove into view, and the hiatus had placed my impending orgasm on hold. I jumped from my bed, rushed to the window, and dropped to my knees. Captain Allen's magnificent erection, a thick, darkly complexioned, and hooded cock stood waiting for me. I closed my mouth around it and let it slide over my tongue.

I gripped Captain Allen's shaft, as Brother Slim had taught me, so I wouldn't gag. I worked the head of his dick, and as I used my tongue and lips, jacking him between strokes with my mouth, I jerked my own cock. I spit into my hand again to lubricate my swollen dick, and then I sucked hard on Captain Allen's dick. I heard him moan, and I wondered whether he was still sliding his paintbrush over the old boards of our house.

My dick grew heavier. At the same time, I felt Captain Allen soften slightly, and then grow diamond hard. He was approaching orgasm at the same time I was. I vowed to make us come together. I sucked his cock with all my might, torturing the foreskin of his dick while I squeezed the tip of my own. Orgasmic tingles rushed through the head of my cock. I was committed to come, and I heard Captain Allen moan, "Oh, you cocksucker."

Somehow, I liked the sound of it: Ben Marshal, cocksucker. It had an official ring. Maybe I should have business cards printed. That thought was erased as I tasted semen, spicier than Brother Slim's custard, but flavorful still. My tingles had increased, turning into waves that crashed down my cock so that my pelvic muscles contracted and a burst of my jism splattered against the wall under the window.

Captain Allen's cum hit the back of my throat, and I let it go down. I wanted his sperm in my stomach. I wanted to eat his load, swallow him whole. He came, moaning, hanging on a ladder fifteen feet in the air, and quivering from my cock-sucking power. I sucked his cock until he had come his all, and while I sucked, I shot my own load on the wall and onto the floor.

While my memories swam before my exploding consciousness, I continued sucking Jeff's cock. I was hard, but I did not masturbate. Why not, I cannot really say, except that Larry and Chip were watching. There is no logic to that cause; I can only state it.

By then, Jeff was grabbing the back of my head as tightly as I was gripping his butt. He was fucking my mouth, and I was fucking his dick with my lips, tongue, and throat. As Jeff's dick reached the back of my throat, I swallowed hard, time after time. I tried to swallow his dick. At the same time, I slid my finger into his asshole, which was hot and tight, but lubricated with the weird water of the volcanic pond. I was using the hot, slightly radioactive volcanic mud to lubricate his asshole so that I could slide my finger inside. More and more, I opened him up until my entire forefinger was rubbing against his prostate.

"Oh, the way you suck me, Ben," Jeff moaned loudly. "Oh, man, I'm gonna come."

I could hardly answer, since his dick was fucking my throat, but I pressed harder against his prostate, massaging the little gland enough to drive him to distraction.

"Oh, god, here I come," Jeff howled. I kept swallowing, his cock's head penetrating into my throat. I knew that he was shooting his semen down into my esophagus, but there was no more hope of my tasting it. He was coming beyond reason, beyond compassion, beyond compare, and beyond any rationality whatsoever. I was the master of his cock, the ruler of his orgasmic universe. I had only to suck him, and he must obey.

"Oh, Ben," Jeff moaned. "I can hardly stand it. Your mouth is so good. Ah, Ben."

I met Chip when I signed up for a summer English course at Clark College, in Vancouver, Washington. That summer I was staying with my Aunt Donna, who insisted that I "better myself" rather than lounging around the house. Chip was taking the same course, and when

I found out that he was the President of the Gay Penguins, I asked him about the club. The club didn't have regular summer meetings, but he suggested we have lunch at Burgerville.

After we collected our food, Chip led me to a table occupied by his two friends, Jeff and Larry. We talked for a few minutes about the local scene. (All three said that it was better to go across the river to Portland, Oregon). Before the meal ended, the guys told me that they were going on a weekend camping trip and hike around Mount St. Helens.

"Want to come along, Ben?" Chip asked.

"Sure," I agreed readily, never having taken a camping trip nor hiked more than a mile and a half in my life.

Right after class on Thursday, we piled into Larry's jeep and set out for the mountain. We parked in a remote location, loaded our gear, food, and water onto our backs, and set out over rough terrain. By the time we camped for the evening, I was half-dead. I hurt all over, but we still had to pitch our camp, build a fire, and fix our food before we could eat and sleep.

Every rock that had spewed out of the 1980 volcanic eruption must have found its way under my sleeping bag. If the rocks weren't enough to keep me wakeful, my dread of a rattlesnake or mountain lion attacking me while I slept would have. I spent a night in near agony, and decided that morning could not come soon enough.

Morning came far too early. I have to admit that breakfast was good: eggs, ham, and flapjacks cooked over an open fire. The food restored me, so that I set out with high good spirits that lasted an hour. By the time we stopped for lunch, I didn't think I could walk another step. Nevertheless, I would have died rather than admit my weakness. Almost immediately after lunch, we ventured upon a landscape where the vegetation had not yet returned. The air reeked of rotten eggs, and great chalky deposits streaked the rocks. We passed a vent where steam and gas spewed out of the ground, testament to the molten lava beneath the thin crust.

Larry said that the white streaks were mineral deposits and the smell was a combination of hydrogen sulfide and sulfur dioxide, which escaped in the venting steam and bubbled up in the pools. Shortly thereafter, we came upon the small pond, about five feet across. The water looked like greenish milk, and as I stared at it, a smelly bubble broke the surface. Larry tested the bottom with a stout stick, finding it to be only about four feet at its deepest point. After he had tied a thermometer to the stick and measured the temperature at all depths, he pronounced it safe.

"Safe from what?" I asked, staggered that these guys seriously planned to get into that hellbath.

"We don't want to get scalded," Jeff said. "People have lost legs from wading into geothermal pools, those who weren't killed outright."

"The water is heated by the molten magma just beneath the surface. If we waded in and the crust was so thin that we broke through, well, it would just be too bad."

None of this information motivated me to soak in that pond, but the guys were already getting naked. I glanced at Jeff's thick cock and Chip's sculpted ass and the chest and arm muscles that Larry had worked for in the gym. For a moment, the reeking air nearly overcame me. I felt a minute of dizziness, and I was having trouble getting a breath. The air seemed to be burning my lungs. Then I glanced down and saw that I had completely undressed myself. The guys were already squatting down in the hot pond, so I waded in behind them.

When I pulled my mouth off Jeff's dick, Jeff dropped back into the pond as if someone had biffed him. His hands slipped under water, and I knew that he was groping his dick and balls to make sure they were still attached. Jeff wasn't the only one feeling his dick. My cock was swollen with desire. Chip had risen to his feet so his erection jutted toward his stomach. He fingered the head of his cock, not really jacking, but simply fondling and petting his toy. Larry was beating his meat furiously.

Jeff was still staring about with wonder. "That was the best," he moaned, "the blowjob of a lifetime. Man, nobody has ever sucked me like that."

"Better than the blow jobs I deliver?" Larry said looking wounded to the core. He stopped jerking off in order to study my mouth.

"Ben, please, man," Jeff pleaded. "You just gotta do these guys. It's the only way they're gonna believe me."

I could feel my mouth widening into an ingratiating grin. "Sure," I agreed, mildly abashed that my new chums regarded me an oral whore.

119

"I could suck dicks all day," I added, trying to sound like a sophisticated gay man, and sounding more like a cock-crazed newbie.

"Larry is closer to getting his rocks off, Ben," Chip offered. "You better suck him first."

Larry rose from the water. His cock was smaller than Jeff's, but it had a ferocious look. Vowing to tame the wild critter, I touched my lips to it. Chip dropped to his knees beside me, placing his face close so he could see. I bobbed my head upon Larry's cock and worked his dick head with my lips. Larry moaned loudly. By that time, Jeff had recovered from his shattering orgasm, so he too pressed close.

I wrapped my tongue around the underside of Larry's dick and fucked him with my mouth. Meanwhile I grabbed his butt with one hand and started jerking off my own cock with the other. Chip pulled my hand away from my dick. "Save it, Ben," he urged. "We have a surprise for you later."

Making Larry come took no time at all. Within a minute, he was shooting his semen onto my tongue. It was warm and sweet, and I let it slide down my throat.

Chip took a little longer, but not much. His cock was longer than Larry's, but not as thick as Jeff's. I'm partial to the thick ones, personally, but I enjoy sampling every size and shape. I swallowed the head of Chip's cock into my throat and let him shoot his spunk straight down. When he pulled out of my throat, I felt a distinct wooziness. I staggered, and the fellows caught me.

"Come on, guys," Larry urged. "We better get away from these volcanic fumes. We've breathed enough of this sulfur. Especially you, Ben."

"But what about my surprise?" I protested as the guys loaded our packs and hiked naked over the hot landscape.

"Your surprise will come later," Chip assured me, taking me by the arm and forcing me to walk a little faster.

We did not have to hike far before we left the thin crust and the volcanic vents behind. We found a meadow where the wildflowers had returned and there was a grove of young aspens. We pitched camp there, and after breathing in the pure air and enjoying a hearty supper, the guys proved that they were not like my first two lovers. Brother

Slim and Captain Allen had been takers; my new friends took and gave joyously.

"You passed the test, Ben," Chip said. "You're one of us now."

"Ben, you've noticed," Jeff began, "that everybody got his rocks off today – except for you."

Here comes the surprise, I thought. The guys giggled with anticipation. "Who gets to suck Ben's dick, or do we take turns?" Chip asked.

Jeff shook his head. "I had something else in mind," he said. "Something I'll bet Ben has never done."

A funny feeling came over me. What was he going to propose?

"You just want his cock up your ass, Jeff," Larry taunted. "We're onto your wicked ways." He giggled again when he said it, so I guessed that it was a running gag.

"Like you guys don't?" Jeff taunted. "However, Ben sucked my dick first, so he gets to fuck me first. He can do your asses after mine, if he feels up to coming three times. How about it, Ben?"

My first impulse was to claim that I was an exclusive cocksucker. After all, I'd never done anything else. But my hands remembered the feel of Jeff's firm ass mounds, and my cock stiffened. I was hard to fuck his ass. I followed my second impulse. "Yeah," I said. "I want to fuck you, Jeff."

Jeff positioned himself face downward, and raised one leg toward his chest. The invitation was obvious, but I was not sure how to proceed. Eager to teach, Chip and Larry grabbed my dick, which was rock hard. They lubricated my cock and slipped on an extra-strength condom. They lubricated the outside of the condom, nearly driving me to raptures as they rubbed the lube onto my wrapped dick. I wasn't sure that I could hold out until I slipped my cock into Jeff's ass.

Surprisingly, I did hold out. The unfamiliar territory unnerved me sufficiently so that while I pushed my cock between Jeff's butt cheeks, my mind reeled at the novelty.

"Slide it in, Ben," Jeff urged. Chip and Larry watched with hot, eager eyes. When I pushed downward, I heard Jeff draw a deep breath. He opened readily so my cock slipped into his hot, tight chute. I pushed it in to the hilt, pulled back, and plunged home again. His ass felt like a thousand hands and mouths massaging my cock.

"Oh, that's good," I moaned, fucking like a real man for the first time. I thrust and rose, lifting my bare ass and plunging down, riding the push and pull of the flesh, and savoring the tingles in my cock as I fucked Jeff's wonderful ass.

"Jeff's ass is a great ride, Ben," Larry laughed as the throes of orgasm struck me hard.

Chip added, "My ass is better."

As I wrung the last drops from my swollen cock, I looked forward to many happy outings with this group.

("The Second Impulse" originally appeared in *Ultimate Gay Erotica 2009* from Alyson Books)

When Wade's Woody Was Running

To my way of thinking, *Gidget* was the great film of 1959, so I went to the theatre daily while it was playing. Unlike the thousands of American boys who lusted after Gidget, I had no interest in cuddling up to Sandra Dee – I wanted to be Gidget – so I could get a Moondoggie of my own. After blissfully watching the movie eight times in four days, I withdrew my total $50.00 savings to buy a 9'4" balsa wood surfboard, and nearly dislocated my shoulder trying to balance upon it on my bed. I believed that if I could only master the board, rise to my feet, and dance upon the waves, I would end up doing a wildly different dance with Moondoggie in the surf shack.

I imagined that Moondoggie and I would kiss romantically, which would inevitably lead to heavy petting. He would cup my ass with both hands, and whisper in my ear that I had a great butt. Then we would kiss more deeply. Moondoggie's tongue would push into my mouth. He would be aggressive and urgent in his need to master me, and I would be happy to let him take me.

"Oh, Tony," Moondoggie would moan. "I have to fuck you now."

"Yes, Moondoggie, take me any way you want me."

As I reclined upon my bed, thinking of Moondoggie, my hand slipped into the waistband of my Jockey briefs. My other hand felt up my own ass. I pushed my underwear into my ass crack as I rubbed my dry cock. Meanwhile, I imagined Moondoggie pushing me down on his cot in the surf shack. His cock would be hard and thick when he pulled off his surf trunks.

"Take me, Moondoggie," I urged, spitting into my hand and flogging my cock wildly. Moondoggie would need no urging. He was horny as hell and ready to shoot his load into me. Thumbing the head of my dick, I tried to guess whether Moondoggie preferred my mouth or my ass. Sometimes I would blow him, and his imaginary cock would push through my lips and slide along my tongue. Other times he would prefer to fuck me, and I would lie upon my stomach while Moondoggie parted the cheeks of my ass and pushed his thick surfer cock into me. My fantasies were sadly lacking in detail because, as yet, I had not even kissed another boy, nor held hands with one, much less moved to the advanced stages of fucking or sucking. I knew about butt fucking and cocksucking, though, and I tried to flesh out my fantasy life while I furiously pounded my cock.

My fantasies lapsed while I surfed the wild waves of orgasm that began as minute ripples in the head of my cock but churned with potent rollers that deposed my senses. Explosions of light and color blasted my conscious contemplation, my breath came in heavy rasps, and my heart raced. My lips quivered, my nipples crinkled, and my eyelids fluttered. My jism drenched the front of my briefs and scented the air with the smell of spilled semen. Then I lay in a half-awakened state, revisiting the shreds of my boy-Gidget fantasy and staring dreamily at the movie poster thumb tacked to my bedroom wall. After a while, I arose and stepped into the shower, cleaning my pubic zone, and soaping and rinsing my undies lest Mom should discover the evidence of my secret joy.

In Southern California, summer is Gidget time. Summer is when the Moondoggie college boys come out to play. I jumped the gun. Five weeks before I was due to graduate high school, I bought a new cabana set consisting of a red and yellow jacket with matching swim trunks, and hit the beach at Malibu – by getting my mom to drop me off with my surfboard. Life at Malibu Point was not as I had envisioned it. First, there was nobody making and selling boards on the beach, nor were there a bunch of hungry boys living in a surf shack. The authorities had stationed lifeguards along the beach to make certain nobody violated ordinances, lit bonfires, built shacks, or threw alcoholic luaus.

The beach was so crowded that I couldn't believe my eyes. Even worse, there must have been about a hundred boys (and a significant number of females) trying to ride surfboards. The movie had attracted every college coed, her sister, brother, boyfriend, and father to Malibu. Still, those sun struck fellows looked good to me. I spotted one with real Moondoggie potential, sidled up to him, and struck up a conversation.

"Bitchin' surf."

He looked at me as though I were some weird squishy sea creature and said nothing.

"Nice combers," I tried again, trying to conceal my budding erection by shifting my board to my other arm, but dropping it on his toe instead. He let out a howl that brought stares up and down the beach. "Do you want me to stop annoying you?" I asked ruefully.

"I want your heart to stop beating," he suggested.

I decided that I would have better luck with these boys after I showed off my potential. After all, I was a member of my high school swim team – how hard could surfing be? Surfing had looked easy in the movie. I soon discovered that I had no more idea how to surf than a jackass does. I could hardly paddle the board, and ended up gripping my rails as the waves washed me backwards toward the beach. I consoled myself that I was riding a surfboard, even though I was lying down. No sooner had I congratulated myself for that small victory, than I wiped out – meaning I rolled off my board, lost it in the surf, and flailed back to the beach. I looked more like a drowning sailor than a skilled swimmer.

Coughing, wheezing, spitting, and gasping, I continued cutting a poor figure on shore. I figured that I would earn the nickname Wipeout at best, but I wasn't good enough for the real surfers to notice. They ignored my pathetic attempts. Nor did any of them call each other by fancy surfer names – not within my hearing. There was no Kahuna (where was Cliff Robertson when I needed him?), but only Bill, Biff, Chuck, Dave, Mike, Sam, Tom, and Wade.

I decided that my failure had to be rooted in the cabana set. I tossed the jacket and wore the trunks but I still couldn't catch a wave, much less paddle out to one, and the other surfers yelled to me to get out of the ocean. I called my mom from a pay phone and went home tired, waterlogged, miserable, and blaming my condition on the cabana set. With the right clothes, I would succeed where I had failed before.

Mom's friend Beth sewed me a pair of custom trunks in a classic Hawaiian print. Beth assured me that the cotton fabric would hold up nicely when I fell off the board. I looked damned good in the surf trunks, but they didn't help me ride the board, and riding the board was my ticket to riding a surfer. Once again, I placed my board upon my bed with the fin hanging off the edge just as Gidget did in the movie and sprang to my feet. I promptly toppled sideways as the board shifted.

The next morning, Mom drove me back to Malibu. I paddled out and watched what the other surfers did. They turned their boards and climbed onto their knees. To my horror, even climbing to my knees was too much for me. I slipped off my board and didn't see it again until I washed up on the beach.

I ended up sitting about forty yards from The Pit, with a group of wannabe surfers, smoking cigarettes, and telling about how we'd be riding the tube except for the war wound that crippled us. One of the real surfers walked by, looked us over, and mouthed, "Faggots." I jumped to my feet, grabbed my board, and headed for the water. I passed the surfer on the way. "The next time you call me a faggot," I said to him, "you better have your cock out."

His eyebrows raised and his eyes popped. I kept stalking toward the never-ending surf, but he caught me, grabbed my shoulder, and swung me around. Having learned one lesson, I kept a tight grip on my surfboard so I didn't drop it on his toe.

"You really want to learn how to surf?" he asked. Something electrical passed between us, something that was more than the touch of his hand on my shoulder. I felt an explosion deep down, and I knew that this surfer boy was destined to be my Moondoggie. His was the face that launched long boards for me.

"Yeah," I said. It was true. I had to ride the board. Riding the board, dancing upon the wave, and walking upon the froth were the keys to everything I thought I wanted. Skill upon the rolling sea would lead to romance and pleasure. "Yes," I said. "I have to do this."

"Lay your stick down," he insisted. "Wait here." He ran off, and in a minute, he was back with a borrowed board without a fin. He laid the board upon the sand and told me to kneel upon it.

"I'm Wade Walker. Sometimes called Waterwalker."

"I'm Tony," I told him, relieved to hear surfers really bestowed each other with nicknames. The movie wasn't entirely fiction.

"Okay, Tony," he said with a generous smile. "There's a few basics you gotta learn – like paddling, duck diving or turtle rolling, catching a wave, popping up, and positioning."

My heart would have sunk, but Wade was looking yummier by the second. "That's a lot," I admitted, almost breathing into his ear.

"The hardest thing is popping up, so I'm gonna teach that first. Lie down on your stomach."

Now that order sounded encouraging. However, I realized that he meant I was supposed to lie on the surfboard, so I assumed the position. Then Wade took me through the steps of rising to my knees and then popping up onto my feet so that I was standing sideways on the board. After an hour, my arms were throbbing with the effort. "Boy, oh boy," I said. "I'm a competition swimmer. I thought my arms and chest were stronger."

With a laugh, Wade swatted my ass. "You're doing great. You're using your muscles differently, but you'll get used to it. Let's get wet."

After returning the borrowed board, Wade taught me paddling and positioning my body on the board. Of course, as a swimmer, paddling came naturally to me. Still, by the end of the day, I didn't feel that I had improved much, but Wade said that I had great potential.

"You're gonna be a fine surfer, Tony."

I brightened, and my exhaustion slipped away.

"Are you free tomorrow?" he asked, as we stood in the waist deep water.

"Sure." I was in love. Never before had any boy paid so much attention to me.

"In the morning I'll teach you how to get through the waves so they don't push you back." I was holding on to my own surfboard and nodding my head when I felt Wade press his palm against my outer thigh. It was no accident. He didn't pull it away, but moved it around so that his hand slipped between my legs. My cock stiffened, and after a surprised hesitation, I reached for his dick.

"Aren't you the boy who called me a faggot?" I asked, feeling the outline of his cock through the cotton fabric.

Wade grinned, but he glanced around rather apprehensively. "That was meant for Scooter's benefit," he said. A couple of swimmers were paddling our direction, so Wade stepped back. The fear of denunciation, arrest, and prison affected me too.

"Do you have your car here?" he asked.

"Oh, I caught a lift," I breezed, not wanting to admit that I'd been getting my mom to drive me to the beach.

Wade brightened. "Come on," he urged. "I'll give you a lift." We let our erections deflate before we left the water. Wade picked up his board and led me to a 1938 Pontiac station wagon. Though Wade had painted the hood and fenders red – with a paintbrush – wood covered most of the body. "Here's my Woody," Wade offered, lifting up the back door and sliding in our surfboards. Mine slipped sideways.

"Damn," he said. "We don't want to ding it." Jumping into the back, Wade realigned our boards. His butt stuck out, and I could not resist the rounded mounds. I climbed in and ran my hands over his taut surfer's ass.

"Oh boy," he said. He shivered with pleasure at my intimate caress. I let my hand glide down his ass crack and push between his legs. I felt the hot underside of his balls through the cotton. Wade's crotch pulsed and quivered beneath my probing fingers. Then I again explored the generous mounds of his butt until he twisted and wriggled into my arms.

"Are you okay with kissing me?" he asked hesitantly.

My fingers combed his sun-bleached hair as our lips pressed. I could scarcely believe that I was finally kissing another boy. I could feel his hard cock poking against mine as I pushed my tongue into his hot mouth. Wade sucked my tongue and stabbed it with his own, his lips hot, his body squirming against mine. My cock felt as if it were going to rip through my swim trunks. Trying to adjust it, I pushed my trunks down so my cock popped free.

"Wait," Wade gasped, drawing away from me. He twisted and pulled the back door shut. With our surfboards blocking the salt-encrusted windows, no one could see us. Wade pulled my trunks over my bare feet. Then he pushed off his own trunks. Naked together, we kissed again. My mind reeled, not only from the fast shift in my fortunes, but also from Wade's passion. His enthusiasm for my body was beyond flattering.

My hand was on his naked cock. His skin was smooth and hot. The circumcised head swelled hard like a billowy mushroom. As I squeezed it, a munificent quantity of thin fluid leaked out, slicking my hand. Bathed in this pre-ejaculate, my hand could pound more freely on Wade's cock. For the past months, I had been dreaming of sucking a surfer's cock or taking a blond beach boy's thick dick up my ass. However, Wade wasn't ready for that step.

"Let's jerk each other off," he suggested, his eyes shining with anticipation.

I would have been a heel to disappoint him. I never leaked much fluid before I ejaculated, but Wade was dripping enough to give us both slippery palms. Soon he was jerking my cock with his semen slick hand while I beat his meat. And even as we stroked, rubbed, squeezed, and fondled cock, we kept on kissing.

As we grew close to shooting our all, we began fucking each other's fist. We sprawled face to face, humped our asses toward each other, and let our free hands roam. Wade's hand gently slipped over the mound of my ass as I thrust into his fist.

"Oh, that's nice, Wade," I moaned, pulling my mouth from his.

"Yeah," Wade said. "I haven't done this with a boy since . . ." He stopped as though it would wound me to learn I was not his first jerk-off buddy. I, on the other hand, would have loved to hear more.

My cock seemed to grow heavier, and as it did, Wade's cock pulsed and thickened in my hand. Tingles rushed through the head of my dick, while Wade's cock leaked enough fluid to fill a beer can. Then the full throes of orgasm struck me. I rode the waves without a board, wave after wave of intense pleasure. I felt the muscles contract the underside of my balls and spasm throughout my pelvis. The first contraction was hard and tight, but so intense was the burst of pleasure that I could not feel the jism squirting from my dick. I did feel the hot spunk striking my own pubic hairs and even splattering high onto my stomach.

I squeezed Wade's dick tighter, directing it up as I did so, and something hot and wet slicked my right nipple. Even as Wade's contractions stilled, mine continued, and I became more aware of the spurts from my tortured dick that splattered against Wade's skin, decorating him with my spunk nearly to his chin. Suddenly, the back of Wade's Woody smelled of spilled jism, and we broke apart, gasping for breath and laughing at the same time.

"Isn't that better than jacking your own?" Wade hooted.

"Oh, yeah," I agreed. "That's the first time I ever did it with another boy."

"I did it a couple of other times," Wade confessed.

"Tell me about it," I urged. He hesitated, but I tweaked the head of his cock between my thumb and forefinger. "Come on, Wade. I'm not gonna be jealous. I want to hear about it."

Wade told me about his high school friend Charles. In the back row of a dark movie theatre, Wade and Charles started whacking off. One thing led to another until they had their hands on each other's dick. "Chal only let me jerk him off twice," Wade said. "He acted kind of ashamed after we did it the first time, and after the second, Chal said that we shouldn't do it anymore."

"He thought playing with your dick was wrong? It didn't feel wrong to me."

"Me, neither. Besides, there was another problem with Chal."

"What was that?"

"He didn't surf. He couldn't even swim."

Then I knew that I had to learn how to surf if I died in the attempt. If it would please Wade, I'd work my ass off to become the best surfer on the beach.

Wade and I tried to clean up with a towel as best we could. Then he drove me home. I invited him in, but he shook his head. "I better not meet your mother while I've got streaks of your cum on my stomach. I'll pick you up tomorrow morning."

Leaving my surfboard in the back of Wade's Woody, I rushed into the house and up the stairs. I heard Mom shouting something, but I called down, "Let me shower first, Mom. I'm covered with salt and sand." If she only knew, I thought, grinning to myself as I stood under the spray. I washed extra good and soaped up my swim trunks too, since they bore telltale spots.

My arms were exhausted, but I did fifty push-ups and fifty pull-ups that evening. If I was going to get up on that surfboard, I was going to need more than swimmer's muscles. I surprised myself by sleeping rather well, but I woke early. Wade was picking me up at eight, and I wanted to be ready for him.

"What's the matter, Tony?" Mom yelled when she heard me rummaging around in the kitchen.

"I'm getting breakfast," I called.

"It's five o'clock in the goddamn morning," she moaned. "You've never got up this early in your life."

"Wade's picking me up. We're going surfing."

Mom staggered into the kitchen pulling her bathrobe around her and firing up a Pall Mall. After sucking in a morning lungful of unfiltered smoke, she looked at the five strips of bacon and the four eggs I was frying in bacon grease.

"I need protein," I said. "I gotta get my strength up."

"Holy shit," Mom said and dumped a third of a cup of grounds into the old percolator.

Wade pulled up in his Woody about five minutes before eight, which meant that I had been eagerly ready for only an hour. For reasons I could never fathom, Mom escorted me to the curb, smoking, slurping her coffee, and prying into Wade's background. By the time I had planted my ass in the passenger seat, Mom had found out Wade's address, his parents' names, his school, his general state of health, his immunizations records, his surfing skills, and his family's political affiliations.

Red faced, I said, "Good morning," as we left Mom firing questions from the curb about Wade's upcoming graduation.

"My mother would have done exactly the same," Wade confessed, making me feel a lot better. I loved Mom, but she could be embarrassing. I could not imagine what she would do if she guessed my true feelings for Wade or found out what we had done together.

Wade and I carried our boards into the water, where we went over the basics of paddling again. I could hardly believe that paddling alone could be so complicated. "If you can't paddle, you'll never catch a wave," Wade warned, which inspired me to paddle until my arms were ready to fall off. When I began to get the hang of paddling, he showed me how to balance while sitting on my board. I promptly leaned too far to the left and fell off. On my next valiant attempt, I leaned too far forward and planted my face in the ocean while my surfboard shot out behind me.

However, I have a natural gift of balance, so it didn't take long before I got the feel of my surfboard's little tricks. We went back to paddling, and Wade taught me how to swim through a wave rather than attempting to ride over the crest of it. Duck diving came easy for me, so we called it a day.

I was hoping that we would head for Wade's Woody, but Wade led me to The Pit, where the surfer boys hailed him. "Waterwalker, who's your friend?"

"I'm Tony," I said.

"I'm Pop Hardy. I've been watching your goofy foot stance," one boy said, referring to my tendency to balance with my right foot forward. "You're gonna be a great surfer, Tony Goofyfoot."

With that declaration, the surfers in The Pit claimed me as one of their own and I possessed a surfer's name. Since The Pit was strategically located out of lifeguards' line of sight, Pop Hardy handed me a can of Coors, and I lit a Camel. Eventually the churchkey made its way around, and I popped two holes in my can and took a sip. Sitting beside Wade, I let the boys' tales of bitchin' surf roll over me like giant combers, as they described their passion for wave riding, not to mention their escapes from the boneyard.

The sun was setting over the Pacific when Wade and I stumbled back to his Woody. Our need unspoken, we climbed into the back and hastily pulled off our trunks. My mouth found Wade's, and I sucked his tongue. His cock rubbed against my thigh as I flicked my tongue against his. Then his hand found my dick. He gripped my shaft and rubbed the head of my dick with his fingers. Moving his thumb over the tip, he attempted to unscrew my dickhead as though opening a jar. A delirious rapture shot through me, so I grabbed his cock and squeezed it hard.

We jacked each other as we had the previous day, but before we could climax, I suggested, "Let's switch positions."

"You want to?" Wade moaned. "I've wanted to try that." With obvious eagerness, we shifted so that we were facing each other's cock. I felt Wade's hot mouth upon my cock. So eager was he to suck me, he had my dick half way to his throat before I had a chance to kiss his soaring erection. "You're so hard, Wade," I murmured just as I touched my lips to his cock head. A shock went through me, something akin to what the electric chair must feel like to those who reached the top ranks of Murder, Incorporated, and I took his cock deep into my mouth. I was enthralled.

Do cocksuckers surf? Do surfers suck cocks? Those questions raced through my consciousness like the musings of a French existentialist. Unknown pranksters burned a swastika into the real life Gidget's parents' driveway – because she was Jewish. What would surf culture do to Wade and me if they learned we were something even more frightening – faggots?

Yet as I took Wade's cock deeper into my mouth, letting it slide along my tongue as it leaked a delicious fluid, and opened my throat, swallowing so that it would pass my uvula and fuck my whole mouth, I knew that we were free. We were surfers. We rode waves. We had sat in The Pit, drinking Coors and smoking Camels with the greatest of the greats. In fact, Wade Waterwalker, the boy whose thick cock was growing heavier in my mouth, was already one of the big names along the coast, and I was soon due to add my own name to the list of legendary surfers.

Sucking Wade's cock was everything I had imagined it would be. His cock was so thick I couldn't wrap my tongue around the whole underside. I tightened my lips upon it, and agitated the head with my lips and tongue. It felt so smooth in my mouth that I wanted to keep it always. However, even as I thrilled from the cock in my mouth, my body was passing through states of arousal toward orgasm. Wade stimulated my cock with his lips and fingertips. He titillated my cockhead with his tongue, and even nibbled lightly.

I groaned around Wade's dick when I fluttered past the point of no return. I was going on that red-hot tube ride, and Wade was the fervent wave. I tasted Wade's hot cum in my mouth, and I felt his dick clamoring with his ejaculations. Twitches of pleasure swept through me. The jolts were bitchin'. Wade's hand was stroking my ass as the rollers of ecstasy claimed me. The waves of delirium washed out my conscious thoughts until I was merely a sucking organism and a spurting orgasm.

Drained at last, we rolled apart panting and chortling. "That was a fantastic orgasm," I howled.

"Like surfing a fifteen foot wave," Wade agreed. "I love the taste of your cock."

"I love your cum."

When Wade dropped me off, we stole a quick kiss with our dick-puffed lips. The body of the Woody blocked the neighbors' view, but I could only hope that Mom wasn't watching out our window. However, I heard her working in the kitchen as I floated inside and ascended to my bedroom. I checked myself in the mirror, half expecting that I would look different. But it was the same freckled visage grinning back at me, though my eyes sparkled with happy mischief.

The next morning I was eagerly awaiting Wade's arrival when the phone emitted its sharp notes. "Hello," Mom said. "Oh, yeah, Tony, it's for you."

"My Woody blew a gasket when I started it up," Wade grumbled inconsolably. "I'm gonna have to skip the beach today."

Wade's Woody wasn't running! The awfulness of that calamity swept over me like a seventy-five foot roller.

Fortunately, I suffered only one day of misery. Wade had his Woody in good repair by the next morning, and we headed for Malibu. Wade patiently taught me everything he knew about surfing, and my determination to learn, not only to please him, but to fulfill my own ambition, combined with a natural ability and a total disregard for life and limb, soon had me standing on my board.

On the morning of our fourth week together, Wade and I paddled side by side, duck-dove through the approaching surf, turned, and waited for a wave. We saw a nice roller, and since I was the closest, Wade waved me toward it. I caught the wave and popped up on my board.

"Shoot the curl," the boys called. "Shoot it, Tony Goofyfoot." And shoot it I did, right foot forward, my surfboard going faster than it had ever gone. After my ride, I paddled in the shallows while Wade caught his wave.

When we reached the beach, the crowd hailed me: "Tony Goofyfoot. Tony Goofyfoot." I was a surfer, and later in the Pit, smoking my Camels and sucking down Coors, I told my own tale of riding upon the mist. Later, Wade and I sneaked off to his Woody to hone our other skills.

Wade and I had a blast that summer, on the swells and in his Woody. We met the night of our respective high school graduations, night surfed for the first time under the brilliant moonlight, and sucked each other off in a secluded spot under the bluff. Ultimately, we did everything two boys can do together, and that summer set the pattern for our lives. Of course, there were those inevitable dark days when Wade's 1938 Woody broke down, but we had bitchin' fun when Wade's Woody was running.

(A shorter version of "When Wade's Woody Was Running" originally appeared in *Surfer Boys* from Cleis Press)

The Day I Got Gang Banged

As I bicycled across Rickenbacker Causeway, my Brazilian swim shorts gave my ass a girlish look. I had purchased my new swim shorts that morning, and even the salesman had gasped when he saw how the rear seam cut between my buttocks and lifted my rump. Arriving at the beach, I chained my bike to a coconut palm, spread my beach towel, and baptized my new swimsuit in the warm water.

When I returned, the stranger sitting on my towel queried, "Who are you?"

"I'm Ong." The words drooled out of my mouth. He was yummy with almond skin and Mediterranean eyes. "You're sitting on my towel."

He didn't offer to move. "Ong. That's a Thai name?" Without waiting for my response, he offered, "I am Sayid Mujtaba Ali bin Thuwaini of the Sultanate of Oman."

"Sayid?" I asked, planting my ass beside his. I could feel the heat of Sayid's body. He was wearing skin-tight cut-offs with the rear pockets removed. His cock swelled as I pushed close to him.

"I like your swim shorts, Ong. They accentuate your buns."

"They enhance definition," another voice echoed. I turned to see a young charmer emerge from the shadows, his skin the hue of Victorian furniture. His package filled the front pouch of pink hibiscus Speedo briefs. His rear jutted too, always a gratifying sight.

"Right ho, Cobber," the newcomer offered, extending his hand. "Adam Shillingford of the Commonwealth of Dominica."

Cobber? I blinked at that peculiar appellation. "Are you guys together?" I asked, my heart sinking. If they were lovers, I was odd man out.

"The three of us, Cobber," Adam said waving toward a tall, redheaded fellow in green trunks. "Meet Sinclair Harrison of the Biloxi Harrisons."

"Hot diggity, Ong," Sinclair exclaimed. "Them's snazzy cookie cutters snakin' up ya'll's ass."

"Are you chums gay?" I asked. "I'm just asking."

"Damn tootin' we're gay," Sinclair said. "Been so since I were knee high to a grasshopper. I do love tight asses, and I'm always hotter than a half-fucked fox in a forest fire."

"Sinclair puts it colorfully," Sayid twittered, his fingers brushing my buttocks. Wild heat shot through me. "But truth to tell, we passed you on the causeway. We could not help remarking your superior *derrière*."

I may have blushed, but the greatest warmth arose from my crotch.

"Can you guess what is uppermost in our minds?" Adam asked.

"And it sure ain't whether Jimmy Carter will whoop President Ford's ass in November," Sinclair added helpfully.

"You boys would like to slip your cocks into me?"

"Ong, I'm fixing to come like a horny gator."

"Right ho."

"It would be a pleasure."

My heart was racing. Three guys. Three dicks. Of course my old lover George Peterson and I had gone for seconds often, and I'd found the second butt fuck better than the first. But three? And with Sinclair swinging a cock that looked like a policeman's truncheon. Of course, I could start with Sayid who looked rather small, take Adam's average sized cock second, and so work up to Sinclair's monster.

"How're you lads fixed for lubricants?" I asked.

"Cocoa butter," Adam chirped, displaying the container.

"You won't hurt me?"

"We'll make it good for you, Ong."

"We will make you come."

"When my ole tallywhacker gets to thumping your bunghole, you're gonna shoot cum so hard it'll blow yore hat inter the creek."

That was all the inducement I needed. My dick was stretching my new swim shorts, and the guys' raging hardons were twitching. "Let's do it under the bridge," I suggested, leading the way into the cool shadows.

138

Concealed from the prying eyes of swimmers, Sayid slipped his fingers in the waistband of my swim trunks. "I'm first."

Once I got the zipper of Sayid's cut-offs down, I saw that he had no underwear. Sayid's cock was achingly hard as I slicked it with cocoa butter. I barely rubbed my fingers over his circumcised cock, but the touch was enough to make him leak. I grinned at the fluid oozing from him and asked, "How do you want me?"

"Hands and knees," Sayid suggested.

"Poke 'em, doggie," Sinclair yelped, but, to my joy, Sayid slicked his fingers with cocoa butter and probed first one, then two, into my ass. I pushed open for him, popping my asshole open the way my uncle had taught me back in Thailand. Sayid twisted his fingers inside me before he mounted me.

"Are you ready, Ong?"

"Sure. Slide it in, Sayid," I offered, pushing hard with my asshole.

"Oh, here it comes, Ong," he grunted, thrusting forward. My asshole dilated, and the familiar fullness invaded my rectum. I smiled with pleasure.

Sayid thrust forward, pulled back, thrust, and moaned. "Oh, mercy, Ong," Sayid moaned. "I shan't last a dozen strokes. Ah, here I go. I shall now shoot hot cum up your ass."

"Let it fly," I urged, gripping his cock with my anal sphincter. His dick trembled and surged as he passed through orgasm into mindless spurting.

When Sayid pulled out, having shot his all, I grinned at Adam. "Stand up, grip your thighs, and stick out your ass," he suggested.

Rocketing to my feet, I complied. Adam thrust his cock into my asshole until his lap bounced off my buttocks. "Oh, you do possess a bounteous set of hunkies, Ong," he murmured.

My cock dribbled a thin stream as Adam's cock milked my prostate. Then Adam's cock bucked against my anal sphincter, while before my eyes Sinclair slicked his big banana with cocoa butter.

"How 'bout ya'll take me face to face, Ong?" Sinclair howled as soon as Adam pulled out.

Needing no further encouragement, I threw myself onto my back on the cool sand and raised my legs. Sinclair pressed his whopper against my wet asshole. I was so slick after taking two cocks that his dick head slipped right in. My asshole dilated as he pushed his shaft deeper into me. With the entrance of his thick cock came intense feelings. My cock grew stiffer, and Sinclair's hard abdominal muscles rubbed the underside of it.

A moan slipped out of my mouth. No man had ever made me moan before that day.

"Sinclair shall fuck the cum out of Ong," Adam announced, fingering Sayid's cock. Inspired, Sayid started jacking Adam's dick as they watched Sinclair hump my butt. I felt deep pride just before the seizure of orgasm struck me. The tingles rippled up my ass and down my cock.

"Jiminy, Ong, here I come," Sinclair yelped. He humped me faster, which threw me into full orgasm. My cum splattered onto his stomach and my own as he unloaded in my ass. Adam and Sayid were jerking off on us as we came, and their cum rained upon Sinclair's back.

A few minutes later, we washed in the sea. "Hot damn, Ong," Sinclair effused, "Y'all oughta come live with us. You got the best ass I've ever fucked."

I moved into their apartment the next day, and for three wonderful years, I remained the group's faithful fuck toy.

("The Day I Got Gang-Banged" originally appeared in the now out-of-service online periodical *Tommyhawk's Fantasy World*)

Each Sacrifice Brings Its Own Reward

February 14, 2009

I had gotten fucked hard, no doubt of that. Lars's thick cock hammered up my ass and his hard loins pounded my buns until I got my rocks off right along with my attacker. However, during the traditional Valentine's Day worship service, Preacher Prout wasn't telling the church the true story about how I became a motorcycle gang leader's anal angel. Preacher Prout claimed that God had put forth His hand and saved my virgin sister from getting raped. And there was my sister, Mary Alice Worth, sitting beside the pulpit, looking holier than a sacred cow. From the expression on her face, she thought her farts were incense.

I shifted in my chair. Three days after the butt fuck, I was still feeling Lars's thick cock, which had stretched my asshole wide open. Lars was the leader of the gang, and he had loaded me up just right, and left me gaping and dripping. He'd left me with something else too, something I hadn't known about myself: I liked getting filled with his cock. I enjoyed that rough butt fucking, and I wanted to feel that wild sensation again and again. But that wasn't anything I was going to tell the preacher and the congregation. They didn't know that I'd taken the cock that was meant for Mary Alice – the simpletons thought God had rescued her.

Preacher Prout went yammering on about how the gang abducted Mary Alice and me, and since he'd gotten the story from Mary Alice, he had the details dead wrong. Mary Alice sat in her white gown, radiating virginity and purity, while Elder Booter, Deacon Tate, and Deacon Dink stood next to her in their shiny black suits.

"Yea, truly, brothers and sisters," thundered Preacher Prout, "our saintly sister was riding in an open automobile with her brother at the wheel, as they swept over the highways and byways of God's green land to a convocation of saints at the Holy Retreat."

I stifled a laugh. Mary Alice's holy retreat was a fat farm where she was going to get them to liposuction twenty pounds off her gut. I twisted my buttocks on the hard pew while the preacher rattled on. My flesh retained the memory of the hard dick that had opened me, opening me to the gratifying thrill and prodding me so hard that I could still feel Lars's dick inside of me, opening me, filling me, and anointing me with his seed.

"Sad to say, the devil was abroad in the form of a gang of sinful motorcyclists. The brother lacked the automotive skills to evade the gang, and thus our beloved sister was taken captive. The gang conveyed the sister, with her brother, to their headquarters, where after a time spent in an orgy of alcohol and drugs, the gang were ready to rape our chaste sister."

"Noooo," the congregation moaned, Elder Booter being the loudest.

As Preacher Prout spoke, pictures of everything that happened in the gang's headquarters filtered through my mind. What happened last was the most vivid memory, and I shifted again as my cock hardened in my underwear.

"However, just as the leader of the gang prepared to insert his prodigious equipment into our sister's virginal utensil, the Spirit of the Lord intervened. God came down in the shape of a lightning bolt, smiting the roof of the gang's headquarters. The gang started back, sore amazed, and brother and sister ran outside to find their own car had been transported to a place before the gang's headquarters. Yea, brothers and sisters, God Himself lifted that car from one place to another, providing the means of escape so our beloved sister can sit before us today as a testament to the heavenly miracle of virginity."

The congregation rose then to sing a psalm, again Elder Booter being the loudest – though Booter was tone deaf and couldn't carry a tune. Still he was a Pillar of the Church, besides being the obnoxious, self-promoting owner of the biggest used car lot in town. I held the hymnal low to conceal the major boner I was sporting. Funny thing was, since Lars's massive prick reamed my anus, whenever I got a hard-on, I felt the need for something significant up my ass. In the middle of church, with the congregation singing praises to the glory of God, I smiled as I thought about the things I'd done the night before.

February 13, 2009

Near to midnight, I was lying in bed, half-dreamy and all-horny. I couldn't fall asleep, and I knew my sleeplessness wasn't due to excitement over the Valentine's Day People Who Love the Lord church service scheduled for the next morning. I could only think about the sensation of Lars's big prick pushing into my ass.

I was wearing our sect's traditionally modest pajamas with the divinely approved underwear. The garments seemed to bind me like barbed wire. I climbed out of bed and rummaged through my secret stash – the one my mother didn't know about – and pulled on the special underwear I'd ordered through the mail. I pulled them on, and they fit my contours like a friend. I stroked my own ass, feeling my hard, muscular buttocks beneath the smooth fabric.

My cock was rock hard by then, which pulled the seam of my underwear even tighter up my butt. I liked that sensation. I felt slutty, and I liked feeling slutty. I rubbed my dick through my underwear. I felt up my ass with one hand and screwed the head of my cock with the other. Within a few minutes, I was getting close to coming. I stopped – I was just getting started.

I opened my window and picked up the garden trowel I had placed upon the windowsill for easy access. Earlier in the day, I had carefully washed the trowel with soap and water. As I washed, I concentrated on the smooth wooden handle. The handle curved toward the center and expanded to a greater diameter as it approached the metal implement. I pulled off my special underwear and replaced them in my secret stash. Then I took out the bottle of personal lubricant that I had sneaked into the house.

I jacked my cock a little bit, lubricating it as I jerked it. Then I slicked up the handle of the trowel. Ever so carefully, I pushed the handle against my asshole. I drew a deep breath, as Lars had taught me. I pushed with my ass to dilate my hole and slid the trowel into my ass. It slid in rather easily. I giggled with pleasure as I flogged my dick some more while concentrating on the sensation of the smooth handle in my ass. After a few minutes, I pushed the handle in deeper.

"Ah, I'm taking it," I moaned softly. "I'm taking your big cock."

In no time at all, I had the trowel handle in all the way and proceeded to fuck my ass with it. As I slid it in and out and twisted it back and forth, it sent pleasing sensations through me. The trowel wasn't as good as Lars's dick, but it was better than nothing. I tried squeezing it with my asshole as I pounded my dick.

I was squeezing the trowel out with my anal sphincter and pushing it back in with my hand, and twisting the head of my dick with my fingers when I felt the powerful sensation that signaled approaching orgasm. I pushed the trowel deep into my ass and tried to hold it there while I pounded my cock. I placed my opposing palm under the opening of my piss hole so I could catch my semen in my hand. If my mother ever discovered cum-stained sheets, there would be holy hell to pay.

I fantasized about Lars pounding my bare buns. I pictured his thick cock slamming up my ass. I imagined his thick cock spurting inside me. Orgasmic tingles rippled through the head of my dick, but the tingles felt different. Somehow the tool up my ass changed the texture of my orgasm. My pleasure was deeper, more exotic, and terrific. My dick throbbed, but so did some organ within my rectum. My dick grew heavy with my rising cum, and I tingled all over. I felt deliciously slutty. I whispered, "I'm an anal angel."

My muscles at the base of my penis contracted sending semen into my hand, and my asshole contracted around the trowel handle. I could hardly hold it inside of me as my dick erupted with thick spurts that created a puddle in my palm. I milked my dick until I could squeeze out no more. Then I touched my tongue to the semen in my hand. It did not have much taste; certainly, it was not unpleasant. It was sort of like the taste of sweet cooked mushrooms. I licked it up and swallowed it. I continued licking my hand until it was clean. Then I pulled the trowel out of my ass, examined it for evidence, and replaced it on the outer windowsill.

When I was certain that I had left no emblem of my activities, I dressed again in the approved underwear and pajamas. With a sigh, I climbed into bed again. I felt lonely and a little sad. Maybe it was only a fantasy on my part that Lars would come for me. Perhaps he had forgotten me already. Perhaps he was already choosing his next anal angel. A single salty tear dripped onto my pillow as my satiated body drifted into sleep.

February 11, 2009

Mary Alice was reciting scripture as we sped along the highway toward the fat farm. I had the top down on my roadster, which let me drink in the golden February day while the rushing wind blew away Mary Alice's boring prophecies before they could reach my ears. I wanted to enjoy the sudden spring-like weather, the seventy-degree air that was rapidly melting the snowdrifts that lined the highway.

The so-called motorcycle gang was only five big hogs, and the guys were just out for a ride. They showed no interest in us until Mary Alice stood up on the car seat and started screaming that they were all bound for Hell for their sinful ways. Even then, they would've laughed off her ravings if she hadn't bombarded them with religious tracts. A tract slapped against their leader's faceplate and nearly wrecked him.

I was yelling at Mary Alice to sit down and shut up, and she was telling the bikers about the destination of the unrighteous when two motorcycles pulled in front of us, two alongside, and one in back. As they reduced speed, I was forced to follow suit in spite of Mary Alice demanding that I drive on.

When I was completely stopped, a burly, bearded biker reached in, turned off my engine, and took my car keys. Then I regretted that I'd been driving with the top down. The open car made me feel completely vulnerable. My feeling of helplessness mingled with my feeling of fury at Mary Alice. Of course, it wasn't in my sister's nature to accept responsibility. All troubles originated from the devil or they were somebody else's fault – usually mine.

"This is your fault, Joey Dan," Mary Alice said. "How could you let this happen?"

"Just shut up and they'll let us go," I advised, though I should have saved my breath. Mary Alice had never listened to me, not once in our entire lives.

The leader of the motorcycle gang had climbed off his machine. He was wearing black boots, a black leather vest with silver studs, and butt-hugging jeans. His jeans showed off his round muscular ass, and his cock formed an obvious bulge in the front. I gasped quietly at the sight of that bulge. I could imagine how thick his cock must be to make such a protrusion. My own cock tightened ever so slightly. I wanted to

145

adjust it, but Mary Alice would pitch a conniption if she caught me handling my crotch.

Another guy climbed off his motorcycle and approached the roadster from the passenger side. The leader looked at me. "You ought not to be throwing trash at people on the roadways. Now we're just gonna watch you two pick up that litter, and then we'll go our separate ways."

"We will do no such thing," Mary Alice shrieked, seizing my arm as I prepared to pick up her tracts. "Once God's word has been flung forth upon the bent world, it is not to be called back." She stood up in the seat again and pointed directly at the leader. "Especially not by order of Satan's agents."

That accusation made the leader laugh, but it pissed off the rest of his gang. "Let's take 'em down to the roadhouse," one suggested. "Throw a little scare into the bitch."

The leader nodded uncertainly. "You two climb out of there. You're taking a ride with us."

I didn't like that idea. I was wearing an expensive shirt and light gray flannel slacks, and Mary Alice was wearing a filmy white dress. All her clothes were white, though most of the time she pranced around in choir robes. However, I had no choice, especially after they pulled Mary Alice out of the car and set her prissy ass on the back of a motorcycle. In spite of it being a bad moment, it was the time in my life when I most wished I had a camera.

"You're going to sit behind me," the leader said, pointing toward his motorcycle. I could tell that he was feeling a little out of his depth. They hadn't planned on abducting us; Mary Alice had provoked them, and now the leader was off script. He was playing events by ear, which meant that anything could happen.

"My name is Joey Dan," I said, with a shy smile, however unintentional.

"Okay, Joey Dan, plant your ass behind mine." He gave my butt a friendly pat to urge me along. "Red Bob will bring your car directly. And my name is Lars."

Lars was so big there was hardly room left on the seat for me. I had to spread my legs around his muscular ass. My cock was pressed against his ass crack, and the heat of it made me hard. It was a funny

146

sensation, this heat from the proximity of a rough biker's body. I had never been aware of my lust for other men, springing as I did from an isolated community in Eastern Oregon, founded by an obscure religious sect whose traditions lived on in our society. Though our father was one of the wealthiest ranchers in the state, we had been sheltered from worldly views.

When we reached the roadhouse, we found more bikers inside. They were boozing and smoking gigantic hand-rolled cigarettes. I could guess what was in them.

Never one to spread oil on troubled waters, Mary Alice dropped to her knees, lifted up her hands, and beseeched God to preserve her virginity. I whispered that getting on her knees might give the gang ideas, and shouting about being a virgin was like waving a red flag in front of a bull. She didn't pay attention to me, and kept praying loud enough to arouse the dead.

"Let's gang bang the bitch on the pool table," one of the gang yelled.

A cheer went up, but I stepped in front of Mary Alice. "I can't let you rape my sister," I screeched.

The roadhouse fell deadly silent. "You gonna fight all of us, boy?" the one who'd called for the gangbang drawled.

There was no way I could go home to our parents and admit that I let Mary Alice get raped by a drunken gang. Our parents thought Mary Alice was a gift from Heaven.

"I can't fight you, so I'll fuck you," I offered in desperation. "Take me instead of her."

"Now the party is getting interesting," Lars said.

Suddenly big sweaty bikers were lifting me onto the pool table and pulling off my flannel slacks. Of course, that was the day I'd first worn my new white underwear with the seam up the butt and the pouch in front. Despising our community's divinely approved undergarments, I'd rented a post office box in a nearby town and ordered the body defining underwear though the mail. At the time I placed the order, I was responding to urges I couldn't quite understand.

"Who-ee, will you look at these cookie cutters this pup is wearing," a biker howled.

"Man, what an invitation. His skivvies done got a tight seam right up the crack." A rough finger traced the seam. The finger sliding up my ass crack was the most intimate experience I'd ever had. It made me feel hot and prickly. I liked the way they were handling me, treating me like a sexual being for once in my life.

The hard-handed manhandling driving me wild to get it, I found my mouth begging for it. "Fuck me," I moaned. "Fuck my ass."

Suddenly, Lars's face was close to mine. In spite of his rough appearance, his breath was sweet. "You ever been butt fucked before?"

"No," I answered honestly. "This will be my first." In truth, I was as much a virgin as my sister, though she wanted hers and I was eager to shed mine.

Without warning, Lars's lips pressed against mine. As he kissed me, I kissed him back, sliding my tongue into his mouth. My cock was so hard it was nearly tearing through my soft briefs, and coarse, sweaty men were feeling up my ass and rubbing my cock. The reality of kissing another man while still more men groped me with lascivious abandon excited me wildly. None of Mary Alice's promises of a heavenly paradise could compare.

Lars pulled his mouth away and whispered in my ear. "You're gonna be mine alone, Joey Dan," he promised. "I ain't gonna let you get a rough fucking from the whole gang. I'll turn your ass out right. I'll take you just the way I took the rest of these boys. That'll make you one of my gang. Would you like that?"

"Yes," I agreed without hesitation. He was offering something I'd wanted my whole life, though I would not have been able to define my need until that moment. "My ass is yours for the taking, Lars. Take me now, but then you have to do one thing for me."

"Anything," he agreed, his tongue driving in my ear no sooner than the word was out.

"Let me drive my sister home." Resisting an evil temptation to offer Mary Alice to the gang, I added the words, "virginity intact."

With a chortle of agreement, Lars chased the other men off me. "I'm going to fuck his pussy ass," he said. "I'm gonna turn him out nice – just like I done you fellows. Where's the sky pilot bitch?"

"She run outside."

"Then leave her ass alone. You guys do each other like I trained you, while I teach Joey Dan what that hole in his ass is really for."

With winks and nudges as if I were joining the gang, the fellows fell to groping each other, pulling off their clothes, kissing, hugging, stroking ass, rubbing cock, licking and tonguing without the slightest inhibition or consciousness of shame.

"Freedom," I shouted, pulling off my underwear and throwing them to Lars. He placed them against his face and sniffed audibly. The scent excited him so that he tossed the underwear aside and buried his face in my butt crack. I had never imagined such a thing. I nearly exploded with rapture as his tongue slid up my crack, driving deeper and deeper.

"Oh, oh," was all I could say. My cock was throbbing for release so I grabbed it and fingered my dry dick head. A thin stream leaked onto my hand, which I used to lubricate my cock. Always before I'd had to masturbate in great secrecy; to handle myself openly, to gratify my carnal instincts in front of a group of men who were rapidly sinking into an orgy of sucking and fucking, to indulge my instincts was the ultimate in liberation.

Always I had denied my homosexual impulses, though my fantasies had long hinted at my true self. Suddenly, I was released from the captivity, and I could be joyously man-hungry. These emotions and half-formed thoughts were whirling through my brain as Lars's hot tongue slipped into my asshole. I jerked my cock all the harder, unable to believe my good fortune.

Lars pulled his face away from my ass and held up a bottle of lubricant. He poured it into his hand, and then slowly slid one lubricated finger into my ass.

"That went in easy," he said. "You positive you ain't never done this before?"

"Never," I said.

"Then you're clean. So am I. I ain't got no diseases, so I'm going bareback."

My heart was beating fast, thundering in my chest. I had to trust him – what other choice was there? Before I could respond, he had two fingers in my ass, twisting them to and fro, opening me for his cock.

"Yeah, fuck my gay ass," I begged. "I want you inside of me. I want you to come inside of me."

Lars arranged me on my face on the pool table, drawing up my left leg until my knee was almost to my face. "This will make it easier, Joey Dan. You tell me if'n it hurts. Now you take a couple of deep breaths and push with your asshole, and you're gonna have a good time."

As I felt the head of his cock positioned against my asshole, I drew three deep breaths, letting the air out slowly. As the pressure increased on my asshole, I pushed as though I was trying to push his cock out, but the harder I pushed the deeper he came in. There was no pain, only an incredible sensation of fullness.

"You're a born butt boy, Joey Dan," Lars exclaimed. "You're taking it all the way. My cock's so wide at the base that some guys in my gang can't take but half. I got it balls deep in you. Man, your butthole is a natural cock canal. You're an anal angel."

I was already flying with lust and excitement, and his words filled me with pride as well. I wanted to tell him that I loved him, but what I said was, "Come on, Lars, get to humping."

He did so, and my eyes must have popped open even wider than my asshole as the sensation of pure bliss filled me. I tried to slide my hand under so I could continue fisting my cock, but Lars was nailing me so hard that I couldn't. Still the head of my dick was getting friction from the cloth on the pool table. I was sliding a tad as Lars reamed me and something else was driving me toward release; something hidden up my ass was getting milked off by Lars's thrusting dick.

"Oh, fuck, that's good," I moaned. "Oh, man, fuck me like that. You're making it good for me, Lars."

"Ah, Joey Dan, your ass is tight. You're gonna make me blast my load. Ah, fuck, yeah, your hot grainy hole is practically fucking my dick."

Suddenly, even as my hands gripped the sides of the pool table, I felt the weight of approaching orgasm. My dick grew heavier, swelling harder against the green cloth.

"I'm gonna squirt, Lars," I shouted. "You're gonna make me come."

"Guys always come when I fuck them," Lars bragged, his words coming in gasps. "Oh, shit-fire, Joey Dan, I'm gonna go too." His dick felt like it thickened, stretching my asshole even more. Explosive tingles rippled through the head of my dick, radiating upward, even as I felt my asshole trying impossibly to contract. The muscles at the base of my dick could contract, and they blasted loads of jism out of my pee hole. I moaned and grunted as I decorated the top of the pool table, and Lars pounded harder and harder as his own orgasm shook him and he shot his hot semen into my anal canal.

Our contractions stilled slowly, and Lars pumped his cock in me for a few more strokes. We were both slippery with sweat and still linked together like a bolt and a nut. My breath was raspy, and I could hear my fast heartbeat combined with the thunder of Lars's own pump.

"Thank you, Lars."

A low chuckle proceeded from his throat. "You're welcome, Joey Dan. I oughta be thanking you. Your ass is a damn fine ride." With a sudden effort, he pulled his cock out. I gasped at the sensation. My ass made a popping sound as Lars's dickhead exited. Lars laughed and rolled onto his side. "Bet you didn't reckon when you started off today that you'd be getting your first butt fuck."

"No," I agreed. "Is it the first? Meaning there will be more?"

Lars patted my fresh-fucked behind. "You bet your sweet ass, Joey Dan. There'll be more."

My roadster was sitting in front of the roadhouse with Mary Alice in the passenger seat. She was reciting proverbs with furious intent. "You left me sitting here, Joey Dan," she accused. "God will punish you for your neglect."

"Don't you believe in sacrifice, big sister," I said, thoroughly disgusted with her attitude. "I took a cock up my ass so you wouldn't have to." Like it was a hardship.

Mary Alice acted as if she hadn't heard; she made no comment, but returned to reading her scripture. I shifted in the car seat, feeling the wet stickiness in my ass. My asshole felt stretched, a little sore, perhaps, but in a good way. In spite of having my sister in the car, I'd never felt so happy in my life.

"What are you smiling about, Joey Dan?" Mary Alice demanded. "You should be praising the Lord because He saved us from those evil men."

"The Lord?" I protested. "I saved you. I offered myself in your place, and they accepted the offer."

"Joey Dan, you wicked imp! I'm going to pray extra-hard for your soul, not that it will do any good. You're a Hell-bound sinner. Now take me home since you've made me miss my appointment at the spa."

In spite of Mary Alice denying what had actually occurred, I felt fantastic. I'd enjoyed the butt fuck as much as Lars had, maybe even more, and he'd assured me that I was a scrumptious piece of ass. He uttered the half-assed compliment for the gang's amusement, but there was a love light burning in his eyes that fired a lascivious dream in my psyche and a burning love in my entrails.

Before the gang let me go, I told Lars where I lived. "Now that you've found my ass, come and get me," I pleaded, pulling up my underwear.

"I'll come, Joey Dan," Lars promised. "On Valentine's Day, just like we agreed."

February 14, 2009

The congregation finished the psalm and sat again, for which I was grateful since I still had a raging boner. Remembering Lars's cock plunging in and out of me had inflamed me with lust. I wanted to get filled that way again. If I could not open my ass to hard cocks, then life would be meaningless. I looked around the church, studying the cow-eyed countenances still rapt upon my sister. Not a one of those pathetic men was man enough for me. I strained my ears, hoping for the roar of approaching motorcycles.

I had lost touch with what was happening in the front, for when I looked again I discovered that Mary Alice was standing behind the pulpit. Dim in distance a strange thunder rolled. When she read out an apocalyptic scripture, her voice took on a mad stridency that I had heard hints of before. The sound of the thunder seemed to be growing louder.

Mary Alice's eyes were glowing with religious fervor as she pronounced, "My brothers and sisters, fathers and mothers, saintly men and pious women, sin is always among us. Rank evil is the viper in our bosom. I urge you to purity, to chastity, to a restoration of innocence. But how do we claim innocence when one among us has committed the sin of Sodom." Here she pointed directly at me. Oh, oh, I thought. Lars, this would be a good time for you to show up.

"My own brother, Joey Dan, has confessed to being a sodomite." Many members of the congregation gasped, and our parents pulled back from me in horror. "He is fallen, this wanton dog, this perverted abandoner of the natural use, this layer with mankind."

Mary Alice's accusation alone was sufficient to condemn me in the congregation's eyes. They required no proof, though I tried to explain, tried to calm down the mad pack that reviled me. However, I felt no fear because over the roar of the worshippers, another roar could be heard, as if a terrible tornado of wrath were bearing down upon the church. As my own parents pushed me out of their pew, the roar grew louder.

"I did it to save her," I shouted, stalling until my rescuers arrived. Hit the gas, Lars! "I told them to take me instead of her. I traded my ass for hers."

"God saved our sister," Preacher Prout thundered. "Do not profane a holy miracle with tales of your twisted lust."

Talking to these diehards was no use. With a twisted grin, I threw defiance in their faces. "Twisted or not, Lars's big dick felt great up my ass," I shouted. "I enjoyed it, Mary Alice. I like getting fucked. I can't wait until next time."

My mother collapsed upon the floor. My father leaped up and uttered imprecations like an Old Testament father. "You son of a wicked woman," he said, looking a lot like King Saul. "You got your perversions from your mother's side of the family. You're no product of my loins."

Elder Booter, Deacon Tate, and Deacon Dink held me tight while the rest of the congregation pulled at my clothing. My shirt ripped down the back. My own father pulled the shoes from my feet. Looking down, I watched Preacher Prout unfasten my belt and pull down my zipper.

"What do you have in mind, preacher?" I sneered. The roar was growing much more distinct, but the congregation did not seem to notice. The preacher was tugging at my pants. Soon they were gone, and I stood in my underwear.

The sound grew so loud that even some of the churchgoers were becoming aware of it.

"That sounds like motorcycles," Deacon Dink commented with a puzzled expression. I envisioned Lars leading his gang toward the town. Confident that they would arrive in time to save me, I smirked at the congregation and wiggled my butt at the preacher.

"Where did he get that soft, stretchy underwear?" my mother wailed from her place on the floor.

"From Hell!" Mary Alice answered. Even as she spoke, the elder and the deacons bustled me toward the street. In the doorway, Preacher Prout booted my buttocks with the left foot of Christian charity, and I sprawled onto the dusty pavement.

"Hey," I protested. "Stripping me is one thing, especially if you're planning to fuck me. Makes me feel like the Poor Man of Assisi. Kicking my ass is quite something else. You might have ripped my underwear." The reference to St. Francis was lost upon Preacher Prout and his followers. They were too ignorant of their own Christian history to get the allusion.

"Fetch a rope," Elder Booter summoned. I only laughed at him. The rope was not long in coming, but before the maddened mob could tie it into a noose, my deliverance arrived in a roaring cloud.

"It's the Second Coming," Deacon Dink shouted as a thunderous haze of dust that resembled a desert sandstorm ripped through the streets.

The congregation drew back as a hundred bikers circled the church. The air was filled with ice pellets, sand, and bits of greenish sage. The noise was beyond imagining. As I picked myself up, a hand reached for mine.

"Climb aboard, Joey Dan," Lars shouted, pulling me onto his motorcycle in front of him. The congregation cowered back before the wrath of the motorcycle gang, though Mary Alice broke forth and demanded that I repent.

"Fuck you, asshole bitch," I yelled.

Through my contoured underwear, I could feel Lars's thick cock hardening against the seam up my butt. A warm good feeling filled me, a thrill beyond description. I ground my crack against his dick to goad him into action.

"Haul ass, Lars," I urged.

And off we thundered. I felt as if I were riding Lars's cock as much as I was riding the motorcycle. We roared up hill and down, along sweeping curves where the snow still lay in banks, and through tunnels of dry air blowing off the mountain snowfields. At length, we reached the gang's headquarters, the roadhouse where Lars had opened me to new joys.

"You reckon them assholes will follow us?" Lars asked me as we sauntered arm and arm into the roadhouse.

"Not a chance," I assured him. "The church doesn't really care about me – not enough to come after me anyway."

My church clothes had stayed at the church, and my only garment, my white underwear, was looking pretty filthy after the hard motorcycle ride. Also my throat was dry. "Here, wash out the dust, Joey Dan," Lars offered, handing me a brown bottle. I had been born and raised in a "dry" county, since our sect did not approve of alcohol, so I had never tasted beer. This one was called a Bachelor E·S·B. I took a sip and made a face that gave Lars a big laugh.

"Swallow it, Joey Dan," he urged.

"Swallow it, swallow it, swallow it," the bikers chanted. I swallowed. Without actually intending to, I took another healthy swig. I could see how a taste for beer could grow upon one.

Still laughing, Lars lowered his jeans and pulled off his underwear. I was startled to see that he was wearing new underwear, exactly like the "cookie-cutters" I was wearing. He pulled them off and his big cock popped free. It rose immediately. Lars sat down on a chair and rubbed the head of his cock. He smiled at me, and his meaning was obvious.

"Swallow it, swallow it, swallow it," the bikers chanted.

I must have appeared puzzled, because several of the bikers decided to demonstrate. One dropped his pants and sat while another touched his tongue to his fellow's cock. I watched as the swollen cockhead disappeared into the biker's mouth. Others followed suit, several offering their dicks while sitting, some while standing, and others while reclining on the floor. Two guys began sucking each other on top of the pool table. Watching the 69 action was one of the most exciting things I'd ever witnessed.

Meanwhile, the first cocksucker was taking more and more of his companion's cock. He craned his neck and went lower. He seemed to be taking the cock right into his throat. "See how he does it?" one biker asked me. "See how Crusher is swallowing Grundy's cockhead? He keeps swallowing and that way he can fuck Grundy's big dick with his throat without gagging on it."

"Give it a try, Joey Dan," Lars urged.

I dropped to my knees and placed my hands on Lars's thighs. My heart was racing as though it would fly out of my mouth. I had taken Lars's cock in my ass, and I had gleefully received his semen, but this step seemed more significant to me. Was I a cocksucker? On both sides of me, bikers were sucking cock and enjoying it.

"Oh, fuck, yeah," the biker sitting next to me was moaning. "Here it comes, Gig. I'm gonna blast my duck butter down your throat."

Gig pulled his head back so his lips were brushing the piss hole of the biker he was blowing. The first shot of semen painted his lips. Gig's tongue flicked once; then he lowered his head all the way on the erupting prick. He tucked his chin so that the cock must have been coming into his throat. I realized that Gig had to swallow; spitting was a stark impossibility. He had positioned his head so that the warm cum had to shoot directly into his throat.

"See, Joey Dan," Lars murmured. "Blowing dicks ain't nothin' to be afraid of."

"Oh, fuck, yeah," the biker repeated, rocking his hips in the chair. "Fucking shit, Gig, my cream is going hot down your throat. Fuck, that's good."

The performance was so inspiring that I hesitated no longer. I touched my tongue to Lars's cock. "That's the way, Joey Dan," Lars said encouragingly. "Just take a little taste of my cock."

I took a little taste, and then I took a little more. I licked down his shaft and he raised his hips so I could lick his big hairy balls. "That's it, Joey Dan. Lick the sweat off my nuts."

Gross as the offer sounded, the reality was pleasant. Lars's balls were hairy and had a pleasant salty taste. I only meant to give them a little lick – just to please him – but I found myself licking them and even sucking on them. After a while, I was slurping up his cock shaft until I reached the head of his dick. It was like a big knob. I slurped it. I mouthed it. I kissed it. Finally, I let it pass over my lips. I pushed my lips over my teeth so I wouldn't bite him, and his cock slipped along my tongue.

"Put your hand on the shaft, Joey Dan. Grip it low," Lars instructed. "Just suck the top part. Don't try to take it like Gig just did. That's for experienced cocksuckers. Later, I'll teach you how to throat fuck a cock like Gig did."

I heeded Lars's good advice. I clutched the base of his cock so my lips could not pass beyond the width of my hand. Still Lars's big dick filled my mouth. He extended almost the length of my tongue, but his dick head did not reach my uvula. I was able to suck him off without gagging.

What surprised me most was the sense of power I felt. I had a cock in my mouth. I could make it come. I could drive a man into a state of agonized ecstasy. You will be mine, Lars. You are my sex slave. I suck your cock. I'm your Anal Angel. Yet I am the master and you are my slave. I hold you in thrall.

It was true. Lars almost screamed as I brought him closer and closer to orgasm. I wiggled my ass in my tight road-stained briefs as I sucked his dick. I was going to take him. He would have to come in my mouth. I would leave him no choice. He would come at my command. I massaged his stiff dick with my tongue, and I tortured it with my swollen lips. When I heard him moan, I worked him harder.

"Mother fucker, Joey Dan," Lars howled. "Oh, my, fucking, oh – shit – yelp – ah!"

Lars's cum was shooting into the back of my mouth, but some was landing on my taste buds. Mushrooms that cost fifty dollars a pound had a similar flavor. Except that the semen in my mouth cost me nothing – save for a few minutes of pleasant labor.

I could not have spit out the cum if I had wanted to, but I didn't want to lose a drop. I wanted Lars's semen inside of me. I wanted his cum in my stomach, just as I had wanted the wet present in my bowels. Give it to me, Lars. Give me your hot spicy spunk. Shoot it onto my tongue. Spew it down my throat. I'll take every drop you can shoot. I'll empty your big, hairy, sweaty balls.

When Lars had shot his last, and he sat drooping, red-faced with exertion and gasping for breath, I threw back my head and laughed. Too bad you weren't here, Mary Alice. Too bad you didn't watch the way I sucked Lars's dick. Maybe it would have done you good. Perhaps it would have freed you from a future of false faith, frigidity, and fat.

Lars recovered quickly. "You ain't come yet, Joey Dan," he remarked thoughtfully.

"I feel great, Lars," I said, wiping my mouth.

"Yeah. Still," he said thoughtfully. I noticed that his cock was rising again. "Maybe you better sit on it. Better a butt orgasm than jerking off. I'll bang your joy buzzer until you pop your cork."

I pulled off my underwear and dropped them on the floor. "I'd like that, Lars," I agreed. "Fuck my horny ass."

"No, Joey Dan, you fuck your own ass," Lars said, tossing me a jar of anal lube. "Sit on my cock and ride it."

The way Lars said it presented a challenge. His cock was hard and flying again. After fingering a glob of anal lube into my hole, I lowered my ass onto his lap. The slick head of his cock brushed my left butt cheek. I shifted until it slid into my crack. I pulled my buns apart and let my asshole touch his dickhead.

"That's the way, Joey Dan," Lars offered. "Now sit on it."

Another biker whispered in my ear while I considered the logistics. "Gravity is your friend. Just let it happen."

I dropped an inch lower, so that Lars's cockhead was opening my asshole. It felt as good as our first fuck, though different. This time I was on top. This time, I would initiate the anal action. "It's time for man-to-man penetration," I proclaimed, letting my ass sink lower. My asshole opened and accommodated Lars's cock. I was quickly passing the point of no return. I was not yet strong enough in the legs to rise completely off of his cock. Another inch and I would be committed to take the whole thing. A leer of pure wickedness painted my face as I lowered my butt that inch – and more. Slowly I sank downward, taking Lars's cock into me.

My own cock was flying as I lowered my ass. Lars's dickhead hit my prostate and inflamed feelings of imminent anal orgasm. "Oh, Lars," I moaned. "Your dick is going to make me come."

"Yeah, ride it, Joey Dan," Lars howled. "Ride my dick until you get your rocks off."

Ride it I did. I rode hard, and my cock tingled as I bounced upon Lars's prodigious member. My asshole swelled, dilated as it was, and every nerve in it sent signals to my cock. My prostate jangled with the hard penetration, and it too sent demands to the head of my dick. Deep tingles commenced, and the tingles increased in intensity until they became overwhelming stings and goosy prickles. The stings and prickles grew into madcap flames, blood-and-thunder ruffles that blasted all conscious thought.

My dick grew heavy, tightened, thrilled, and tolled. My bell rang. I gonged. My muscles sent gouts of cum up my cock and out the hole. I flung semen across the room as my horny ass rode Lars's cock.

"Ride it, Joey Dan," Lars groaned. "Ride the pleasure."

I screamed aloud with joy as Lars ejaculated a second time, shooting his wet spunk into my anal canal. Meanwhile, I continued to fly big squirts across the roadhouse. I bounced upon his dick until I could come no more. Gradually my exertions stilled and I sat quietly upon his cock.

"Man, Joey Dan," Lars wailed. "That was a hell of a fuck."

After a few minutes, two of the gang lifted me off Lars's dick. I staggered to the bathroom and scrubbed in the sink. I washed my sweaty armpits and my sticky asshole and my semen twisted dick. Then I heard the door open behind me.

"I bought you some stuff," Lars said. "I got them day before yesterday." He held out a fresh pair of slinky briefs, just like those I had before, except the new ones were crimson. I pulled them on and adjusted the seam in my butt crack. "Man, you look like a Thursday night fuck," Lars said, and he meant it to please.

He stroked my buns, two moons with a crevice that had brought so much pleasure. Then he gave me the black jeans with silver studs. I pulled them up and they fit my ass like a glove. The seam pulled between my butt cheeks to accentuate my curves. He handed me the heavy socks and the leather biker's boots. Then the leather vest, worn without a shirt, and the long black coat with the dangling silver chains.

I dressed in the outfit and examined myself in the mirror. I looked damned sexy and damned scary. Mary Alice should see me now, I thought, and turned to kiss Lars. As his lips met mine and I tasted his breath again, I looked forward to a future in which Lars would mount my ass again and again and give me a lifetime of hard anal pounding. Inspired, the whole gang of sensual spirits would fall into joyous orgies of cock jacking, butt fucking, and dick sucking. When Lars slipped his tongue into my mouth, and his hard, loving hands caressed my ass through my new biker jeans, I knew that I had found a tribe and a home.

February 14, 2014

I never returned to the old hometown, though I read newspaper accounts about some of its doings. Mary Alice married Deacon Dink and from a photo printed about two years later, I deduced that she had swelled up to three hundred pounds. Preacher Prout lies buried in the graveyard at the state penitentiary where he was incarcerated for molesting a fourteen-year-old girl. Elder Booter founded a white supremacist and anti-gay movement, but so many groups sued him that he bankrupted his car dealership and ended up surviving on food stamps in a tiny rust-hued trailer on the edge of town.

For five blissful years, I have ridden with the gang, enjoying a hedonistic existence of happy debauchery and voluptuous freedom. I ride with Lars, and I love being his anal angel. When I think about how Lars freed me from that spiritual prison, I kiss his lips and ride his cock until the faces of Mary Alice, our parents, and Preacher Prout become pale images that fade from my memory like the rising dust from our motorcycles that diffuses in the sky.

Author's Note

Readers will note the Biblical allusions in the story. The one most worth consulting reads as follows: "Then Saul's anger was kindled against Jonathan, and he said unto him, Thou son of the perverse rebellious woman, do not I know that thou hast chosen the son of Jesse to thine own confusion, and unto the confusion of thy mother's nakedness?" (1 Sam. 20:30).

I am indebted to E. M. Forster for his short story "The Torque," printed in *The Life to Come*. The devices of "the Goths" kidnapping the brother and sister, the Goth leader raping the brother in place of the sister, and the church's honoring the virginal sister stem from Forster's story. I always thought that instead of being raped, the brother should offer himself as a "voluntary sacrifice" in place of his sister, and hence "each sacrifice brings its own reward."

("Each Sacrifice Brings its Own Reward" originally appeared in the now out-of-service online periodical *Tommyhawk's Fantasy World*)

The Fruits of Fantasy

"For a long time now, I've been entertaining myself with a rape fantasy," I confessed, settling my buns in the enveloping chair and sipping from the glass of pale ale my host had provided.

My host was a horny weasel, a derisive, leering con artist named William Winchell, who took pride in his small-but-gym-sculpted body and his frank sexual accessibility. For reasons bypassing all common sense, William preferred being called Wolfie. Wolfie was the gay community's most repugnant example, but he was also my best friend. For some reason, Wolfie trusted me, instinctively knowing that I neither wanted nor expected anything from him in spite of his having inherited something in the neighborhood of a hundred million. Wolfie could have had many false friends, but the instinct that comes with wealth told him whom he could trust. If only Wolfie, himself, had been as trustworthy.

"Entertaining yourself, girl?" Wolfie snickered in response to my opening. "You mean you've been jerking-off to your daydream."

"Ugh," I stuttered, hating to be called girl. I am thoroughly gay and thoroughly male, and I didn't want to be anything else. The lewd way he described my masturbation fantasies made my face burn, though his description was insightful.

"Are you embarrassed?" Wolfie howled. "Girl, I know you beat your meat. Everybody does it, Kevin." To demonstrate, Wolfie reached into the waistband of his cotton shorts and rubbed his cock. "Come on, girl, tell Wolfie your fantasy."

He was so uninhibited that I had to smile, but I knew I couldn't trust him. Anything I said he would bark all over town. I might as well confess my little secret to a television news reporter as tell Wolfie. Still...he was my best friend and I was weak.

"It starts in different ways," I mused. "Sometimes I get captured by a group of men who tie me in the back of a van and haul me to a secret location. Sometimes I'm in a shop or a doctor's office where some beefy guys push me through a secret door and bind my arms and legs. My fantasy can even get cultist – I get abducted by space aliens bent on homosexual implantation, or thrown into the fairy dimension where sex forces my body into the beautiful fairy form, or tossed into the underworld with domineering demons with big round asses and thick hard-ons."

"Let's keep it down to Earth," Wolfie protested. "I don't want to hear about you sucking off pixies or getting fucked by tentacles. Tell me a regular story, Kevin."

"If you insist," I agreed, knocking back the rest of my ale. "But I need a refill first."

When Wolfie rose, his outrageously distended shorts spoke volumes. Even in the dim light, I could see the feral lust written upon his face. I wondered how my own face looked. The sun had set, but instead of turning on the lights in his living room, Wolfie lit three candles. The flames created an atmosphere of heightened eroticism. As Wolfie refilled my glass from a green bottle, his swollen cock bobbed in front of my face. I wondered whether he expected me to grab it; however, the moment passed. After pouring ale into his own glass, he flounced onto the couch just opposite my easy chair and wiggled his hard butt into position. His eyes glistened at my crotch as I began speaking.

"I'm in the changing room in a department store. The hot-eyed sales clerk has sent me there with a pair of charcoal flannel slacks. After slipping out of my shoes, I pull down my jeans and check out my physique in the full-length mirror. I'm wearing thong underwear that heightens the shape of my ass, and when I pull up the flannel slacks, I see that they look stupendous – they flatter my buns like no pants I've ever owned. However, as I eye myself in the mirror, my cock growing somewhat heavy as I inspect the goodies, I feel a falling sensation. I cannot imagine what is happening. I hastily remove the flannel slacks, but before I can grab my jeans and shoes, the room stops with a lurch, the door is thrown open, and two powerful men seize my arms. The men are wearing white, form-fitting Lycra shorts and nothing else except for some barbaric jewelry, and they are incredibly well hung – not-to-mention, muscular beyond credence.

"I'm too dumbfounded to speak. I stand mute and helpless as they rip my shirt off my chest and tip me up to remove my socks. Wearing naught but thong underwear, I'm led out of the dressing room. However, the scene has changed. The dressing room has descended to a covert sub-basement, and my abductors lead me silently down a corridor painted with pagan images of satyrs and centaurs engaged in homosexual orgies. On sylvan mountains and by the shores of pristine lakes, men and creatures struggling to be men penetrate each other so wantonly that I cannot help feeling aroused. My cock tightens in my thong, pulling the back deeper into my cleft.

"'Where are you taking me?' I gasp, but my captors grin lasciviously and say nothing. Yet something in their manner reassures me. Even as I struggle to break free, they handle me gently and one pats my ass with loving promise."

"Girl, where can I find that department store?" Wolfie interrupted.

"Only in my imagination. Have you heard enough?"

"Are you shiting me?" He refilled my glass with ale – as if he was trying to get me tipsy. "Keep going."

"There is a red door at the end of the corridor, and painted in script upon it are the words, 'All ye who pass this portal must submit to the lust of man for man.' The two men who hold me do not pause for an instant. They open the door and haul me through as though my fate had been decided from the beginning of time. My heart beats faster as the red door closes, for they have led me into a dimly lit place peopled with shadows. Rows of candles outline a path along the tiled floor, and toward the far wall flaring torches alternately reveal the shapes of waiting men.

"'Bring the victim forth,' commands a deep and booming voice, and my guards lead me along the path. Sitting on a leather chair is a man with pure white hair that hangs thickly below his shoulders. He stands at my approach. He is over six feet tall; his shoulders are broad, his chest chiseled, and his arms brawny. He wears a silver thong that threads between outstanding buttocks. However, his most appealing feature is his thick cock, magnificently revealed through the thong."

"Oh, baby," Wolfie exclaimed. He was rubbing his cock openly, and so contagious was his uninhibited masturbation that I found my own hand massaging my erection. Wolfie laughed at my realization; his cock jutting, he ran to his bathroom and returned with two bath towels and a bottle of jack-'n-glide personal lubricant. He threw me one of the towels, arranged the other on the couch, and pulled off his cotton shorts and briefs. "Keep going," he urged, so I continued telling my fantasy.

"'You have been selected,' the white-haired man announces. 'We observed you through our spy holes, and our machinery delivered you. You have no power to resist. You will serve our needs as we demand.'

"His words electrify me. I am confident that I will not be harmed – so long as I submit to their every lust. I drop to my knees before him (somehow I know that I'm supposed to do that), and I kiss his cock through the stretchy silver cloth.

"'He has knelt before us,' intones the leader, and the voices of many men implore, 'Let him suck.'

"My guards strip the thong from the white-haired man's body, and his cock instantly hardens to a full erection. The gigantic dick head bounces before my lips. I know what is demanded, so I touch my tongue to it. A thrill runs through me like an electric shock; my own hard-on rages within my thong.

"I open my mouth to receive his erection; I close my lips around the head of his cock and tickle it with my tongue. I cannot resist as he fills my mouth deeper and deeper, and soon my mouth is a hot hole fucked by his magnificent dick. His cock slides along my tongue and touches the back of my throat. I pull my head back until I can again work the head of his dick with my lips. I worry it, suck it, tease it, and torment it.

"The white-haired man cannot resist my lips. As he trembles with his approaching orgasm, I feel my power. He had watched me change in the dressing room. He had sensed my vanity, and he found it exciting. Then he ordered me brought to his realm. However, he cannot master me, even though he kidnapped me. He is my slave, and I am his master. I let his cock ride along my tongue again while the ripples of orgasm pierce his cock head. I cock my head so his dick enters my throat.

"I take him deep into my throat before I pull back. His cock bucks in my mouth, he cries out in the fierce agony and rapture of orgasm, and his cock spurts as I worry it with my tongue. As I taste his cum, I push my head forward again so he shoots his next spurt into my throat. I let his hot spunk slide down my throat. I take him until he is drained and quivering."

"Don't end it now," Wolfie yelped, his hand pumping wildly.

"Slow down, Wolfie," I urged, merely toying with my own cock. "I enjoy teasing it out. There's a lot more to come." I swigged ale to

166

moisten my dry mouth and added another spurt of lubricant to my hand. Then I continued the story.

"'That was done well,' the white-haired man says when he can again speak. 'You have passed the first stage. Are you prepared now to receive the second?'

"'I am prepared,' I assure him without doubt or reservation. 'I live to serve.' I laugh within at the suggestion. My abductors will serve my pleasure.

"'Mount the platform and position yourself for reception,' he commands.

"I turn, and revealed by the torches' glare is a platform rising seven steps above the floor, and mounted in the center is an oddly shaped table. My guards and the white-haired man, who I have guessed is the owner of the department store, mount the steps at my side. At the top, I study the narrow table. Its operation is obvious. I am to lie face down upon it. The convex center will raise my ass for easy access and the slit will accommodate my tumescent cock. Velcro straps will hold me in position while the men have their way with me.

"'Disrobe now and mount the place of penetration,' comes the command.

"Disrobing consists of removing my thong underwear. I step out of them and press them into the proffered hand of one of my guards. He takes my underwear and displays them reverently. A deep moan rises from the assembled men. At the sound, I can wait no longer. I turn to my guards to assist me, but they shake their heads. Unassisted, I must make the ascent and offer my ass.

"I have to scramble onto the table, but I find a foothold that places my groin directly upon the smooth rotundity that seems perfectly engineered for my proportions. My swollen cock fits neatly into the slit, and there is a comfortable padded ring for my face. No sooner am I prone than a man tightens a Velcro strap across my lower back. Two other men fasten down my wrists and two more my ankles. In this prone position, I am vulnerable to anything they might do if the whim suits them. I am helpless and restrained. My heart pounds in anticipation, but I am not afraid.

"'You are now positioned for lubrication and penetration,' the white-haired man intones. 'Expect no mercy. The cocks and semen of many men will fill you. We will fuck your ass until you have enjoyed three anal orgasms, and by the time we have finished, you will be our fuck toy for life.'"

Wolfie abruptly released his dick and regarded me with alarm. "No condoms? Are you gonna let them shoot cum into your unprotected ass?"

AIDS has ravaged all of us, if not in our bodies, then in our psyches. Even a fantasy involving unprotected sex had awakened such fear in Wolfie that it had shattered the mood.

"I'm making this story up, Wolfie," I assured him. "In my fantasy world, AIDS never happened. There are no sexually transmitted diseases in the land of make believe."

"Oh, baby, I get it," he said. His cock had softened, but it glistened brightly from the Jack-'n-glide. "Let me grab a couple more ales, and you can keep telling the story."

"Another ale and I won't be able to drive home," I protested.

"You've already had too many to drive, and besides this is a jack-off party now. Let's get sloshed and beat our meat."

"Okay, Wolfie," I agreed, and after he had paraded naked from his kitchen with two ales in his dick-slick hand, I began talking where I had left off.

"I can no longer see who approaches me from behind. However, my ass is raised and my legs have been spread. I feel hands feeling up my butt, hands attached to bodies eager to blast their seed into my rectum. The lubricant they pour into my crack is pleasantly warm. I feel a finger carefully opening my hole, and the warm lubricant flows into me. Yet the finger is not done; it explores to its extent, twisting and turning and probing as the lubricant makes my channel slippery and flows deeper and deeper. Then the finger withdraws and reenters doubled in thickness. Two fingers are now inside me, and I moan with quiet pleasure. The men are opening me to receive their hard, thick cocks.

"'The first chosen shall mount him,' commands the voice now so familiar. The table is sturdy. I know that a man is climbing onto it only by the sound. Then his hands touch me, his legs brush mine, his hands caress my ass. He climbs atop me, the head of his cock pressing my asshole. I draw a deep breath in anticipation just as he begins to slide it in. My ass opens easily and without discomfort, and soon his entire weight is pressing down upon me and I feel an intense fullness from the thick dick penetrating me.

"'Yes, I love how you fill me,' I moan, unable to move except to hunch my ass rhythmically. I have never been so thoroughly dominated as I am by this strange man who has entered me, and I submit to him with all my will. My only thought is to bring him to overwhelming pleasure.

"'You submit well," the white-haired man approves. 'You will now receive his seed.'

"Even as the leader speaks, the man fucking me groans and begins humping me faster. I feel his cock stiffen harder than before; then that pulsing organ bucks within me. The man moans in the throes of orgasm, his noise like the shout of a turtle. He fucks my ass wildly, and his waves of pleasure travel through my body for my own cock feels near to spurting its bounty. However, the man fucking me has ejaculated his last burst. He lies gasping atop me. As he withdraws, I feel a deep sense of loss, almost of betrayal.

"However, my disappointment is not long. A second man ascends the table, and he mounts me even more assuredly. I open my ass to his hard shaft; the opening is long and wide. Gasping with joy, I push my ass upward as much as possible until he is banging my buttocks with his lap. As he thrusts, ripples of pleasure tease my cock. Every thrust into my ass arouses me deeper. I cry out with the approaching orgasm, but my cry is lost in unison with the cry of the man fucking me. He comes as I come, matching me spurt for spurt until he collapses in exhaustion. In extremis, our bodies throb as one."

"Oh, girl, here I come!" Wolfie shouted, his head lolling back and his eyes twitching even as his hand pounded his cock. Spurts of his jism decorated the towel he had strategically placed.

Seeing Wolfie ejaculate and combining that physical sight with the psychic vision of my fantasy, I sensed my own orgasm approaching. My cock filled and grew heavier. I watched Wolfie, yet my daydream played on to the next man mounting me and thrusting his cock into my ass as the leader ordered another man to remove the face pad and fill my mouth. Ripples of pleasure rushed from the head of my cock, which became unstoppable waves as the powerful muscles at the base of my penis contracted again and again to throw my juices into the air. My own spurts missed the towel entirely, but decorated my chest and stomach, my thighs, and even the underside of my chin.

For several minutes, I sprawled supine and wet with my eyes tight shut and my imagination aflame. Finally, I heard Wolfie stand up and I opened my eyes.

"Wow, Kevin, you sure did blast a load," Wolfie said admiringly. He looked at the cum on my naked body, and his eyes followed a trail that dripped from the arm of the chair to the Persian carpet.

"We better get that now," I said. "Do you have a paper towel?"

"Don't worry, girl," Wolfie said with a laugh. "The housekeeper will clean it up in the morning. She's used to mopping up semen. If the chair or the rug is stained, I can afford new ones."

I wiped my stomach, chest, chin, and thighs with the towel, and Wolfie showed me where to place it in the hamper. Then he asked, "How does the fantasy end?"

"Who knows," I admitted. "I never make it to the end."

"You ought to write it up and submit it to a magazine," he suggested. "Lots of guys would be interested in reading that fantasy."

"Let them think up their own," I suggested. "Writing is too much like work."

Wolfie giggled in response, and there we let the fantasy lie. We drank a bit more ale than was good for us, ordered a gourmet pizza, and ended up sleeping chastely in Wolfie's bed. The next morning I returned to my own apartment where jerking-off with Wolfie was just another happy memory.

Wolfie and I and other friends chatted on the phone every day, but nearly two weeks passed before Wolfie and I arranged an outing. He called me on Saturday afternoon and suggested I drop by his place. He hinted vaguely at plans for dinner and a movie. After promising to come right over, I changed my clothes, locked my door, and walked down the fifteen steps that led from my apartment to the landscaped courtyard. When I reached the bottom of the stairs, I saw a man who took my breath away. I assumed that he had just emerged from another apartment, for he came from the direction of the mailboxes.

What struck me – besides his divine chassis – was his attire. He was dressed in clinging white-spandex short-shorts resembling those in my fantasy. However, he was also wearing a red vest with white piping and matching red boots that rose nearly to his knees. I could only assume that he was wearing a new gay-scene style. I could not help but smile at him. In his turn, he cocked his hip, revealing a shapely buttock.

"Are you new to the building?" I asked.

"Just visiting," he said with a winning grin. "Are you Kevin Homewood?"

"Yeah," I admitted, pleased that he knew my name. He moved close, took both of my hands in his, and gazed deeply into my eyes.

"What luck," I whispered. "Wolfie will have to find another date."

Abruptly, the beautiful stranger's hands tightened on mine, and as he pulled me off-balance, another man behind me – whom I had not noticed – yanked a ball-gag into my mouth and fastened it behind my head. I struggled as both men seized my arms and cuffed them. However, they delayed in binding my legs so I caught one a vicious heel to the shin.

"Yipes!" he cried.

"Careful, Kevin, the game is called sodomy, not war," the other admonished as if I weren't playing fair. If only I could have questioned him, protested, voiced my terror, or announced my objections, but the ball gag prevented those solutions. I struggled as the two men – the one hobbling – half-dragged me down the paved walkway under the maple trees. The man I had kicked, who was attired exactly like his fellow, slapped my ass. Shying away from his hand, my hip brushed the bulging crotch of the first man's spandex shorts. At that point, I began to doubt the reality of the situation.

Though my heart continued thudding wildly, instinct told me that this abduction was not what it seemed. I held onto that hope. My captors pushed me into a van that sat waiting in the parking lot. Climbing in behind me, they shut the windowless side door. When a faint blue light came on overhead, I realized that three other men were awaiting me in the back. I could see a man sitting in the passenger seat and the driver. They were all wearing the same uniform: red boots, vest, and white shorts. The men in back made short work of stripping off my shoes, socks, and pants. After inspecting my underwear, they shook their heads sadly over my briefs.

"You're supposed to be wearing a thong."

I tried to talk through the ball gag, but I could only make meaningless sounds. One of the men took my chin in his hand, looked into my eyes, and asked, "If we release one of your hands, will you cooperate?"

After I nodded my head, someone unlocked the cuff on my right wrist. I instantly lashed out, bashing one captor's ear and making him yelp. "Yike!" I discovered later that he was the same luckless fellow who had received my heel on his shin. The violence bought me only a few seconds. I had the sliding door half open and was trying to throw myself onto the street when my captors dragged me back.

"Get his underwear off." Two pulled on my legs while another dragged down my underwear. "Get him into this thong. He's got to look the part."

I felt the thong underwear being pulled up. Someone adjusted my basket and pulled the thong between my buttocks. The experience was so erotic I forgot to be scared. My cock stiffened as the van transported me through the dark city streets.

Did I suspect that Wolfie had a hand in my abduction? Of course I did. This capture was precisely the sort of inane, demented, psychopathic, troubling idea that would occur to Wolfie. Moreover, he had the money to hire actors and stage a scene to "give me a thrill." He would imagine me enjoying my fantasy played out upon the stage of life and flesh, never thinking of the real life terror an actual kidnapping would invoke.

If I had known for sure that Wolfie had planned the experience, I could have gone along with the joke – providing it didn't go too far. Getting gang banged in a masturbation fantasy was one thing; receiving seven cocks one after another sounded like a ghastly prison experience.

When the van stopped, my captors placed a blindfold over my eyes and handcuffed my hands again. Since they had removed my shoes and socks along with everything else, I couldn't kick without breaking my toes. They dragged me out of the van, and I felt cold concrete beneath my feet. I wondered how many people were watching me being led, gagged, bound, blindfolded, and attired in only an extremely sexy, and not-to-be-doubted, obviously homoerotic thong undergarment. In spite of my fear, the thong tightened as my cock arose unbidden.

Through the blindfold, I could see that we entered a brighter area. I could hear sounds around me, some of them familiar. A buzzing neon light, doors opening and shutting, the humming of a vending machine, a weird tumbling that might have been an ice machine. I heard the men walking in their red boots until the concrete became carpet beneath my feet. At last, I heard the whoosh of an elevator door. A sensation of movement followed, but I could not say then whether we were traveling upward or downward. They led me out of the elevator, through an area of bright light in which there was a current of cooler air, and into a place of darkness. I heard a door thud shut behind me. Then I felt hot hands on my body; someone was stroking my ass.

"Are you prepared to mount the platform and position yourself for reception," a voice asked. At the same moment, one of my guards released the ball gag so I could reply.

"If I get out of this alive, you bastards are heading for the penitentiary."

"That's not what you're supposed to say, girl," Wolfie complained.

Laughing, my guards stripped off the blindfold and released my hands. There were thirty or more men leering at me, all flamboyantly gay, most of whom I knew. To a man, they were wearing sexy underwear. Most were already half-drunk. As I stood blinking in the dim light, they began to cheer.

"Surprise," Wolfie said, pushing a glass of some sweet alcoholic beverage into my hand.

"You did this to me?" I accused. Wolfie seemed taken aback.

The guy I'd met at the bottom of my steps spoke up, "Wolfie, I don't think Kevin knew it was rigged. Like he thought he was really being kidnapped and was gonna get raped. He kicked poor Gary here and after that tried to take his ear off. Look at the lump on Gary's leg."

Gary obligingly pulled down his red boot, which bore an obvious scuffmark from my heel. Wolfie looked at the actor's shin in a show of mock sympathy, though there wasn't much to see. The boot had protected Gary's leg so I had not broken the skin; nonetheless, I had raised a goose egg along his shinbone. His ear was only slightly pink. "I'll pay your doctor bills, girl," Wolfie offered blithely, as though that assuaged the pain.

Gary stared at Wolfie with amazement. "I'll be jiggered," he managed at last.

I tried to make Wolfie understand that there was a difference between reality and fantasy, and that I hadn't known the abduction was a game, nor for a few minutes, did the actors he had hired to shanghai me. I told him that I could have jumped out of the van and broken my neck, or that I might have seriously injured one of my captors in my struggles. However, Wolfie was incapable of understanding. He kept pointing out that we were a bunch of nearly naked gayboys partying in a luxury hotel suite and that the alcohol was flowing freely.

I couldn't stay angry with Wolfie, any more than I could stay angry at an animal that inadvertently clawed in its eagerness to get petted. Wolfie was an animal in his own way, lacking in responsibility or the ability to empathize fully. In his enthusiasm to make my dreams come true, he had caused pain, but he could not comprehend the wrongness of his conduct.

Making it up to Gary was another story. "How can I make it up to you?" I asked.

"You can't," Gary said. Did I detect a faint teasing tone in his voice? Did he want me to beg him?

"Come on, Gary," I scoffed. "You did kidnap me."

"But you didn't have to lash out at me," he countered. "You deserve a first-rate spanking."

"Huh!"

"Yes, that would be a fitting retribution," he said, dropping his ass into a chair. "Just drape yourself across my lap. I'm gonna paddle your ass."

"A spanking, a spanking," my friends howled with delight.

Wolfie helped push me over Gary's legs so I was bottom up in his lap. I was still wearing the thong, which was tightening in my crack. My dick hardened against Gary's thigh. Did I want him to spank my ass?

Whether I wanted it or not, Gary's hand slapped down on my bare ass cheeks. The slap stung – though more pleasantly than I would have imagined. The next slap followed, and I nearly came in my thong. Guys were laughing and clapping their hands as Gary gave me six swats, bringing me closer to full-blown orgasm with each one. However, before the ripples in my dick could reach the point where I was committed to ejaculation, Gary stopped swatting me and let his hand glide lovingly over my upturned butt.

"If I swat you another lick, I'm gonna come."

"Me, too, and I'd rather you came in my ass."

"Fancy that!" Gary moaned. "Normally, guys are petrified of my phenomenal prick."

Suddenly, numerous hands were helping me stand. "Butt fuck Kevin while we watch," Wolfie demanded. It was the first sensible thing he'd said all evening.

Gary jumped from his chair. His colossal cock made a thick loaf in his briefs. A wet spot betrayed where it had leaked while he was spanking me. "I won't fuck you without kissing you first."

"Fine by me," I whispered hoarsely. Gary pulled my face to his and our lips pressed. His tongue slipped through my lips, over my teeth, and met my tongue. The deep kiss drove me wild with passion, and when Gary's hands glided over my buttocks, I wiggled with desire.

"Butt fuck, butt fuck, butt fuck," the crowd was chanting, Wolfie loudest of them all.

"Are we going to oblige the voyeurs?" Gary whispered.

For an answer, I reached into his briefs, freed his cock, gripped it with my hand, and stroked it. Then I pushed down his briefs so he had to step out of them. His prodigious cock stood proud and free. I gasped at the sight of it. "That's a whopper."

Wolfie had thoughtfully provided bowls of condoms and lubricants. Gary pulled out an extra-strength condom, and I lubed it from a package. I lubed the outside until it was glistening with the slick jelly. Drawing a deep breath, I turned away from it and thrust back my ass.

"I can see you want my dick, Kevin. You want it bad," Gary crooned as he slid a slick finger up my hole. He added more and more lubricant. He twisted back and forth before giving me a second finger. He lubricated me and opened me up to receive his monster cock, while I wiggled my horny ass.

"You're ready, Kevin," Gary assured me, removing his fingers. "Take a deep breath." I felt something tremendous pressing against my asshole and felt a moment of wild panic.

"Deep breaths, Kevin," Gary urged. I felt an incredible pressure, followed by a mind-boggling fullness. Then excruciating pain.

"Oh, god, you're killing me," I cried. "It's too big. Pull it out."

"Rest your butthole, girl," Wolfie yelled from the cheering section. "You're taking it just fine. No problem."

Sure, no problem of yours that I'm going to split in two, I thought. But even as that thought flitted through my brain, the pain subsided. Gary's cock was starting to feel good.

"You can push it in a bit deeper now," I suggested.

"Happy to oblige, Kevin," Gary said. "Hey, fellow, is this your first time?"

I laughed. "Not in the least. Every time I've been fucked I liked it, but it's the first time I took one as big as yours. Everything's okay. I'm taking it easily now."

"You're built to take the big ones, Kevin. I got it deeper into you than any other guy I've ever fucked." So saying, he gave a thrust; the pressure increased, but the pain did not return. As his lap pressed against my buns, I felt as though I was about to shoot my load.

"Kevin, I'm in all the way," Gary shouted. "You're taking my whole cock. You're the first guy who ever took the whole shebang."

Gary started rocking back and forth, fucking me with a steady rhythm. Reaching around with a slick hand, he grabbed my cock and jerked it as he pounded my ass. As he fucked me, his cock milked my prostate, and that combined with my extreme arousal – not to mention his firm fist pumping my dick – brought me toward the edge of orgasm. I was fast approaching ejaculation.

"Oh, Kevin, I'm getting close," Gary moaned. I ground my ass back to meet Gary's quickening thrusts. He manipulated my movements by stroking my cock shaft, in between squeezing my dick head between his fingers. As he thumbed my dick, I banged my ass hard against him, impaling my rectum deeply. In the head of my cock, I felt the first tingles that signaled the approaching storm of pleasure.

"I'm gonna come," I moaned. "You're making me come, Gary."

"Wow," he managed, thrusting maniacally. Already, his animal urges had overthrown his conscious self.

His hand and his cock got me off. I rode his cock like a trooper, thrusting and grinding on it while he banged me forcefully and jacked my dick. The tingles in my dick rose into a crescendo of sensation, a pleasure subterranean and delicious, forbidden and fantastic, dangerous and sublime. Then I was coming; yet the semen did not spring from my cock, but leaked thick and cruelly, milked rather than flung. My spunk splattered upon the carpet at my feet while Gary continued to thrust faster and faster. I heard his breath rasping in my ear. He squeezed my dick head, and then I did let fly. My cum rose in a wet arc, splattering our audience.

"Come in me," I urged. "Give it to me, Gary. Shoot it up my ass."

"Ah, man," Gary managed, his gasps hot and frantic. "Ah, here I come."

I thought that I would feel the hot spunk being spurted into the condom, but I only felt his cock in my asshole, his flesh striking my buttocks, and the continuing deep massage of my prostate that caused me to fling my own fluids onto the crowd. After a longer time than I would have imagined, Gary slowed his thrusting. He pushed his cock in and out a few more times, slowly, ever slowing; then he drew it out altogether. My asshole made a popping sound as he withdrew his cockhead and we both laughed.

"Oh, Kevin, that was great," Gary whispered. "Yours is the best ass I've ever had."

"We sure do fit together nicely," I agreed, my head swimming. I was in love.

I must admit that Wolfie had thrown an extravagant party. It was my first gay-guys-get-wasted-in-their-underwear soiree, and after a couple of hours, the sex was popping as freely as the drink was flowing. The fellows were pairing off every which way. Gary and I cuddled on a couch and watched the action. I got a little drunk, and ended up going home with Gary. He and I have been an item ever since.

("The Fruits of Fantasy" originally appeared in the now out-of-service online periodical *Tommyhawk's Fantasy World*)

The Solipsism of Narcissus

Resolved to let my naked reflection surprise me, I turned bit by bit. One wall of my bedroom is all mirror; it gives back the room: bed shaped like a swan, pink walls, black flowered draperies. Two candles burned upon my highboy dresser (like the bed, a thrift shop find). The mirror caught the curve of my ass, luscious, desirable, perhaps a more flagrant lure than any guy's ass should be. Long hours at the gym had chiseled my muscles, not into that hard soldierly look, but into classical perfection. My face had a hint of softness, an almost feminine beauty.

My cock jutted, hard, tight, plump with juice. I touched the circumcised head with my finger. My skin was smooth, and that single touch released a silvery drop of semen. "I am so in love with myself, I come at my own reflection," I whispered to the face in the mirror. That's what ruined the mood. I had to laugh at my foolishness. If I come to know myself, will the knowing destroy me?

Don't we all love ourselves? I slid a hand over the curve of my ass, relishing the solid protrusion. Don't we all know ourselves? Self-knowledge is the essence of masturbation. Self-induced orgasm. I gripped my cock harder, fingering my dick head. A delicious agony, but my hand was dry. I looked at the fluffy pink towel I had spread over my bedspread. I dropped my ass onto the towel and opened the bottle of lubricant on my nightstand. Then my cock was slick, and my hand too.

Lying on my left side, I stroked my cock with my right hand. My reflection was golden in the reflected candlelight. I squeezed the head of my dick between my thumb and forefinger. I squeezed it, and then I twisted it hard. My urgency was almost painful. I rolled onto my stomach and rubbed my cock on the towel. Turning my head, I could see the swell of my buttocks, a golden bowl awaiting the silver rod's arrival.

I rolled onto my side again, and stroked my cock. I thumbed the rim of my circumcision (my mother had called it my scar). Riding the swan bed, I felt the tingles in the head of my cock. The tingles rippled through the head and heated the shaft. Then I was in the full grip of orgasm. Pleasure washed through me. I held my cock down toward the towel so that cum would not splatter my bedspread. My muscles contracted. So careful. I spurted. So planned. The towel caught my spurts. So clean. I could smell my spent semen. And so achingly lonely.

Enclosing Sturgeon Lake and 26,000 acres of farmland, wetland, and wildlife refuge, Sauvie Island basks in the confluence of the Willamette and Columbia rivers, flat in terrain and fertile in production. I bicycled past the U-pick farms where Portlanders were harvesting blueberries, red raspberries, and strawberries. Hagridden by time constraints or laziness, other people purchased their berries from the produce market while their children lost themselves in the corn maze.

As I bicycled past a dog-boarding kennel, loud barking split the morning calm. Across the road, a lone harrier was eating a luckless coot, two juvenile red-tailed hawks soared on the thermals, and three bald eagles watched from the treetops. Continuing along the flat road, I pedaled past the lavender farm and the herbary, along the endangered Sauvie Island Levee and the Sunken Village, the looted archeological remains of a Chinook settlement, and past the family beaches until I arrived at clothing-optional Collins Beach.

I locked my bicycle and helmet to the trunk of an eighty-foot cottonwood, a tree that favors the moist soil along the river. I pulled my beach towel out of my panniers, and deposited my cycling shoes, socks, jersey, and bicycle shorts within. Carrying my towel in my hand, I sauntered naked past a group of nudists playing volleyball, past sun worshipers on the lengthy stretch of hot sand, and past families walking au natural along the riverbank.

The sand was warm under my feet, and the sun warmed my skin. I already had an overall tan, product of a tanning bed, so I walked in a golden aura. Heads turned, young and old, male and female. I strolled to the river's edge. In the Columbia's shallows, my reflection grew. A few more steps and I was looking at my naked body, bathed in golden light, while minnows swam through my reflection.

As I stood, the universe reeled behind me. My reflection doubled. I cast two images in the water, both desirable. What strange magic was this? My breath came hot in my mouth. But it was not from my mouth only.

A whisper of an exhale tickled my ear. My reflection turned toward me while the sun hung still in the infinite sky. *"Comment vous appellez-vous?"*

The voice hung upon the air, floating like a cloud of vapor. If I turned, I would break the spell. He would vanish into the molecules of the atmosphere. Still, I dared. I turned, and his face was so close. His eyes were green with flecks of gold. They were magical eyes. They were far seeing eyes. I knew that he could look right through me. He could see my soul. Yet he had asked my name.

"Derek."

"Derek," he said. "I am Jules." His eyes dropped to my feet and slowly rose, consuming my skin until he met my eyes again. "We might be brothers," he said. He pointed toward our reflections. "There we look exactly alike." He touched my lips with his forefinger. "Here, too. Our mouths are the same." His finger traced down my chin, touched both of my nipples, left a white trail down to my navel. There he stopped. No one had trimmed his foreskin. "Yet I see a difference."

"My mother had me circumcised. On the best medical advice, of course." Why was I discussing my dick with a strange man? My scrotum tightened.

Within a few minutes we were both seated on my beach towel and sharing family histories. "Somewhere, we must be related," I said, dropping my eyes toward his naked cock. "I was born on Smith Rock Way in Terrebonne, Oregon."

"I, too, was born in Terrebonne," Jules admitted. "But my Terrebonne is in Quebec.

"Too strange, Jules." As I spoke, my hand grasped his upper thigh. His legs were hard muscle, as was his provocative ass. "Let me ask this: how did you get here today?"

"I like to swim naked. I like the sun. It's the weekend." He studied my eyes. "Nevertheless, that is not your question, Derek." Could he read my mind? Could I see his thoughts? "What do you want to know? My mode of transportation?"

I nodded, my thoughts whirling. Could he have arrived by bicycle? That would be not coincidence, but kismet.

Jules smiled. "I rode my bicycle." He laid a muscular hand on my thigh. I felt a tug in my cock. I didn't harden fully, but even a blind gayboy could have sensed my engorgement.

Jules' cock thickened as mine did. I scanned the beach. A woman, the mother of the family, snapped a picture of a father and daughter strolling along the shore. The man was corrupted by the ravages of time, while his twelve-year-old child was thin as a lath. His ass sagged while hers was a hard crack with tight swells. The woman, who had hanging fat around her midsection, caught up with them, and the threesome walked arm in arm. Jules and I were in a place of liberation, but not in a place of fellatiation.

"I want to suck your cock, Jules," I said. "Not here. My place. Your place. Anywhere private."

"This is so abrupt, Derek."

My face flushed. I was too forward. Jules smiled slyly at me. "We will bask naked in the sun," he said. "Then we will dress in our bicycle shorts and visit the herb growers where we will purchase aphrodisiacal scents. Thus armed, we shall learn what pleasures the day may hold for us."

We spread our towels in the hot summer sun and stretched on our stomachs side by side. I turned my face to his, and Jules' breath tantalized my nostrils. The hot summer sun, an Oregon sun, kissed my ass. The sun kissed Jules' ass too, a delightful swell that rose from his thighs and dwindled into a narrow waist. His waist was almost unmanly, but was I complaining? His waist mirrored my own, wrested from low calorie intake and countless hours at the gym.

If Jules could be called a sissy, I could be called a worse one. Though who would do the calling, who knew. Over the past three years, I'd done a million squats with ever-increasing weights. I had sweat and lifted, watered and grazed. I had seen my buttocks swell and my waist shrink. Could I condemn Jules for doing the same? He was my hazy double. My soul's *fascia*.

"*Mon semblable*," Jules whispered unexpectedly.

Fifteen minutes crawled away. The next fifteen seemed an hour, and the final fifteen took a lifetime. Jules' body made my mouth dry and my balls ache. The heat radiated from his hip to mine, and I had to hide my erection from passers-by. While public nudity is legal in Oregon, public arousal is not.

"Is your stem hard, Derek?" Jules asked.

"Yes."

"As is mine. How do we reach our bicycles in such a condition?"

We waited anxiously for a clearing, but the beach walkers were numerous. Instead of giving us a break, company inundated us. Then our luck worsened. A group of naked high school girls began practicing their cheerleading routine not twenty feet from us. Clearly, they had chosen that spot with forethought, taunting us. However, their presence had a surprising effect. After watching the girls squat and bounce for several minutes, I realized that my cock had gone flaccid.

"I've lost my erection," I whispered.

Jules laughed and sat up. "So have I. Nothing there for either of us, is there?" His eyes darted toward the teenage girls to indicate the object of our disaffection.

We stood and walked toward my bicycle. The girls had gone quiet. Knowing that they were watching our rumps, I gave Jules' butt a friendly pat. Either that touch would discourage their vacuous teenage souls or our bare-assed homoeroticism would inflame them nearly as much as it inflamed me. As I touched him briefly, I felt the silky skin of his butt cheek, and the solid muscle beneath. The scent of pastures carried on the wind, the pungent fragrance of mown hay and horse shit, but his scent, a sweet, salty whiff forked heat lighting in my brain.

Reaching my bicycle, I dipped a hand into my pannier for my red and gold bicycle shorts. Jules smiled as my cock and ass disappeared into the shorts, which at once adhered to my form. Having studied my body in front of a mirror for hours on end, I knew how I looked in those shorts.

"Where is your bicycle?" I asked as he stood naked watching me pull on my jersey and slip into my cycling socks. Jules led me a short distance to where he had secured his bicycle. His shorts and jersey were two tones of green and fit him even more deliciously than mine did me.

"Would you like to come back to my apartment?" I asked.

"Where do you live, Derek?"

"Portland."

"So far, *mon cher*?" He shook his head at my folly. "I own a cottage here on the island. You must come home with me."

# # # # #

"You live in a barn?" I gasped. Jules' cottage was a three story red barn with white trim and a silo.

"*Oui*," he answered, taking the herbs we had bought along the way and unlocking the door. "I had the exterior restored and then I converted the interior." Inside, the barn swept to the ceiling, creating a single space, vast and playful. Paintings by local artists created explosions of color on the clover-colored walls. A stair spiraled up the silo. Jules had transformed the former hayloft into bedrooms with less privacy than office cubicles.

These wonders engaged my eyes for a blink before my wondering gaze fell into the mirrored wall that gave back our reflection. Standing in our bicycle garb, our colorful, skin gripping shorts and jerseys, we were of a pair of bookends. Jules' eyes followed mine. I touched his hand, and a spark of lust crackled between us. Then his mouth was on mine, our lips pressing. I tasted his lower lip, raised my mouth, and let his tongue in.

My cock was swelling my shorts. Jules' hands were on my back. He caressed me, his hands gently sliding down my back until he was gripping my ass. His hands glided over the mounds of my rump and slid along my crack. I slipped my right hand between us and touched his cock through his shorts. He was solidly erect, and as I tweaked his hooded head he leaked copiously.

"*Je te veux*, Derek," he whispered into my ear, and his tongue followed his hushed breath. I nearly ejaculated then, but I held on. He placed his left hand behind my head and pulled my lips to his. His right hand stroked my ass while he licked my lips. No man had ever touched my ass in that way. His tongue pushed through my lips and licked the inside of my cheek. I met his tongue, flicking the tip of mine along the underside of his.

Taking the bottom of his jersey in both hands, I lifted it to his neck. Jules laughed as he raised his arms so I could pull it over his head. The skin on his chest, covering developed muscles, was as creamy indoors as out. I licked his shoulders and bit his neck. Lowering my head to his nipples, I sucked first one and then the other.

I kissed his stomach, which was hard and flat. My hands found the sculpted mounds of his ass. His ass was firm, solid, and protrusive. It filled the seat of his bicycle shorts, creating a yummy silhouette that the mirror gave back. The deep cleft between his swelling, almost feminine buttocks, was shadowed in the silver mirror image.

"Yes, Derek, stroke my ass," Jules begged. "I love to have my ass touched."

I groped his ass as I scooped his navel with my tongue. Soon my fingers arose as if of their own accord and found the waistband of his shorts. Then I had them sliding downward. I slid them off his ass, and his cock finally popped free, jutting before my face. I pushed his shorts down to his ankles, and he lifted one foot at a time, so I could strip him utterly.

When I touched my lips to his cock, it thickened but did not grow longer. I was delighted to find that he was fully erect at five and a half inches, the perfect length for my mouth. Naked in the evening's liquid light, his body could be my own – save for our one significant difference. Yet I could not suck my own cock. I touched my lips to his cockhead again and pushed my tongue under his foreskin.

Remembering that he liked having his ass stroked, I gripped him again. I stroked both taut cheeks while my mouth rode his cock down to the root. Pulling back, I popped my lips over his dickhead, and he rewarded me with a sweet leakage. Jules' precum tasted of persimmon. It was sweet as fruit with a tart aftertaste. My tongue tingled as he released more cum upon it.

"Oh, Derek, *je t'adore, mon cœur*," he moaned. "*Je t'adore, mon cher.*"

Did he truly love me already? Or did he truly love what I was doing to him? I did not care. I sucked him harder. I worked the head of his cock with my tongue and twisted it with my lips. I mouthed his head with my firm lips, took his cock to its full length, once, twice, thrice, and mouthed his hooded head again.

He burst into a series of feral moans, unable to control the sensations flooding his cock and radiating through his body. His cock lost its tautness for a pregnant second as it prepared to spurt. Then it hardened to fullness again, swelling even thicker than before. I felt the vibration in his cells and the quickening of his blood. He shuddered and a creamy spoonful of his cum sprayed along my tongue. I swallowed and took spurt after spurt.

His contractions quieted, but I was trembling. Did this beautiful fellow find my mouth to his liking? Had he had better? I was proud of my cocksucking talent, but his supernatural beauty and raw silence filled me with doubt.

"*Merci*, Derek," he gasped. "*Merci très beaucoup.*" I was still gripping his sculpted buttocks and giving his cock an occasional lick. After a while he took my arms and lifted me to my feet. "Come." He led me up the winding silo stairway to the bedrooms, where he switched on a Lotus Swirl Tiffany reproduction lamp and found two green silk robes with a dragonflies-over-cattails design. He pulled one around himself, tying it at the waist. The robe stood open to his navel and barely covered his bare ass.

I dropped my bicycle shorts and jersey (we had removed our shoes at the door), and dressed in the other robe. Then he led me to another mirrored wall where we stood side by side, touching, and studied our reflections. To our left a wide window revealed the last rays of the setting sun off the glaciers of Mount Adams and Mount St. Helens.

Jules turned toward me, and as the mirror reflected the swell of his ass under his thin robe, I caught my breath. He smiled, reading my whole history in my face. In all of my affairs (really two) I had taken the role of the bottom, servicing my lover with my mouth. My enjoyment had come from masturbating while I sucked, for neither of my lovers had serviced my needs. To my surprise and Jules' delight, I was panting over his ass like any top, and wondering how it would feel to slide my cock between his enticing swells.

"What do you want from me?" he purred.

"I'll tell you soon."

"But of course. You hesitate to speak of your secret longing."

"It's not that," I lied, which brought a knowing smirk to his face.

"Come. We will have an appetizer."

"Cum – I just had that snack," I quipped, but Jules did not laugh. Instead, he took my hand and led me downstairs.

Jules bade me sit, and he returned shortly with a platter of grape leaves stuffed with beef, dill, and fresh mint; olives stuffed with almonds; a board of blue stilton; a warmed loaf of honeyed bread; and foaming glasses of sweet, dark stout. "This beer will strengthen your cock."

"Why?"

"So you can do that thing that you dare not mention."

I gurgled. Was he reading my mind? "What do you think I want?"

"You want to fuck my ass. You cannot stop staring at it. You cannot leave off touching it."

I nearly choked on an olive. "How do you feel about that, Jules?"

"It is the thing I enjoy the most. I would relish your cock inside of me."

"I've never done that. Either way."

"It is easy. I have received many, many times – and given as well."

My heart nearly stopped at the implication in his words. Did he intend to slide his cock up my ass? I must have reddened for he hastened to reassure me.

"I expect you to fuck me – only. If, someday, you wish to receive in the same way you give to me, then we will proceed. Only then."

"Do you have condoms?"

Jules grinned, knowing that he had me. His face was elfin with mischief. I could not help but give back that smile, and the mirror on the wall gave back my face: tightened lips upturned sharply with monkey business sparking from my eyes.

"*Oui, Monsieur Derek*," he said rising from the couch. His erect cock pushed through his robe. My mouth went dry. I took a hefty sip of the stout and discovered that I was sporting the erection of a lifetime. My cock would have pierced steel plating.

"Wait here," Derek commanded and raced up the staircase. His robe rode over his firm ass as he leaped from step to step. I took another swig of the stout. I swear that it worked. My cock grew even stouter. I had to plow it into something, and my double's ass was the most alluring object in the Pacific Northwest, if not the nation.

Jules was back in a jiffy, bearing extra-strength condoms and sexual lubricants. I was stunned by the degree of his preparations, as well as the extent of his enthusiasm. Dropping to his knees, he lubricated my dick and slipped a condom over it. Then he lubricated the outside of the condom. I nearly shot my load into it while he slicked the outside, but Jules took care not to allow me a slip beyond the coming place.

Doffing his silken robe, Jules gripped the back of a chair and pushed his ass back. I stood almost frozen as his butt brushed my cock. Slowly, almost fearfully as though I were about to slide my cock up my own ass, I reached for his buttocks. My hands slid over his quivering mounds, and the effect was an explosion in my brain. Overcome, I pushed forward, pulled his butt cheeks apart, and pressed the head of my cock against his asshole.

A theretofore hidden satyriasis claimed me. I pushed forward and thrust. Jules gasped as I penetrated him forcefully. "I am coming," he gurgled. "*Merde*. One thrust. *C'est impossible*. One thrust – *un orgasme. Fantastique.*"

I hardly heard him. I was thrusting harder, driving my piercing cock up his ass. My whole body was throbbing. My dick tingled and I thought that I was coming, but my sensations fooled me. My tingles went on and on. I had a mild orgasm, followed three strokes later by a second. The third mini-orgasm was stronger. Was I finished? Before that vagrant doubt had filtered completely through my consciousness, those tingles multiplied. My heart skipped a beat as the pleasure deepened.

I toppled into the most intense orgasm of my life. Waves of mind-blasting pleasure washed away my conscious thoughts. For just a second I caught the mirror image: one beautiful young fellow banging the ass of his double. I saw my ass pull back and my cock grow from Jules' buttocks. Just that one flash impinged upon my brain before my first terrific contraction shot my cum into the condom.

I thrust more slowly as I came. I savored my sensations, so lost in the moment that for a wink in time I felt a cock thrusting in my own ass. Did I share the sensation that Jules was experiencing? I only knew that the feeling was wonderful, and so sweetly fleeting. When I pulled my cock out of his ass, and he turned to me with a face wreathed in smiles, drew my lips to his, and pushed his tongue into my mouth, I hoped that the time would come when Jules would fuck my ass in the wonderful way I had fucked his that day.

Later, Jules cooked a spicy ragout while I baked a yeasty bread in his oven. We carried our dinner up to the room at the top of the silo. Four curiously shaped windows revealed the full moon glowing off the mountain glaciers. Jules scooped a chunky dressing full of Roquefort onto our salads. Then he raised his glass of stout to me: "You are so beautiful, Derek. So beautiful that my heart aches to look at you."

"You are like a fantasy within a dream," I said, hoping that I didn't sound too corny. "You're the perfection that subdues my reason." Jules accepted this mush with lovelight sparking from his eyes. "And I still taste your cock – your cum on my tongue."

Jules smiled. "And I feel your cock within my ass. Next time we will not use the condom. I want your cum inside my body, just as mine is in you."

"When I'm ready."

"*Oui.* Tonight you must sleep beside me." He waved his hand to indicate the complete darkness outside. Since I had expected to bicycle home long before the sun set, I had brought no light. "I have ejaculated twice and you once already. We need not come again tonight, although I am willing if you would prefer a second orgasm." His manner hinted that he would relish a third.

"How about we cuddle and fondle each other?" I suggested. "We'll see what happens then."

After washing dishes side by side, we fell into his bed where we cuddled and fondled until we had masturbated each other to orgasm. Jules' hot semen painted my abdomen and wet my nipples. My cum decorated his skin up to his chin. Stuck together pleasantly with wet cum, we laughed with delight before we slipped into sleep.

The next morning I pedaled homeward, still tasting Jules' cum on my tongue, still feeling the firmness of his ass beneath my thrusts. We had made a date for that same evening, but still the previous day seemed so dreamlike that I wondered whether he existed anywhere but in the mirror of my heart.

Author's Note

Sauvie Island exists, as does Collins Beach, one of Oregon's officially recognized clothing optional beaches. That said, anyone familiar with the island will notice that the author took geographic and seasonal liberties. This story is not a picture of reality, but a distorted mirror view of the real. Thus strawberry picking time (late spring) and the corn maze (fall) happen at the same time.

Willie the Wily Woodchuck

While I was going to college, I stayed in Grandpop Baldwin's rickety old house. Grandpop was still living, though his arthritis kept him confined to the first floor. There were just the three of us sharing digs there: Pop, Grandpop, and me. Mom had run off to Nashville, Tennessee, with that no-account country western singer, Sammy Sofa. That was the day after Grandpop went into the storage room for a jug of applejack and caught her sucking Sammy's dick on the freezer chest.

The winter quarter had been running for four weeks when Pop had to fly to Memphis to deal with another of Mom and Sammy's slimy legal maneuvers. Sammy and Mom were trying to get their paws on my college fund, so I hoped that Pop would prevail in the Tennessee court. Pop's departure left me in the house with Grandpop. Despite his age and arthritis, Grandpop didn't need a lot of care because he was an independent old buzzard. Still, I felt responsible for him.

On the first night in February, Grandpop and I baked a chicken, fried a load of potatoes, and tossed a spinach salad. Eating beside the fireplace, Grandpop sucked down a mug of hogback stout, insisted I get a quart for myself, and started telling me about our ancestor, a British officer who enlisted help from the Native Americans during the Revolutionary War.

"You mean our family was on the side of the Redcoats?" I gasped.

"Yes, but that shit's not the point, Ollie," Grandpop said. (Pop always called me by my given name Oliver, an insufferable surname. I didn't mind Ollie). "We have a part of American history that no bastard alive has ever seen."

"What's that?"

"We have Captain Baldwin's journals. He wrote a detailed account of everything he did, Ollie. Every single damned thing. And the whole shitting match is in the attic over our heads. In a wooden chest with our ancestor's name burned onto it."

"Do you want me to bring it down?"

"Hellfire, no," Grandpop swore. "Your father would burn the goddamn journals."

"Burn them?"

"Yes, your priggish father is my beloved son and all that horseshit, but that boy is so fucking straight that he must've been born with a poker up his ass."

Grandpop wasn't making that up. Pop was the most straight-laced man I know, while coming to live with Grandpop and hearing his speech was a real ear banger.

"Nevertheless, you should read Old Bugger Baldwin's journals, Ollie. You're the one descendent of Captain Baldwin who'd truly appreciate their meaning."

I didn't think much more about Captain Baldwin that night, but the next afternoon after classes, my friend Cosmo stopped by as agreed. He had promised to show me an easy way to write a paper for freshman English.

"You type your subject into Google," Cosmo said, doing the same on my computer. "Find some article that looks like the assignment. Copy the whole fuckin' thing and paste it into Word."

"Isn't that plagiarism?"

"Not if you don't get caught. See, you gotta right click on one word out of every six and change it to a synonym. That way, nobody will get wise. That's how I ace every paper."

Following Cosmo's method, I had a two-thousand-word paper done in under an hour. "I feel like a cheater," I admitted.

"That's good," Cosmo informed me. "That's a survival mechanism. Just don't ever admit it to anybody. Swear on a stack of fucking wangels ten feet high that you wrote every word." Cosmo gave me a judicious look. "Just make sure that you read this paper before you hand it in. If you use a word like 'hircismus,' like you did here on your second page, make sure you know what it means when the professor asks you. Otherwise, you're fucked without lube."

"Shit. Hircismus is a stupid word," I protested after checking the on-line dictionary. It means 'stinky armpits.' What the fuck's hircismus got to do with Tippecanoe and Tecumseh?"

"Huh?" Cosmo's familiarity with American history was horrendous but hardly unforeseen considering that he cheated.

192

"Maybe I should be writing about British captains in the Revolutionary War."

"What the fuck are you talking about, Ollie?"

"Something Grandpop said. Come on. Let's check it out."

Cosmo and I slipped up to the attic, which we reached through the unused third floor lumber-room. The whole damn day, Grandpop had been sipping from a bottle of Glenfiddich single malt sweetened with a hint of Drambuie and chanting poetry from an 1850s volume of Robert Burns. He was dreaming of better days by the blazing fireplace, so he wasn't going to disturb us. Cosmo and I had the upper regions of the house to ourselves.

The attic was crammed with old stuff: paintings, books, rolled Persian carpets, longcase clocks, and furniture that would have the staff of Antiques Roadshow shooting loads in their undies. "Who's this James Tissot dude?" Cosmo asked, looking at a painting of a ship with a shitload of rigging and some perplexed looking figures.

"Damned if I know," I said. "Look at this old sea chest." I pointed out an ancient trunk built of shrinking wood and leather straps. "Look, it's got Captain Baldwin's name burned into the top."

Opening the trunk, I found uniforms worn by my ancestor during the Revolutionary War. Unfortunately, they had red coats. There was a powdered wig too, which was yellowed but still could have been worn for a Halloween party. Between layers of a British flag and some regimental flag for the ninth brigade or something, I discovered a thick manuscript. The pages were made of rag paper and were sewn together with a faded blue thread. Opening it up, I discovered that my ancestor couldn't spell worth shit, and he must've thought that punctuation was a plot devised by the continental army.

"Holy shit!" I said. "Captain Baldwin was into gay sex." I glanced at Cosmo to see how he was taking that news. To my surprise, he wanted all the juicy details.

"Read it out loud," Cosmo insisted. I was on my hands and knees looking into the chest, and Cosmo was on his knees beside me. Suddenly he felt alarmingly close. A hot flash shot through me. I sat down on the filthy attic boards and opened the manuscript to its second chapter. The sex scenes started somewhere in there, and Cosmo had no interest in my ancestor's story before arriving in the New World on George III's troop ship.

The Diary of Fergus Baldwin, December 23, 1777

General Grose paced nine times around his office before he uttered a word; meanwhile, I stood at quivering attention until he deigned to notice me. The general reeked of wine and brandy, and I wished the drunken rogue would come to any senses he might possess. It wasn't as if Grose were a bona fide military man. King George had appointed Grose to his position for one reason – to get him out of England. Grose was so bird-witted that our Gracious King preferred to station him across the Atlantic to wage war against the American cacklers.

It was the twenty-third of December, and I was looking forward to Christmas with my fellow officers; eating goose, drinking gin and porter, and plunging my stout Scot's plugtail into some colonial harlot's laced mutton. Little did I ken that those plans were already knocked to flinders. Grose suddenly stopped and regarded me with his dull eyes. I could not tear my gaze from his teeth, which were stained black from drinking Madeira.

"Baldwin, we could lose this war."

"Sir," I gasped. "The British army? Against a bunch of buffle heads? I expect we'll see those traitors Washington, Jefferson, that old devil Franklin, and the rest of those clowes twisted from good British hemp before the spring."

"You're a dupe, Baldwin. We suffered six hundred causalities during the Battle of Saratoga while the colonists lost only a hundred and fifty. We are waging war across a sea, while these rapscallion 'patriots' are fighting on their home ground. There's a rumor that Prussian troops might join Washington at Valley Forge. We need to stir up the savages against the colonists."

"You expect the heathens to help us?"

"Given the alternative – yes. Therefore we're sending you to negotiate with the tribes south of the big lakes."

"Sir, I'm a soldier, not a diplomat."

"This mission requires a soldier, Baldwin. No sane dignitary would undertake the task. Therefore we decided to send a man whose life is of little value to anyone."

That pissed my goose, but I could hardly say so. "As you command, sir," I replied with a bow, but the general lacked the wit for sarcasm.

"Stir your stumps, Baldwin. You must depart tonight."

"Tonight!" I was aghast. "But it's Christmas."

The general regarded me with eyes that looked like two pissholes in the snow. "Forget about swilling rack punch and caterwauling in a whorehouse, Baldwin. Buck up, man. King and Country, what? Dismissed."

Fairly toffee-headed, I picked up my kit and set out for the "Dawn Land" of the savages.

The Diary of Fergus Baldwin, January 15, 1778

The winter village was the largest in the colony. It consisted of three oval-shaped long houses and more than two hundred conical bark-covered wigwams with draping bear or deer skins. Children were sporting in the snow, men were discussing tribal politics and smoking seriously from pipes, and women were roaring over ribald jokes while they cooked thick stews and roasted slabs of venison over open fires.

The village was the most welcome sight I'd ever blinked. I had spent the past three days slogging alone through heavy snowdrifts. I was chilled to the bone, sick from my spoiled rations, and worn to a nub. Not only that, but I had missed Christmas. No bawdy lady's laced mutton for my prick jelly, still less goose, gin, or porter.

"Hallo, English," a fruity voice called in sweetly accented English.

I glanced around expecting greater, but my greeter could only be the approaching apparition. The figure had a sweetly effeminate face with long braids, but he was wearing a man's deerskin top over a colorful print dress that bespoke Paris. I was meeting my first berdache. According to native belief, the berdache's body holds two spirits, one male and one female. A berdache is wise, but foolish; good hearted, but tricky; and magical, but naïve. In spite of my strict Protestant upbringing, I found my soul bewitched by this walking enchantment.

The berdache seized my hands and squeezed them through my thick woolen mittens. "I am Wuchak."

"Wojack?"

"The others of your tribe have called me Willie. You may call me by that name if you desire." Wuchak still had not released my hands, and he had edged closer.

Shivering, I gave Wuchak my name and allowed him to lead me to a wigwam. The hanging bear skins made the inside cozy. A fire blazed in the center, the smoke going out through a hole in the center. Thick robes of hide covered the ground. Wuchak offered me a drink in a clay cup. I sipped, found nothing wrong with the beverage, and tossed it off. "What's in it, Willie?"

Pouring a second stingo, Wuchak displayed an herb with crimson berries. The gnarled offshoots' long stringy haired branches resembled arms and legs. I took the plant and stared at it. I had never seen anything like it. The sight of it made me weak in the knees – or was it the drink itself? I sat down quickly upon a pile of beaver pelts.

Willie helped pull off my boots. The wigwam seemed extremely warm. I stood to struggle out of my uniform coat, and Willie was right there to help me. At some point, he had divested himself of most of his clothing. He regarded me with an elfin smile as I noticed that he was wearing only the traditional breechclout, a single strip of cloth wrapped with two flaps dangling over his nutmegs and bumfiddle.

The heat grew more severe, so I quaffed another drink. Willie poured me a third cup of his magical drink. For some reason, I was not fully cognizant about what was happening. I had been reduced to my small clothes, and Willie was completely naked. In spite of his plugtail and bollocks, he had a shapely, effeminate figure. His pratts jutted, high and tight. His fingers happened to brush my groin, and I discovered that my prickler was tremblingly erect – indeed, had been erect for some time. The wigwam grew even hotter; pleasant feelings coursed through me.

For a moment, I came to myself. I was then buck naked and sprawled upon the pelts. Willie was rubbing a slick compound onto my hard plugtail, and I did not want him to stop. His face came close to mine. His beardless face, his jet black braids, his glossy apple-hued complexion, his soft, liquid eyes drew me in. My lips met his. I found myself kissing Willie, kissing another male in lust rather than friendship. And I liked it.

My rut grew as I kissed Willie, but he pushed away, gave me another elfin grin, and threw himself face down on a pile of blankets. His arse was in an inviting position, and it grew even more inviting when Willie doubled three blankets under his middle to elevate his arse. His reddish pratts invited penetration. Willie pulled his right leg up. "Lie upon me, English," said he. "I shall work my magic and show you delights such as you have never known."

When I ran my hand over Willie's firm mounds, I nearly swooned. My plugtail was flinty, pointing toward the heavens, and dripping as I rubbed it over Willie's alluring pratts. His swells tingled the head of my prickler, so I rubbed it along his bumfiddle. "Stick it into me," Willie urged.

I wasn't peery. I soudsed my dick against his hole and rammed. Willie's arsehole received me like a bitch booby, and I whiddled his whole scrap. No prigging I'd ever done prepared me for that sensation.

"Ah, that's nice," I sighed.

I raised my hips and gave him the blanket hornpipe. Willie's tube was so hot and so tight that my prickler could hardly stand it. Every inch of movement was a torment of delight, a rapturous pleasure that was pain in small doses but a pain I couldn't forgo. All my life, my codhead had itched with an itch that I could never scratch. Willie's anal chute scratched deeper than laced mutton.

"Uh," I groaned. The rapturous distress made me desire more. I clamped my teeth into Willie's shoulder.

A throbbing ecstasy stunned my prickler, and I thrust even harder and faster. "Oh, I'm going to pluck the ribbon. Here it comes. I'm going to jet into your arse."

"Yes, fill me, English."

Pour I did. That throbbing ecstasy tint my reason altogether. My bollocks contracted at the base of my codhead. Humping faster, I jetted my bollock honey into Willie's arse. Willie moaned as I spurted, his arse chute gripping my prickler like a Prussian's fist.

After a brief respite, I popped my drained prickler out of Willie's arse. The berdache sighed with contentment, pulled his legs together, and held my prick jelly inside. After a few minutes, he arose. Crossing the wigwam, he took warm water scented with herbs and washed my codhead thoroughly. Then he had me stand, and he washed me from top to bottom, from ear to ear, and heel to toe. He took away the stink of my journey and left me satiated and sweet smelling.

Night had fully fallen, and the snowfall came with it, blurring sky, earth, and forest. Biding me remain, Willie left the wigwam and returned with wooden platters and bowls of food. Fried fish began our feast, followed by a rabbit stew with carrots, turnips, and sweet potatoes. We picked at slices of roasted venison adjunct to a delicious corn meal bread with wild plum jelly. After we ate, Willie filled a pipe and lit it from the fire.

"Jimson Weed?" I asked, tasting the smoke.

"We call it thornapple." Willie took a heavy lungful, so I did likewise. My head spun as if I had drunk deeply. Willie laid me upon his bed and sat beside me.

"Let me tell you about the woman who married a bear." As I lay naked with his hands caressing me, Willie told me about the woman who loved a bear and bore him a son, who turned out human. In my dreamy state, I saw that Willie's natural world and the human world were the same, unlike the terrible construction of our European culture in which humans war against nature, or seek to conquer it.

Even Willie's name signified his part in the natural world. Wuchak – woodchuck in our English vernacular. Woodchuck the trickster. Oh, he had tricked me into giving my all. I had been in the Indian village only a few hours, but I had already been seduced by Willie the Wily Woodchuck.

# # # # #

I stopped reading and stared at Cosmo. His jeans bore the obvious sign of a major boner. "Don't stop reading," he said. "I want to hear more."

I shifted a bit because my own piercing erection was twisted in my underwear. As I turned my attention to the page, I wondered what Cosmo had on his mind. I sure knew what I was thinking about him.

The Diary of Fergus Baldwin, January 28, 1778

My life has greatly changed since I arrived in the Indian village. I wonder whether I dare return to civilization. The first night I prigged Wuchak, I imagined that I had given all, but I was wrong. There was so much more to give, and the giving brought the greatest pleasure I have ever known. However, speaking of that pleasure to my company would bring disaster. The coves would lay rum glaziers upon me, strip me of my stripes, flog me, and dangle me from a tree limb.

In the thirteen days since I arrived, I jetted my bollock jelly into Wuchak's arse eighteen times. Everyone in the Indian village knew what we were doing, and everyone approved wholeheartedly. Furthermore, Wuchak was a merry grig, and I loved being with him.

Finally came the night when we smoked three pipes of thornapple, which provoked phantasms of the mind, and consumed many cups of Wuchak's special tea, which heightened sexual arousal to a feverish pitch. Wuchak was on his knees before me, nutting my blowen. His firm lips twisted my prickler's head as he squeezed my nutmegs.

"Oh, English," Wuchak simpered, raising his head as I grew close to blasting my honey.

"Do not hesitate in your doing, Wuchak," I moaned. "You leave me in a perilous condition." He sucked at the head a little more, then stopped anon. "What do you want of me, Wuchak?"

"I have given you much pleasure for half the moon's turning?"

"True," I managed. "Your mouth and arse have been better than any wench's."

"Yet I am no wench," Wuchak explained, stroking my prickler. "I am of two spirits. Do you consider my needs?"

It was a suitable question, and I was in a state of high arousal. "Finish me, Wuchak," I promised, "and I shall give you pleasure."

"Oh, English, the moon has turned, and looks to hang fuller. First, you must receive my seed. Then shall your own promise be fulfilled."

Wuchak had been gripping my pratts as he mouthed my plugtail. Without further ado, he slid his hand into my bumfiddle. His touch

The Dream in the Heart of the Forest

provoked tempests within me. The narcotic herbs and drink had so
befuddled my noodle that I spoke forthwith: "Wuchak, slide your
plugtail into my arsehole." I wanted his bollock jelly to bless me from
my bumfiddle to my lips.

I wiggled my arse as I prepared to receive the blanket hornpipe.
Wuchak grabbed my pratts with both hands and touched his prickler to
my arsehole. I pushed my arsehole open, and in he came; his prickler
kept sliding in as my arsehole stretched around it.

"My plugtail is almost all in, English," Wuchak gasped. "You are
receiving it all." With a mighty plunge, the berdache rammed my pratts
with his lap and his nutmegs pressed against mine.

"Oh, yea, that is glorious," I moaned. "Now, prig my Scots arse."

With supreme gumption, Wuchak did so. He drew his prickler back
and reamed my arsehole again. The native berdache stuffed me with his
lunges. I was flooded with pleasure.

"Oh, thy prickler is a marvel, Wuchak."

My beloved berdache rocked back and forth, fucking my arse with a
steady rhythm. As Wuchak prigged me, his thick plugtail pounded me
toward orgasm. "Oh, English, I grow close," Wuchak moaned. I felt
tingles in the head of my prickler that signaled the approaching storm
of pleasure. Wuchak fired my prickler, and those flames rose into a
crescendo of sensation, a tasty, banned, albeit unlikely, pleasure, dodgy
yet transcendent. My bollock honey leaked cruelly while the berdache's
hot breath rasped in my ear.

My own breath was raging in my throat while the words that leaked
around my breath befuddled. "Fuck me harder," I demanded. Every
stroke of his plugtail trilled through my body. I pushed with my asshole
as he thrust his fleshly plug, and squeezed him hard when he pulled
back. My prickler was dripping honey, though I had not touched it with
my hand.

"Ah, English, I'm going to blast prick jelly."

I met his pleasures with my own, wheezing, groaning, and purring
from the superb anguish. Wuchak was going to blast his jelly up my
arse, but I was going to spew before he could. "Wuchak, you're making
me toss honey," I howled.

Tingles of pleasure whiddled my arsehole. My plugtail grew
weighty. The shooting muscles at the base of my prickler sent forth my

200

honey. My prickler jerked as I shot a burst of juice, and my arse clamped down on Wuchak's prigging prickler. Squirt followed squirt as I blasted loads of sticky jelly, my throbbing arsehole milking off Wuchak.

Wuchack gasped as my arse milked him. "Oh, English, I release my spirit into you. You are the only man to receive the magical power of my stick."

Thus did the berdache pour his spirit into me, I receiving willingly the miraculous honey that would alter the course of my life. Colors swirled before my eyes, and I fell into a universe of whirling stars. Throughout the night, I was dimly aware that my body nestled against Wuchak's while he poured into my ears a strange story of two weasel sisters who married two great lights from the starry night.

# # # # #

I wasn't sure at what point Cosmo had pulled off his pants, but he was sprawled on his side in nothing but brilliant yellow sports briefs. "Keep reading, Ollie," he demanded. "I want to hear what Captain Baldwin does next." I could hardly tear my eyes from Cosmo's crotch. His cock looked ready to rip through the fabric.

"How about you read some," I said, handing him the manuscript. As he started to read, I pulled off my shirt. My jeans came off next. While Cosmo read, I toyed with my cock through the fabric of my underwear, a hot bikini in a dip-dyed color print.

The Diary of Fergus Baldwin, February 2, 1778

The morning started with an elaborate ritual. Before sunrise, the village began to gather around, men, women, and children together. Tables had been set up to accommodate the rich food and drink, and the children had decorated the village with moss, ivy, and branches. I gathered with the rest, quaffing black tea and awaiting dawn light. The morning was cold, but I had forsaken my uniform and was dressed in deerskin leggings and shirt, which were soft, warm, and did not itch like wool. I was also wearing a hat and a coat of pelts.

Snow had been falling throughout the night, and the villagers took that for a good sign. However, just before daybreak a wind off the lake began scattering the clouds. The villagers read the sign and muttered darkly among themselves. When the sun painted the morning golden and finally broke out over the tops of the firs, the villagers shook their heads fatalistically.

A celebration of drumming and dancing followed, in which an actor portrayed winter and the dying of the crops, while another played summer with its fruitfulness and plenty. We ate sweet cakes and sipped strong herbal tea while the mummers performed. At the conclusion, the music stopped. Everyone turned expectantly toward a tiny wigwam in which Wuchak had sealed himself the previous night.

Like the rest of the village, I held my breath when the door to the wigwam swung aside and Wuchak emerged. My beloved was nearly naked; he wore only two pelts fore and aft. Wuchak emerged dancing into the sunlight, and his shadow danced with him. Abruptly, he stopped, pointed toward his shadow, intoned words that I could not understand, and scampered back into the hut.

The villagers began talking among themselves, making plans to hunt longer hours for the diminished game, to fish through the ice, and to ration the stored goods. Wuchak had predicted that the long harsh winter would persist for another two moons. For myself, I was delighted; a thaw would have necessitated my departure from this paradisiacal existence to the world of rebellion and war.

The noontime feast was filled with gallows humor. Only Wuchak and I were free from care. As soon as we decently could, we slipped onto our wigwam where we smoked thornapple until our minds were whirling. I undressed Wuchak, and as I pulled away his loincloth his erect plugtail touched my lips. For a moment, I felt as if I had kissed a hot nettle. The sensation of touching my lips to his prickler was boggling. I slid my lips over the head of it and let it ride along my tongue. Wuchak's codhead leaked a thin stream onto my tasters.

The bollock jelly's flavor made me lust for more. It was the best pudding I'd ever tasted, and my mouth formed a halo around his prickler. Closing my fist around his shaft, I nutted the berdache's blowen with my lips and tongue until he rocked his hips as he would prig a wench.

When his contractions settled, Wuchak pulled his prick from my mouth. "Well done, English," complimented he. "Now ye shall prig my arse again. You must spurt your codshead honey into me."

I was not under the hatches. Perhaps Wuchak was a sorry poor tattered fellow, whose breech might be seen through his pocket-holes, had he had pockets, but he had bent over a roll of blankets to offer his pratts and bumfiddle. With that offer, I climbed behind him and slid my prickler into his arsehole. My native lover was burning for my codhead. The head of my prick disappeared between Wuchak's pratts.

I pushed my prickler all the way in until I was whiddling his whole scrap. He received my codshead like a long-lost brother. I reared back and reamed him again, pulling his hair as I rammed his arsehole. Wuchak grunted and moaned, and his throbbing plugtail leaked honey. As I started humping him rhythmically, the native's tight arsehole massaged my prickler like a cow tongue.

The ancestral fires of my clan were burning within me. The jelly rose from my bollocks like molten ore. Rapturous tingles rippled through the head of my prick and vibrated up the shaft. My prick was heavy as the spasms shook me. The muscles at the base of my shaft contracted, and I shot great gouts of bollock honey into his arse.

# # # # #

When my fingers gripped the head of his cock, Cosmo's gasp could have been heard three miles away. I had been watching him rub himself, and the temptation to help him grew too strong. Cosmo dropped the manuscript as I fingered his cock through his underwear.

"Do you know what you're doing, Ollie?" There was a playful tone in his voice.

"What I'm doing is playing with your dick, Cosmo." Only one of my hands was playing with his dick. I was rubbing my own with the other.

Cosmo shifted so that I had better access to his cock. "Are you gay, Ollie?"

"I've never done this before, Cosmo."

"That's no answer, Ollie. Have you ever screwed a girl?"

"No. I haven't ever done a guy either."

"I'm pretty sure I'm gay," Cosmo said, searching my eyes.

"What about your girlfriend?"

"I don't have a fuckin' girlfriend. When I told you that I did, I was lying my ass off."

"Have you ever got your rocks off with a guy?"

"I've jerked off with another guy. Nothing more. Except I dream about it."

"What's it?" I asked, rubbing his cock harder. He pushed my hand away from my cock and began rubbing me.

"Huh?"

I cleared it up for him. "You said you dream about it. I wondered what it is."

Cosmo pushed his underwear down to his ankles. His cock was not so long, but it was tender and looked juicy. Not that it was dinky. He had nearly six inches, and it was pleasantly thick. I pulled off my underwear and grabbed his meat again.

"Have you ever kissed a guy, Ollie?"

A feral rush shot through me. Cosmo was asking if he could kiss me. Oh, how I wanted to kiss him. I wanted to meet his lips so much that my tongue froze in my mouth. I sat tharn.

Without his waiting longer for an answer, Cosmo's mouth was on mine, and his tongue was pushing into my mouth. His firm hand clutched my cock, and his cock spurted a stream that slicked my wrist. I met his tongue with mine. Our tongues played while we fucked our clenched fists. Explosive ripples traveled over my body. A robust explosion scorched my mind, realizing my heart's longing. Cosmo rocked his hips. I fondled his ass as he screwed my hand, and I sucked his tongue, which pushed deeper into my mouth.

Ripples tingled through the head of my cock. "I would do anything with you, Cosmo," I murmured, and, in time, I would do everything with him. I would suck him and fuck him. He would suck my cock, and he would fuck my ass.

My juices were rising. I was going to squirt cum. I pulled my mouth from Cosmo's and whispered in his ear. "I love your thick cock, Cosmo. I love your smooth ass. Come in my hand. Come on me."

"Oh, Ollie, you're making me come."

"That's it, Cosmo," I whispered, inviting him to let fly. "Decorate me with your spunk."

"It's gonna splatter, Ollie."

"That's the way I want it." I gripped his cock with all my might and worked it ferociously. I pounded his shaft and tortured the head of his cock with my thumb and forefinger while my other hand explored his ass's sensuous cleft.

Barely a minute later, Cosmo and I sprawled, wet with cum and discussing when we should try anal sex. I was glad that Pop was in Tennessee, and that Grandpop could not make it up three flights to catch us. Suddenly, a funny feeling came over me. Grandpop knew that I would like gay sex. What's more, he approved.

What had Grandpop said: "Nevertheless, you should read Old Bugger Baldwin's journals, Ollie. You're the one descendent of Captain Baldwin who'd truly appreciate their meaning."

What wonderful strain passed down the generations of my family, I wondered, which passed finally to me? What magic was mine that slipped through centuries from Wuchak's cum to my own?

Cosmo had left long streamers on me, streaks of spunk that wet me from stomach to chin. I slid my finger along a wet strand, tasted Cosmo's cum, and asked, "Could you come again?"

"Now, Ollie?"

"Yeah. You're gonna shoot your next load up my ass. I'm gonna take your whole package."

"Okay. But you gotta do me after."

"Sure. But there's just one thing."

"What's that?"

"We're going downstairs to do it. And we're gonna let my old Grandpop watch. Oh, Cosmo, that old man is gonna love seeing me take your cock."

I had a little trouble convincing Cosmo, but my promise proved true. I told Grandpop what we were gonna do, and he urged us on. Then the old bugger watched me take Cosmo's cock in my ass and called out the most obscene and practical instructions during the whole fuck. By the time we finished, Grandpop had taught me to ride cocks as if I'd been sponging cum anally since the Revolutionary War.

"Hot damn," I swore to Cosmo as I slipped my tortured dick into his anal chute, "Captain Baldwin would be damned proud of us."

("Willie, The Wily Woodchuck" originally appeared in the now out-of-service online periodical *Tommyhawk's Fantasy World*)

Braad Skips Rope at the Bear Festival

The village hunched in Greenwood Forest, shaded by dark firs. Its streets were cobbled, and its houses boasted delicate fretwork. Most of the houses quivered in three stories, though some trembled at four or five. Over fifteen hundred souls, of varied social classes, lived and worked in the village or on its outlying farms. Highest in the society were the Ursine Priests who presided over and judged matters of public morals and government. Below the priests hovered the ranks of the merchants; below the merchants, the craftsworkers; below the craftsworkers, the husbanders.

Each year during the Bear Festival, one youth won the honor of becoming the newest acolyte among the Ursine Priests. The fortunate family that youth left behind advanced its wealth and place in society. It was a boon for a family to have a son initiated into the Ursine Priesthood. So on the first of May following his eighteenth birthday, each boy in the village had his single opportunity to compete for the prize.

# # # # #

During the final week of April, the rains diminished and daffodils burst forth from the awakening ground. Father hitched Toort and Giift, our oxen, to the plow and began turning the dirt for the spring planting. However, unlike the parents of older sons, my parents did not speak of the day when the farm would be mine. Instead, they relieved me of my farm chores and insisted that I spend many hours skipping rope.

"Practice makes perfect," my mother kept saying as I jumped the twirling rope in the onion patch behind the thunderbox. "Now switch to the alternate foot. That's it, Braad. Well done. Now do the criss-cross."

When I stopped, panting and pouring from my exertions, she hugged me enthusiastically. "Oh, Braad, I just know that you are going to be this year's winner. I've never seen a boy who could jump a rope like you do. I have your costume all ready."

"Can I see it? I'd like to try it on."

She laughed. "Not until the morning of the Bear Festival, silly. You have to be ritually purged, bathed, and groomed before you're allowed to see your costume, much less wear it."

"Do I get to keep it after the festival?"

For the first time, I noticed a contrite expression shadow my mother's face. However, she hid her thoughts, and said brightly, "you'll wear your costume for the day of the Bear Festival. After the festival, boys pack away their costumes as keepsakes, and they never show them to the uninitiated. I still have your father's costume."

"Did father win when he jumped rope?"

"Of course not, silly. That would be impossible."

"I don't understand, Mother. Why would that be impossible?"

Instead of answering, Mother handed me the rope again. "Perhaps you need a little more practice jumping side-to-side while keeping your feet together."

I hesitated. "Are you sure that my costume will fit me?"

Mother smiled. "Don't worry, Braad. I made exact measurements. It will fit perfectly, and you will be the most beautiful boy jumping. Oh, I so badly want you to win. Your father does too, though he will not say as much."

My sister Daarla pulled me aside on the morning of the thirtieth of April. "If Father had won the year he jumped rope at the Bear Festival, then he would not be our father." Daarla was twenty-one, so she had already seen three Bear Festivals and knew far more than I did.

"Little brother, I need to tell you something," Daarla whispered, urgently gripping my arm.

"Let go," I yelped. I resented having her call me "little brother." After all, I was eighteen, an adult in the eyes of the Ursine Priesthood.

"Listen to me."

"Okay, I'm listening."

"You need to know what's going to happen tomorrow."

I gasped. The rituals of the Bear Festival were our most important civic secret. No boy knew what happened during the festival until after he attended his first. Girls were also kept in the dark, but they mattered

208

less since they did not compete in the rope jumping. Every boy did compete, but once only, and that in the May after he turned eighteen. After turning eighteen, everyone witnessed the festival year after year, and none ever told the young what they saw. Daarla was threatening to violate the community's greatest taboo.

"You're not supposed to tell me," I said. "It's a surprise."

"It'll be a surprise, sure enough, Braad." She looked around warily. "Mother and Father want you to win the jump rope contest. They can't think about anything but the benefits your winning would bring them. To the family, really. They aren't thinking about you."

"Sure they are, Daarla. Father has allowed me to skip all of my chores, and Mother has been coaching me for months. She's also made my costume."

"Yeah, wait until you see that," Daarla hissed. "Listen, you boys are never told what you are trying to win until one of you wins. Then it's too late. I think the whole setup is horribly unfair. I mean, it's okay if the outcome is what you really want, but what if you don't?"

"That makes no sense."

"I'm not going to argue with you. The boy who wins the jump rope competition gets initiated into the Ursine Priesthood. He eventually becomes a priest himself – for the rest of his life."

I gasped again. The Ursine Priesthood. "How is that bad, Daarla? The Priests run everything. They make all the decisions for the village. They have absolute power. What kind of fellow wouldn't want to be one of them?"

"One who wants a wife, children, family," Daarla protested. "It's a homosexual priesthood, Braad."

A thrill shot through me. Something longed for but never expressed fingered the recesses of my lower consciousness.

"What's more," Daarla continued, "the boy who wins the competition gets his virgin butt fucked. If you win, they'll fuck your tight asshole with everybody watching: Father, Mother, your friends, me. Then the priests will take you away and initiate you. The goddess Keerideen alone knows what manner of indignities they will inflict on you." She licked her lips at her own naughty thoughts. Then, her eyes glowing puckishly, she added, "I'll bet the priests gang bang you until your ass explodes with their cum."

209

The image of a row of tumescent men waiting their turn to fuck my ass sent a hot surge through my loins. "You aren't supposed to be telling me about this, Daarla."

"I thought you should know what you're competing for. You have to compete, but you could throw the contest. Pretend to trip over the rope. Jump badly. Anything to screw up. Let one of your friends take it up the ass."

I pictured the two alternatives. Life in husbandry, working the farm my whole life, marrying and siring children so they too could spend their days in backbreaking farm labor. Or the other path, making decisions for the town, studying the problems of the community, and spending all my days in pleasurable, non-fruitful, sexual activity.

"Daarla, I can't throw this contest. I'm in it to win. Like you said, Father and Mother are counting on me." As I spoke, I knew that I wanted to win more than ever. The idea of marrying and raising children on the farm had always filled me with a sick dread. Then too, I had always felt a quickening in my loins when I swam naked with my friends Boodie and Caasper.

Daarla regarded me with widened eyes. "I think you like the idea of getting fucked. You've never done it, have you? You do have a virgin asshole?"

My scrotum tightened. I pictured Boodie's thick cock and Caasper's round ass as the three of us had often jerked off together in the millet field. "Yes, I have a virgin asshole," I assured Daarla.

"You also have a hard on. I guess you like the idea of getting fucked." She suddenly laughed. "In that case, I hope that you do win. It'll be good for the family."

"I am going to win," I promised her. "Now that you let the cat out of the bag – illegally, I might add – I'm going to give it everything I've got. All I ask is that while the farm prospers for the rest of you, you think of me once in a while."

Daarla suddenly hugged me. "Tomorrow, while you're jumping rope, you'll hear me cheering you on. And afterward, while you're bent over the butt-fuck gallows and the bear priest is opening your asshole, I'll be the one clapping loudest."

The next morning I was standing naked in the middle of Mother's sewing room. I had been purged (any description of that process I'll

210

withhold) and bathed thoroughly, so I was clean inside and out. I had fasted the night before, although I was allowed all the water I could drink. My breakfast consisted of a thick porridge spiced with unfamiliar flavors.

"Open your eyes, Braad," my mother jubilated. "You can see your costume now."

My costume consisted of a yellow kilt so short that it barely covered my buttocks, an armless matching shirt that crossed my chest with ribbons, and red pixie-winged shoes. The kilt and shirt were red trimmed. The pixie shoes had a yellow trim. When I was dressed in this revealing get-up, my mother eyed me with a critical gaze. "Yes, you are beautiful, Braad. I believe that the priests will find you attractive." So saying, she draped a necklace of red and yellow crocus flowers around my neck.

"Mother, aren't we forgetting something important?"

"What?"

I lifted my kilt an inch, which exposed an inch of ass cheek. "Underwear. I can't skip rope dressed like this. The whole village will see everything."

"Braad, there are many things you do not yet know. After today, you will know them. If you lose the contest today, then you will stand with the family through these yearly festivals and see every boy at eighteen skip rope in just such a costume. Without underwear."

"If I lose? I'm going to win, Mother."

"Yes, I believe that you will. Then your world will change." A sudden tear leaked from her eye, but it was not a tear of sadness. My mother wanted me to expose myself before the village, and she hoped to see me butt fucked by the Ursine Priests. "I can say no more, Braad."

"Okay." I had to hear her say it. "Do you really want me to win, Mother?"

"Of course. Why else would I have coached you this past year?" She grabbed a comb and fixed my hair for the third time that morning. "Come now," she said. "Today is your special day. Let's go to the Bear Festival."

I felt some relief when I saw that my best friends Boodie and Caasper were dressed in costumes just like mine, except theirs had different colors. The tip of Boodie's cock hung beneath the hem of his kilt, while Caasper's bountiful ass swelled his outrageously. I suddenly felt outclassed, even though I knew that my own parts were no call for shame.

Boodie and Caasper had been watching the girls dancing wild circles around a tall pole, painted in stripes, and decorated with greenery, flowers, and ribbons. "What do you think of Niisti?" Boodie asked, trying unsuccessfully to lengthen his kilt. He only served to disorder his appearance.

"She's nice," Caasper replied.

"Some fine day I'm going to marry her. If I win the jump rope contest today, maybe the priests will give me enough money so I can ask her tonight."

A sick feeling swept over me. My friends still had no idea about the prize they were seeking. Maybe Daarla was right when she said that the Bear Festival was unfair.

"Have you ever thought about what it would be like if you didn't marry?" I asked.

"Didn't marry? Every boy finds a girl and marries her," Caasper said.

"Not every boy. Suppose you did it with a man?"

"What are you talking about, Braad? That doesn't make sense."

"Haven't you guys ever thought about how it would feel to have a fellow slide his cock up your ass?" I bent forward to illustrate my point. "Fuck you in the ass? Shoot his seed into you?"

My friends backed off three paces and stared at me. "Have you gone crazy, Braad? Have you been sipping from the honey mead jar?"

"Just think about it," I urged. "We three jerked off in the millet field, didn't we?"

"Lots of times," Caasper admitted. "That's normal. It doesn't mean we're going to – uh – do what you said."

Boodie suddenly laughed and slapped my back. "Braad is trying to throw us off balance, Caasper. So he can win the jump rope contest and claim the reward. Nice try, Braad. I'm gonna win this year, which lets you out for keeps."

David Holly

"You know the first thing I'm gonna do when the jump rope event is over?" Caasper chortled, relieved by Boodie's assumption. "I'm going to dive into those meat pies on that table. Along with the ale, and maybe some of the honey mead. Then I'm going to eat as many of those jam tarts as I can hold. That porridge my mother served me this morning was too odd to be filling."

"No kidding," Boodie exclaimed. "I must've eaten the same stuff. Spiced kind of high, wasn't it?"

"It was supposed to give us energy."

The three of us strolled around, examining the tables of food and drink, which we were not permitted to touch until after the jump rope event, and checking out the wares that craftsworkers were selling. Our costumes singled us out, and men past eighteen barbed us with bafflingly suggestive and ribald jests. The girls our age could not stop staring at our short swinging kilts, though they had no more knowledge of what was coming than my male friends did.

Fifteen boys turned eighteen that year, so I had only fourteen competitors. Most years there were more boys jumping. As the noon hour approached, our parents corralled us and pushed us toward the stage. Soon we fifteen stood facing the gathering crowd with the long wooden platform stage behind us. Craftsworkers had erected the stage from scaffolds the previous day, and all of us had dropped by to watch the work progress. The only part we had not seen was the frame erected in the exact center of the stage. The frame had appeared during the night while we tossed in our beds. The frame was a low gibbet of wood with a thick rounded bar at the top. Participants mounted it by climbing three steps.

I tried to imagine how it would work. The boy who won – me! – would climb the steps and drape himself over the frame with the smooth bar under his abdomen. Then the bear priest would ascend, and standing, would be perfectly positioned to penetrate the boy's ass. A funny feeling came over me as I thought again that I was the only one of the fifteen who knew what was coming. I saw Boodie and Caasper glance at the frame with puzzled expressions and then dismiss it as unimportant. Little did they know.

I stood nonchalantly. Some of the boys were fidgeting, obviously ill at ease in their revealing costumes. The sight of one boy desperately trying to make himself invisible brought a smile to my face. Let the crowd stare, I thought, adopting an unflappable demeanor.

A great clamor of horns and drums announced the arrival of the Ursine Priesthood. Young and old, all of the priests were dressed alike: boots with straps that ascended almost to their knees, a pleated white kilt that hung to the middle of their powerful thighs, and a buttonless vest that revealed their muscular chests and flat stomachs. One particularly muscular and youthful priest separated himself from the rest. Unlike his brethren, he was wearing a bear mask that hid his face. He went and stood behind the frame. My heart beat faster at the sight of him.

A short ritual followed, during which the High Priest read out the principal laws of the village and invoked the favor of the deities upon the event about to proceed. Then our names were called one by one, and we made our way onto the stage. Seven boys ended up standing on one side of the frame, and the other eight of us on the other. I was surprised by the roominess. There was plenty of space between the boys on either side of me. Pooge, the boy on my left, grimaced fretfully. I gave him an encouraging grin. I also smiled at the priest who handed me my jump rope.

The community had gathered, every individual except for those under eighteen, the sick, and the invalided. Boys who had jumped rope and lost during the previous years were regarding us with knowing smirks. I was the only boy on the stage who understood the significance of those smirking faces. An expectant murmur sibilated through the crowd. The whole town was waiting to watch one of us get roundly butt fucked.

A blare of horns and a drum roll called us to action. "Jump rope," the High Priest demanded, and we all began to twirl. As I jumped my rope, starting with a basic jump, both feet slightly apart and jumping synchronistically, my kilt flapped up and down, revealing my waggly cock and bouncy ass to the crowd.

Then the ribaldry, the coaching, the catcalls, the cheering, the jeers, the roars, and the applause commenced. "Double under, Braad," my mother shouted, jumping the gun because I hadn't even started the speed step.

I paid no attention, but concentrated on my routine with my whole being. I could hear Daarla shouting. "Look at Braad's ass. He sure has

214

a cute rear." Daarla was trying to direct the priests' eyes to my rump, and my mother encouraged Daarla all the way. I worked at smiling as I jumped harder. My mother had taught me to look happy while jumping, and not as though I was working like a dog.

Working like a dog and pretending to enjoy it, I doubled under, turned it into a triple and then a quadruple. I was leaping high and twirling the rope four times under my feet before I touched down. My kilt was standing almost straight up as I made these powerful leaps, but I paid no heed. I put all my thought into my jumps.

Boodie was the first to get disqualified. He tripped on his rope, grimaced with disappointment, and left the stage. Other boys flopped one by one. Meanwhile, I jumped one legged, first on one foot, then the other. As the competition grew more intense, more boys were disqualified. I tried not to look. I just kept jumping. I didn't even realize it when the crowd sucked in its breath, awed as one, as the last boy left the stage and I jumped on, moving through a rapid series of combination jumps that culminated in a high kick.

"You won, Braad," Daarla shouted. "You won. You can stop jumping."

Then I heard the crowd shouting at me. I grinned weakly as I dropped the rope and stood on wobbly legs. My costume was wringing wet with my sweat. The High Priest wiped my face and shoulders with a towel. Then he placed an arm around my waist and led me to the frame.

The crowd was shouting, horns were blowing, drums were booming, and my ears were ringing as the High Priest directed me to climb the steps to the butt-fuck gallows. I heard Boodie's voice shouting in the crowd, "What are they going to do to Braad?" He sounded alarmed.

Nobody enlightened him. The boys who competed would find out what prize they missed only by witnessing what happened to me.

While I climbed the three steps up to the butt-fuck frame, the crowd fell uncomfortably silent. My legs wobbled once, and the High Priest whispered that I needed to climb unassisted. "You must go to claim the reward under your own power, Braad," he hissed. "Once you have received the prize, we will help you down again."

When I was standing at the frame, the High Priest climbed the steps behind me. "Bend forward," he said. "Drape your body over the smooth pole, grip the front supports, and place your feet in front of the lower rail."

The crowd held its collective breath. I supposed that this was the point where some boys reacted with horror to learn their fate. I grinned at the High Priest. "That will leave my ass in a rather compromising position, won't it?" I teased.

The High Priest tensed, prepared for protest, screams, antagonism, denial, terror, and objection. Doing none of those, I assumed the position he had indicated. Then the village went wild. Loud clamor, horns, bells, chimes, drums, catcalls, cheers, and clapping echoed across the valley and into Greenwood forest. The High Priest stepped close behind me and flapped the rear of my kilt onto my back, fully exposing my bare ass to the village.

More applause and hornpiping followed this event. "What are they doing? What is going to happen to Braad?" Boodie squawked above the howling mob.

And Caasper barked, "This would have happened to any one of us if we had won?"

"You poor fools." Daarla's voice rose above their expostulations. At her words, my friends fell silent and watched.

The High Priest stepped to the front of the gibbet and held an object before my eyes. The object was a thin, polished plug, about four inches long and half an inch in diameter. "I will grease this plug and insert it into your ass," he informed me. "After this one, I will insert a wider one, and then one even wider. This is called the 'First Opening,' which all future priests must undergo."

The plug held no fear for me. It was hardly as wide as the nozzle my mother had used on me that morning as part of my purging. Before my eyes, the High Priest dipped the object in a thick lubricant before he stepped behind me.

"Push with your ass, Braad," he whispered as he spread my buttocks. "You can take it easily."

All of my instincts demanded that I clamp my ass shut, but I resisted my instincts and pushed as the priest instructed. I felt the hard, slick object sliding into my asshole until it was in all the way. "Well taken,

Braad," the High Priest intoned, and the village applauded. The High Priest worked the plug this way and that, widening my asshole for what would follow. The sensation was pleasant, and I found my body stirring.

Stepping in front of me again, the High Priest displayed a larger plug. This he greased and followed the same ritual as before. The second plug was a little harder to take. I drew a deep breath and pushed my asshole with all my might, confident that nothing embarrassing would issue forth. I saw the wisdom of purging a boy who is about to get butt fucked in front of the whole community.

The High Priest kept the second plug in me longer, twisted it more, and worked my ass harder. The plug sent hot shivers through me, and I wondered whether I was becoming aroused. The front of my kilt must have been hanging down, and I wondered whether it would conceal an erection.

The third plug looked gigantic to my eyes, and the gibes arising from the crowd did not reassure me.

"Pop his ass."

"That boy will never close his hole again."

"After Braad opens for that plug, I could drive my whole team up his rectum."

I had to remind myself that I was listening to the mockery of losers. Every man there had taken his turn on the scaffold and had failed to win the prize. I wondered whether all who scorned me spoke true. How many wished they were draped where I was draped and felt what I felt? Who knew?

I was ready for the third plug, even though it was thicker than any human cock could possibly be. The High Priest whispered instructions as he pushed it into me, but the pain was merely a brief flash. Once it was in, my asshole adapted to it readily.

"Does it hurt?' the High Priest asked, pulling out the big plug and then reinserting it.

"It's pleasurable," I moaned quietly. "I feel only pleasure."

"Good boy," the High Priest affirmed. He gestured the assembled Ursine Priests, and I sensed their collective joy. "You are ready to receive the prize."

The High Priest pulled the gigantic plug out of my ass and raised it high for all to see. "Braad is prepared to receive his reward," the High Priest said. With a gesture, he ordered the priest in the bear mask to step forth. The masked priest climbed the gibbet and stood before me. Though the mask hid his face, I could see that he was a young man, probably no more than five years older than I. He was muscled, hirsute, and virile.

"Behold the Bear Sacristan."

Before my eyes, the Bear Sacristan unwrapped his white kilt. His thick cock sprang free and rose until it stood quivering before me. My body went tight as the Bear Sacristan dipped his hand into the lubricant and slicked his cock. His mask heightened my excitement. If I could have seen his face, seen that he was truly human, perhaps I would not have felt the thrill that rippled through me. I gripped my handholds tighter and pushed my ass back. This action was not lost on the crowd. A great chorus of hoorays arose, accompanied by wild clapping. Intermingling with the rah-rah huzzas, echoed a couple of yippees and whoopees, and a distinct element of guffaws, horselaughs, sniggers, and tee-hees.

When the Bear Sacristan walked behind me, the crowd hushed. They had been waiting for this moment. The public had to witness my butt fuck, so all would know when they saw me after that day, I was one of their leaders.

The Bear Sacristan spread my buttocks and pressed his cock against my asshole. The terrific pressure gave me a moment of natural fright. What were the watching townsfolk really thinking? Mother? Father? Daarla? Caasper? Boodie?

"Draw a deep breath, Braad," the High Priest urged. I felt an anal strain, followed by a great heaviness in my ass.

"Well taken, Braad," the High Priest assured me. "Our sacristan's cock is sliding into you nicely. Do you feel any pain?"

Fleetingly, I had felt as though I would split in twain, but that pain subsided, and a pleasing glow swept over me. "The Bear Sacristan can push it in deeper," I urged. "His cock feels good in my ass." A fanfare of horns greeted that remark, accompanied by shouts and calls I could hardly distinguish.

The Bear Sacristan thrust forward; the pressure increased, but the pain did not return. My body fumed with delicious sensations. The Bear Sacristan's lap smashed against my buttocks.

"Braad, the sacristan is in you all the way," the High Priest gloried. "Congratulations."

The Bear Sacristan rocked back and thrust forth: once, twice, thrice. Blazing thrills swept through me. Burning, ruffled, shaken, I gripped my handholds and tensed my legs under the bar. I thrust my ass back to meet his thrusts. The Bear Sacristan started fucking me with a steady rhythm that provoked a pleasure gland in my rectum. I sensed that my cock was jutting in high arousal. Surely, the town could see my erection, while every potent stroke of the Bear Sacristan's cock inched me closer to orgasm.

"Oh," the Bear Sacristan moaned, the first sound I had heard from him. Tensing my asshole, I ground his cock with all my might. His thrusts quickened, and tingles in the head of my cock signaled a gathering gale of gratification.

Feverish pleasure was filling me. The tingles in my dick upsurged; a pleasure vast, yet luscious; remarkable, yet implausible; perilous, yet sublime. Orgasmic vibrations warbled through me. My body shivered with glee. Raptures beyond imagining whipped me into frenzy. My swollen asshole tightened into a pleasure ring around the Bear Sacristan's cock. My nostrils fluttered, my muscles rippled, my nipples crinkled. The trills rolled through my pelvis, meeting other tingles that swept from the head of my cock and mating exquisitely. My dick was alive with a pleasure that sprouted from the Bear Sacristan's cock, the selfsame cock fucking my ass.

At first, I could not feel the wetness of the semen the Bear Sacristan spurted into me, but I did feel the heat. I was also aware of the stroke of his cock in my asshole, his flesh striking my buttocks, and the continuing anal massage that sent clamorous thrills up my cock. After a longer time than I would have imagined, the Bear Sacristan slowed his thrusts. He pushed his cock in and out a few more times, leisurely, sure to milk off the last drops. My asshole popped as he withdrew.

The High Priest and the Bear Sacristan helped me down from the butt-fuck frame. The Bear Sacristan removed his mask. His visage was feral and bearded, long nosed and thick lipped. When he grinned at me, I grinned back. He was more sexy than pretty, more manly than handsome. He and the High Priest helped me readjust my clothing, such as it was, and then both hugged me. I enjoyed the warm embrace of each of the Ursine Priests while the entire community stood in continuous applause. My anal chute felt hot and wet – and pleasantly used.

The High Priest took my arm and whispered in my ear. "Mingle in the crowd. Eat some food, drink a little ale, and say goodbye to your friends and family. While you may leave the temple and visit with your loved ones as much as you need, you are going to be quite busy for the next few years. Your full initiation and training will occupy much of your time."

My mother hugged me, as did Daarla. My father stood somewhat apart, as if my receiving the priest's cock had separated me or elevated me above the family's status. However, when I embraced him, he relaxed and hugged me back.

"Are you ever sorry you didn't win?" I whispered.

Father's eyes widened. "No," he gasped. "I love your mother. I love my children." Then he blanched. "I didn't mean…"

"It's okay, Father," I said. "I believe that I was born to be an Ursine Priest."

I said goodbye to Boodie and Caasper. Boodie had taken Niisti by the hand, and Caasper was downing fruit tarts. We spoke uncomfortably for a time, and I ate a little. Finally, the High Priest signaled me, and I joined hands with the Bear Sacristan. Thus coupled, the Bear Sacristan and I proudly marched to the Ursine Temple where I would begin my initiation and training into the Ursine Priesthood.

("Braad Skips Rope at the Bear Festival" originally appeared in the now out-of-service online periodical *Tommyhawk's Fantasy World*)

About the Author

David Holly lives, moves, and has his being in Portland, Oregon and environs. He is fascinated by the human penchant for odd mythologies, bizarre rituals, diverse religions, forlorn hopes, and broken dreams. He lives in a garish apartment with multihued walls hung with Haitian paintings and shelved with three thousand books. Sharing the apartment are sundry fur-bearing fellow mortals. He is exceptionally fond of strong coffee, red wine, English bitters, rich stout, inverted roller coasters, nude beaches, and hot-looking guys. He wears bright colors, tight slacks, exotic underwear, and slinky swim briefs. He is joyously pagan and loves making merry in heathen celebrations, marching in pride parades, and frolicking naked on Sauvie Island's Collins Beach. Find out more about David Holly and his numerous publications at facebook.com/david.holly2 and gaywriter.org.

aring any underwear. "Excuse me," I said, having a hard time look

inded by that bulge in his crotch, "but don't I know you?" "Maybe

nd of to   bout a

with Ray   God, y

loser?   in?" h

id. "Lik   s stron

ce body   e on G

lly, he l   I eve

up to t   any id

staking   he sam

, I coul   ery lo

ood raci   ne sw

ng with   e in st

we go   behin

ill see   in pu

ed?" he   vent to

rivacy.   grabb

hard. I

k, traci   t, so f

ed it, ha

with m   bing

bbing, I   n cocl

he sound of unzipping filled the small space. I don't know who's h

, but before I knew it, I had his rod in my hand, and mine was in hi

it to do?" he asked, his tone challenging. I knew exactly, and sank